BY BLAKE CROUCH

Upgrade
Recursion
Dark Matter
Run
Abandon
The Last Town
Wayward
Pines

RUN

RUN

A NOVEL

BLAKE CROUCH

BALLANTINE BOOKS
New York

2024 Ballantine Books Trade Paperback Edition

Published in the United States by Ballantine Books, an imprint of Random House, a division of Penguin Random House LLC, New York.

BALLANTINE BOOKS & colophon are registered trademarks of Penguin Random House LLC.

Originally self-published in the United States in 2011.

LIBRARY OF CONGRESS CATALOGING-IN-PUBLICATION DATA
Names: Crouch, Blake, author.
Title: Run: a novel / Blake Crouch.
Description: Trade Paperback Edition. | New York:
   Ballantine Books, 2024.
Identifiers: LCCN 2024008546 (print) | LCCN 2024008547 (ebook) |
   ISBN 9780593874790 (trade paperback) |
   ISBN 9780593874806 (Ebook)
Subjects: LCGFT: Thrillers (Fiction) | Novels.
Classification: LCC PS3603.R68 R86 2024 (print) |
   LCC PS3603.R68 (ebook) | DDC 813/.6—dc23/eng/20240311
LC record available at https://lccn.loc.gov/2024008546
LC ebook record available at https://lccn.loc.gov/2024008547

Printed in Canada on acid-free paper

randomhousebooks.com

9 8 7 6 5 4 3 2 1

Book design by Alexis Flynn

This one is for my readers who have been with me since the beginning.

RUN

The attack was . . . the first recorded instance of lethal raiding among chimpanzees. Until the attack . . . scientists treated the remarkable violence of humanity as something uniquely ours. Scientists thought that only humans deliberately sought out and killed members of their own species.

—RICHARD WRANGHAM AND DALE PETERSON,
DEMONIC MALES

THE tattered wind sock hangs limp against its pole. Weeds erupt through fissures in the runway where she stands, and in the distance, support beams rise from heaps of twisted metal—three hangars, long since toppled upon a half dozen single- and twin-engine airplanes. She watches the Beechcraft that brought her here lift off the ground, props screaming, and climb to clear the pines a quarter mile past the end of the runway. She walks into the field. The midmorning sun blazing down on her bare shoulders. The grass that grazes her sandaled feet still cold with dew. Someone jogs toward her, and beyond them she can see the team already at work, imagines they started the moment the light became worth a damn.

The young man who has come to greet her smiles and tries to take her duffel bag, but she says, "No, I've got it, thanks," and keeps walking, her eyes catching on the colony of white canvas tents standing at the northern edge of the forest. Still probably an insufficient distance to avoid the stink when the wind blows out of the south.

"Good flight in?" he asks.

"Little bumpy."

"It's great to finally meet you. I'm using two of your books in my thesis."

"Nice. Good luck with it."

"You know, there's a few decent bars in town. Maybe we could get together and talk sometime?"

She ducks under the yellow crime-scene tape that circumnavigates the pit.

They arrive at the edge.

The young man says, "I'm doing my thesis on—"

"I'm sorry, what's your name?"

"Matt."

"I don't mean to be rude, Matt, but could you give me a minute alone here?"

"Oh, sure. Yeah, of course."

Matt heads off toward the tents, and she lets her bag slide off her shoulder into the grass, estimating the dimensions of the pit at thirty-five meters by twenty meters, and presently attended to by nine people, seemingly oblivious to the flies and the stench. She sits down and watches them work. Nearby, a man with shoulder-length graying hair buries a pickax into a wall of dirt. A young woman—probably another intern—flits from station to station, filling a bucket with backfill to be added to the mound of grave dirt near the southern edge of the pit. Everywhere that human remains have been exposed, red flags stand thrust into the earth. She stops counting them after thirty. The nearest anthropologist is on the verge of pedestaling a skeletonized body, down to the detail work now—poking chopsticks between ribs to clear out the dirt. Other skeletons lie partially exposed in the upper layers. The remnants of human beings with whom she will become closely acquainted in the weeks to come. Deeper, the dead are likely mummified, possibly even fleshed depending on the water content of the grave. Next to the autopsy tent on the other side, tables have been erected in the grass, and at one of them, a woman she recognizes from a previous UN mission is at work reassembling a small skeleton on a black velvet cloth to be photographed.

She realizes she's crying. Tears are fine, even healthy in this line of work, just never on the clock, never in the grave. If you lose control down there, you might never get it back.

Approaching footsteps snap her out of her reverie. She wipes her face and looks up, sees Sam coming toward her, the bald and scrawny Australian team leader who always wears a tie, even in the field, his rubber boots swishing through the grass. He plops down beside her, reeking of decomp. Rips off the pair of filthy, elbow-length gloves and tosses them in the grass.

"How many have you taken out so far?" she asks.

"Twenty-nine. Mapping system shows a hundred and seventy-five still down in there."

"What's the demographic?"

"Men. Women. Children."

"High-velocity GSWs?"

"Yeah, we've collected a ton of .223 Remington casings. But this is another weird one. Same thing we saw in that mass grave in Denver. Maybe you heard about it."

"I haven't."

"Dismemberment."

"Have you determined what was used?"

"In most instances, it's not a clean break, like a machete or ax strike. These bones are splintered."

"A chainsaw would do that."

"Yeah. So I'm thinking they cut everyone down with AR-15s and then went through with chainsaws. Making sure no one crawled out."

The blond hairs on the back of her neck stand erect, a rod of ice descending her spine. The sun burns down out of the bright June sky, more intense for the elevation. Snow still lingers above timberline on the distant peaks.

"You okay?" Sam asks.

"Yeah. This is my first trip out west. I'd been working New York City up until now."

"Look, take the day if you want. Get yourself acclimated. You'll need your head right for this one."

"No." She stands, hoisting the duffel bag out of the grass and engaging that compartment in her brain that functions solely as a cold, indifferent scientist. "Let's go to work."

There is no decent place to stand in a massacre.

—LEONARD COHEN

THE president had just finished addressing the nation, and the pundits were back on the airwaves, scrambling, as they had been for the last three days, to sort out the chaos.

Dee Colclough lay watching it all on a flatscreen from a ninth-floor hotel room ten minutes from home, a sheet twisted between her legs, the air-conditioning cool against the sweat on her skin.

She looked over at Kiernan, said, "Even the talking heads look scared."

Kiernan stubbed out his cigarette and blew a river of smoke at the television.

"I got called up," he said.

"Your Guard unit?"

"I have to report tomorrow morning." He lit another one. "What I hear, we'll just be patrolling neighborhoods."

"Keeping the peace until it all blows over?"

He glanced at her, head cocked with that boyish smirk she'd fallen for six months ago when he'd deposed her as an adverse expert witness in a medical malpractice case. "Does anything about this make you think it's going to blow over?"

A new chyron appeared across the bottom of the screen—

45 DEAD IN MASS SHOOTING AT A CHURCH IN COLUMBIA, SOUTH CAROLINA.

"Jesus Christ," Dee said.

Kiernan dragged heavily on his cigarette. "Something's happening," he said.

"Obviously. The whole country—"

"That's not what I mean, love."

She looked at him.

For a moment, he just sat there, smoking.

"It's been coming on now, little by little, for days," he said finally.

"I don't understand."

"I barely do myself."

Through the cracked window of their hotel room—distant gunshots and sirens.

"This was supposed to be our week," she said. "You were going to tell Myra. I was—"

"You should go home, be with your family."

"You're my family."

"Your kids at least."

"What is this, Kiernan?" She could feel an angry knot bulging in her throat. "Are we not in this together? Are you having second thoughts—"

"It's not that."

"Do you have any concept of what I've already sacrificed for you?"

She couldn't see all of his face in the mirror on the opposite wall, but she could see his eyes. Gaping into nothing. A thousand-yard stare. He was someplace other than this room. He'd gone deep, and she'd sensed it even before this moment, in the way he'd made love to her. Something held back. Something missing.

She climbed out of bed and walked over to her dress, where she'd thrown it against the wall two hours earlier.

"You don't feel it?" he asked. "Not at all?"

"Feel what?"

"Forget it."

"Kiernan—"

"Fucking forget it."

"What is wrong with you?"

"Nothing."

Dee pulled the straps over her shoulders as Kiernan glared at her through the cloud of smoke around his head. He was forty-one years old, with short black hair and a two-day shadow that reminded her so much of her father.

"Why are you looking at me like that?" she asked.

"You and I are not the same anymore, Dee."

"Did I do something or—"

"I'm not talking about our relationship. It's deeper. It's . . . so much more profound than that."

"You're not making sense."

She was standing by the window. The air coming in was cool and it smelled of the city and the desert that surrounded it. A pair of gunshots drew her attention, and when she looked through the glass she saw grids of darkness overspreading the city.

Dee glanced back at Kiernan, and she'd just opened her mouth to say something when the lights and the television cut out.

She froze.

Her heart accelerating.

Couldn't see anything but the flare and fade of Kiernan's tobacco ember.

Heard him exhale in the dark, and then his voice, all the more terrifying for its evenness.

"You need to get away from me right now," he said.

"What are you talking about?"

"There's this part of me, getting stronger every time I breathe in, that wants to hurt you."

"Why?"

She heard the covers rip back. The sound of Kiernan rushing across the carpet.

He stopped inches from her.

She smelled the cigarettes on his breath, and when she touched his chest, felt his body shaking.

"What's happening to you?" she asked.

"I don't know, but I can't stop it. Remember that I loved you."

He put his hands on her bare shoulders, and she thought he was going to kiss her, but then she was flying through darkness across the room.

She crashed into the dresser, stunned, her shoulder throbbing from the impact.

Kiernan said, "Now, get the fuck out while you still can."

JACK Colclough moved down the hallway, past the kids' bedrooms, and into the kitchen, where four candles on the granite counter-top and two more on the breakfast table made this the brightest room in the house. Dee stood in shadow at the sink, filling another milk jug with water from the tap, the cabinets surrounding her thrown open and vacated, the stovetop cluttered with cans of food that hadn't seen the light of day in years.

"I can't find the road map," Jack said.

"You looked under the bed?"

"Yes."

"That was the last place I saw it."

Jack set the flashlight on the counter and stared at his fourteen-year-old daughter. She was sitting at the breakfast table, her purple-streaked blond hair twirled around her finger.

"Got your clothes?" he asked.

She shook her head.

"Naomi. Go. Now. And help Cole pack. I think your brother got distracted."

"We aren't really leaving, are we?"

"Now."

Naomi pushed back from the table, her chair shrieking against the hardwood floor. She stormed out of the kitchen, down the hall-way.

"Hey!" he shouted after her.

"Cut her a break," Dee said. "She's terrified."

Jack went to his wife. The night beyond the windowpane was moonless and unmarred by even the faintest pinprick of light. It was the city's second night without power.

"This is the last jug," Dee said. "Makes eight gallons."

"That isn't going to last us very long."

From the battery-powered radio on the windowsill above the sink, an old woman's voice replaced the static that had dominated the airwaves for the last six hours. Jack reached over, turned up the volume.

They listened as she read another name, another address over the radio.

"They've lost their fucking minds," Jack said.

Dee turned off the tap and screwed a cap onto the final jug. "You think anyone's actually acting on that?"

"I don't know."

"I don't want to leave, Jack."

"I'll take these jugs out to the car. Make sure the kids are getting packed."

— — —

Jack hit the light switch out of habit, but when he opened the door, the garage remained dark. He shined the flashlight on the four steps that dropped out of the hallway. The smooth concrete was cold through his socks. He popped the hatch to the cargo area, il-lumination flooding out of the overhead dome lights. He set the first jug of water in the back of the Land Rover Discovery. Their backpacks and camping equipment hung from hooks over the chest freezer, and he lifted them down off the wall. Pristine, unblem-ished by even a speck of trail dust. Four never-slept-in sleeping bags dangled from the ceiling in mesh sacks. He dragged a workbench over from the red Craftsman tool drawer and climbed up to take them down. Dee had been begging for a family camping trip ever since he'd purchased three thousand dollars' worth of back-packing gear, and he'd fully intended for their family to spend every other weekend in the mountains or the desert. But two years had passed, and life had happened, priorities changed. The gas stove and water filter hadn't even been liberated from their packaging, which still bore price tags.

He heard Dee shout his name. He grabbed the flashlight, nego-tiated the sprawl of backpacks and sleeping bags, and bolted up the steps and through the door to the house. Past the washer and dryer, back into the kitchen.

Naomi and his seven-year-old son, Cole, stood at the opening to the hallway, their faces all warmth and shadow in the candlelight, watching their mother at the sink.

Jack shined the light on Dee.

She pointed at the radio.

"They just read off Marty Anderson's name. They're going through the humanities department, Jack."

"Turn it up."

"Jim Barbour is a professor of religious studies at the University of New Mexico." The old woman on the radio spoke slowly and with precision. *"His address is Two Carpenter Court. Those of you near campus, go now, and while you're in the neighborhood, stop by the home of Jack Colclough—"*

"Dad—"

"Shhh."

"—a professor of philosophy at UNM. He lives at 1414 Arroyo Way. Repeat: 1414 Arroyo Way. Go now."

"Oh my God, Jack. Oh my God."

"Get the food in the back of the car."

"This is not—"

"Listen to me. Get the food in the back of the car. Naomi, bring your and Cole's clothes out to the garage. I'll meet you all there in one minute."

He ran down the hall, his sock feet skidding across the dusty hardwood floor as he rounded the turn into the master bedroom. Clothes everywhere. Drawers evacuated from a pair of dressers. Sweaters spilling out of the oak chest at the foot of the bed. Into the walk-in closet, stepping on shoes and winter coats. He reached for the highest shelf on the back wall, his fingers touching the pistol case and two small boxes of ammo, which he crammed into the pockets of his khaki slacks.

He returned to the bedroom, dropped to his knees, his stomach, crawling under the bedframe until he grasped the steel barrel of the Mossberg, loaded and trigger-locked.

Then back on his feet, down the hall, through the kitchen, the living room, foyer, right up to the front door, the light beam crossing adobe walls covered in photographs of his smiling family—vacations and holidays from another lifetime. Beside the door, from a table of wrought iron and glass, he grabbed his keys, his wallet, even his phone, though there'd been no signal the last twenty-four hours. Jammed his feet into a pair of trail shoes still caked with mud from his last run in the Bosque, not even a week ago. He didn't realize how badly his hands were shaking until he failed on the first two attempts to tie his shoelaces.

Dee was struggling to fit a sleeping bag into a compression sack as he came down the steps into the garage.

"We don't have time for that," he said. "Just cram it in."

"We're running out of space."

He grabbed the sleeping bag from her and shoved it into the back of the Land Rover on top of the small cardboard box filled with canned food.

"Throw the packs in," he said as he laid the shotgun on the floor against the backseat.

"You find the map?" Dee asked.

"No. Just leave the rest of this shit. Here." He handed her the plastic gun case and a box of 185-grain semi-jacketed hollow points. "Load the Glock."

"I've never even shot this gun, Jack."

"Makes two of us."

Dee went around to the front passenger door and climbed in while Jack closed the cargo hatch. He reached up to the garage-door opener, pulled a chain that disengaged the motor. The door lifted easily.

Cool desert air filled the garage. The spice of wet sage in the breeze reminded him of cheap aftershave—his father. A lone cricket chirped in the yard across the street. No houselights or streetlamps or sprinklers. The surrounding homes almost invisible but for the gentlest starlight.

He caught the scent of cigarette smoke the same instant he heard footsteps in the grass.

A shadow was moving across the lawn—a darker silhouette of black coming toward him, and something the shadow carried reflected the interior lights of the Land Rover as a glimmer of silver.

"Who's there?" Jack said.

No response.

A cigarette hit the ground, sparks scattering in the grass.

Jack was taking his first step back into the garage toward the open driver's-side door, realizing everything was happening too fast. He wasn't going to react in time to stop what was about to—

"Don't come any closer." His wife's voice. He looked over, saw Dee standing at the back of the SUV, pointing the Glock at a man who had stopped six feet away. He wore canvas shorts, thong sandals, and a cream-colored oxford pollocked with blood spatter. The glimmer was the blade of a butcher knife, and the hands that held it were dark with blood.

Dee said, "What are you doing here?"

Kiernan smiled. "I was just in the neighborhood. Been driving around, making some stops. I didn't know you owned a gun. Been looking for one myself." Kiernan looked at Jack. "You must be Jack. We haven't met, but I've heard a lot about you. I'm the guy who's been fucking your wife."

"Listen to me," Dee said. "You're sick. You need—"

"No, I'm actually better than I've ever been." He pointed the butcher knife at the Land Rover. "Taking a trip?"

Tires screeched, an engine revved, and a few blocks away, head-lights passed behind a hedge, light flickering through the branches like a strobe. A succession of distant *pops* erupted in the night.

Jack said, "Dee, we need to leave right now."

"Go back to your car, Kiernan."

The man didn't move.

Jack took a step back and eased himself into the driver's seat.

"Who's out there, Daddy?" Cole asked.

Jack peered into the backseat at his children.

"Naomi, Cole, I want you both to lay down."

"Dad, I'm scared."

"I know, baby. Hold your brother's hand. You all right, Cole?"

"Yeah."

"Good man."

He started the engine as Kiernan receded into the darkness of the front yard.

Dee jumped in beside him, slammed her door, locked it.

Jack said, "You sure know how to pick 'em."

"Do we have everything we need?"

"We have what we have, and now it's time to leave. Stay down, kids."

"Where are we going?" Cole asked.

"I don't know, buddy. No talking, okay? Daddy needs to think."

The dashboard clock read 9:31 P.M. as Jack shifted into reverse and backed out of the garage and down the driveway, nothing but the reddish glow of taillights to guide him. He turned into the street, put the car in drive. Hesitated, fingers searching for the au-tomatic window control. The glass hummed down into the door. Over the idling of the Discovery's engine, he heard another car ap-proaching at high speed, headlights just becoming visible in the rearview mirror.

He floored the gas pedal, the Discovery accelerating through pure darkness.

"Jack, how can you see?"

"I can't."

He made a blind turn onto the next street, drove for several blocks in the dark.

Dee said, "Look."

A house burned on the corner up ahead, flames shooting out of the dormers, the branches of an overhanging cottonwood fringed with embers while molten leaves rained down on the lawn.

"What is it?" Naomi asked.

"A house on fire."

"Whose?"

"I don't know."

"I want to see."

"No, Cole. Stay down with your sister."

They flew up the street.

"I'm going to run us into something." Jack flipped on the head-lights. The console lit up. "You're kidding me," he said.

"What?"

"It's on empty."

"I told you it was getting low last week."

"Are you not capable of pumping gas into a car?"

Three houses down, the headlights swept over two trucks that had pulled into the front yard of an adobe house.

Jack slowed.

"That's the Rosenthals' place."

Through the dark living-room windows: three loud, bright flashes.

"What was that, Dad?"

"Nothing, Nay."

He gunned the engine and glanced over at Dee, a death grip on the steering wheel to keep his hands steady. Nodded at the gun in his wife's lap.

"Wasn't even loaded, was it?"

"I don't know how."

The university campus loomed empty and dark as Dee ripped open a box of ammunition. They passed a row of dorms. The quad. The student union. A squat brick building whose third floor housed

Jack's office. It occurred to him that today would've been the deadline for his bioethics class to hand in their papers on euthanasia.

"There's a button on the left side behind the trigger," he said. "I think it releases the magazine."

"Are you talking about a gun?" Cole asked.

"Yes."

"Are you going to shoot somebody?"

"It's only to protect us, buddy."

Jack watched Dee thumb another hollow-point round into the magazine.

"How many will it hold?" she asked.

"Ten. No, nine."

"Where are we going, Jack?"

"Lomas Boulevard, then the interstate."

"And then?"

"I don't know. I'm trying to work that—" A pair of headlights appeared in the distance.

"You see them, Jack?"

"Of course I see them."

"What's happening, Dad?"

In the rearview mirror, a third set of headlights rushed up on their bumper.

"Jack, do something."

His foot eased onto the brake pedal.

"Jack."

"Sit up, kids."

"What are you doing?"

"Give me the gun."

Dee handed over the Glock, which he stowed under his seat.

They were nearing the roadblock.

"Jack, tell me what you're—"

"I don't know!"

A large oak had been felled across the road, the middle section excised and two pickup trucks parked in front, blocking passage, their high beams glaring into the night.

Dee said, "They have guns."

Jack counted four people standing in front of the vehicles, silhouetted by the headlights. One of them came forward as the Discovery closed within ten yards—a man wearing an Isotopes baseball cap and a red windbreaker. He trained his shotgun on the Discovery's windshield and extended his right hand for Jack to stop.

Jack shifted into park, locked the doors.

The third truck pulled up within several feet of the Discovery's back bumper, its headlights halfway up the glass of the back hatch so they shone directly into the rearview mirror. The man with the shotgun produced a flashlight and circled the Land Rover, shining the beam through every window before arriving back at Jack's door, where he tapped the glass and made circles in the air with his pointer finger.

Jack noted a cold trickle of sweat gliding over the contours of his ribs. He lowered the window eight inches.

"Hey, what's going on?" he said, and it came out naturally enough, like he'd pulled over for a blown taillight, just some annoying traffic stop in the flow of an otherwise normal day.

The man said, "Turn the interior lights on."

"Why?"

"Right now."

Jack hit the lights.

The man leaned forward, the sharp tang of rusted metal wafting into the car, Jack watching the eyes behind the square, silver frames. Those eyes took in his wife, his children, before settling back on Jack with a level of indifference, verging on disgust, that prior to this moment was completely alien to his experience.

"Where you off to so late?" the man asked.

"What business is that of yours?"

When the man just stared and made no response, Jack said, "Look, I don't know what this is all about, but we're going to move on here."

"I asked you where you're going."

Jack tried to wet the roof of his mouth with his tongue. It had gone dry as sandpaper.

"Just up to Santa Fe to see some friends."

The driver's-side door of the truck behind them opened. Some-one stepped down onto the pavement and walked over to join the others at the roadblock.

"Why do you have packs and jugs of water in the back of your car?"

"We're going camping. There's mountains up that way if you hadn't heard."

"I don't think you're going to Santa Fe."

"I don't give a shit what you think."

"Give me your driver's license."

"Fuck off."

The man racked a fresh shell into the chamber, and the awful noise of the pump action set Jack's heart racing.

"All right," he said. He opened the center console, took out his wallet, spent ten seconds trying to slide his license out of the clear plastic sleeve. He handed it through the window, and the man took it and walked over to the trucks and the other men.

Dee whispered, "Jack. Look out your window at the other side of the road."

Where the light from the trucks diffused into the barest strands of illumination, Jack saw a minivan parked in a vacant lot, and just a few feet from it, four pairs of shoes poking up through the weeds, the feet motionless and spread at forty-five-degree angles, toes pointing toward the sky.

"They're going to kill us," she whispered.

Jack reached under his seat, brought the Glock into his lap.

The man was coming back toward the Discovery now.

"Dee, kids," Jack said as he shifted into reverse, "when I clear my throat, get down as low as you can into the floorboards and cover your heads."

The man reached Jack's window. "Everyone out. Except the boy."

"Why?"

The shotgun barrel passed over the top of the window, stopping six inches from Jack's left ear. So close he could feel the heat from recent use radiating off the steel.

"This is not the way you want to handle this, Mr. Colclough. Turn off the engine."

The other men were walking over.

Jack cleared his throat and jammed his foot into the gas pedal, the Land Rover lurching back, a winch punching through the rear window, glass spraying everywhere. He grabbed the smoldering shotgun barrel with one hand and shifted into drive with the other. The blast ruptured his eardrum and blew the glass out of a window, the recoil ripping the barrel out of his hand along with several layers of cauterized skin. He could hear only a distant ringing, like a symphony of old telephones buried deep underground.

Muzzle flashes and the front passenger window exploded, shards of glass embedding themselves in the right side of Jack's face as he pushed the gas pedal into the floor again and cranked the steering wheel to miss the branches of the downed oak tree.

The Discovery tore through the vacant lot, the jarring so violent at this speed Jack could barely keep his grip on the steering wheel. He turned up a grassy slope and took the Land Rover through a six-foot fence at thirty miles per hour, into the backyard of a brick ranch. Plowed over a rose garden and birdbath, then broke through the fence again near the house and sped down the empty driveway and onto a quiet street.

He hit seventy-five within four blocks, blowing through two-way stops, four-way stops, and one dark traffic signal until he saw lights in the distance—the fast-approaching intersection with Lomas Boulevard.

He let the Discovery begin to slow, finally bringing it to a full stop on the curb and shifting into park.

Darkness in the rearview mirror. No incoming headlights.

He tried to listen for the sound of approaching cars, but he heard only those muffled telephones and the painful bass throbbing of his left eardrum. He was shaking all over.

He said, "Is anybody hurt?"

Dee climbed out of the floorboard and said something.

"I can't hear you," he said. In the backseat, he saw Naomi sitting up. "Where's Cole?" Dee squirmed around and leaned into the backseat, reaching down toward the floorboard where Cole had taken cover. "Is Cole okay?" The murmur of voices grew louder. "Would someone please tell me if my son is okay?"

Dee returned to the front seat, put her hands on her husband's face, and pulled his right ear to her lips.

"Cole's fine, Jack. He's just scared and balled up on the floor."

— — —

He drove six blocks to Lomas Boulevard. This part of the city still had power. The road luminous with streetlights, traffic lights, and the glow of fast-food restaurant signs that stretched for a quarter mile in either direction like a glowing mirage of civilization. As Jack pulled through a red light and into the empty westbound lanes, the gas tank's reserve light clicked on.

— — —

They were driving through the university's medical campus when someone stepped out into the road.

Jack had to swerve to miss them.

Dee said something.

"What?"

"Go back!" she shouted.

"Are you crazy?"

"That was a patient."

He turned around in the empty boulevard and drove back toward the hospital and pulled over to the curb. The patient was already halfway across the road and staggering barefoot like he might topple—tall and gaunt, his head shaved, a scythe-shaped scar curving from just above his left ear across the top of his scalp, the kind of damage it would have taken a couple hundred stitches to close. The wind rode the gown up his toothpick legs.

Jack lowered his window as the man collided breathlessly into his door. He tried to speak but he was gulping down breaths of air and emanating the hospital stench of sanitized death.

At last the man raised his head off his forearms and said in a voice gone soft and raspy from disuse, "I woke up several hours ago. The doctors and nurses are gone. What's happening?"

Jack said, "How long have you been in the hospital?"

"I don't know."

"You're in Albuquerque."

"Yeah, I live here."

Jack shifted into park, eyeing the rearview mirror for approaching vehicles. "It's October fifth—"

"October?"

"Things started about a week ago."

"What things?"

"At first, it was just bits on the news that would catch your attention. A murder. A hit-and-run. But the reports kept coming, and there were more every day and they got more violent and harder to understand. It wasn't just happening here. It was all over the country. A police officer in Phoenix went on a shooting rampage in an elementary school and then a nursing home. There were fifty home invasions in one night in Salt Lake. Houses were being burned. Just horrific acts of violence."

"Jesus."

"The president gave a televised speech last night, and right after, the power went out. Cellphone coverage became intermittent. The internet too jammed up to use. By this afternoon, the only functioning line of communication was the radio."

The man looked away from Jack as gunshots rang out in a neighborhood across the street.

"Why is it happening?"

"I don't know," Jack said. "The power went out before any consensus was reached. They think it might be a virus or something."

Dee leaned across the console. "Do you know how you were injured? I'm a doctor. Maybe I can—"

"I need to find my family."

Jack saw the man look into their car, and he thought he was going to ask for a ride, wondering how he would tell him no.

But then the man turned suddenly and limped off down the road.

There were lights on inside, but no customers, no cashier. Jack swiped his credit card through the scanner, waiting for authorization as he watched the ghost town and listened over the dwindling telephones in his head for the threat of approaching cars.

All but super premium had run dry. He stood in the cold pumping twenty-three and a half gallons into the Discovery's tank and thinking how he should've brought the red plastic container that held the lawnmower gas.

As he screwed the cap on, three pickup trucks roared by, pushing ninety down Lomas. Jack didn't wait for a receipt.

Another mile and I-25 materialized beyond some dealerships, cars backed up from the on-ramps on either side of the overpass. Streams of red light winding north through the city, streams of white light crawling south.

Jack said, "Doesn't look like they're getting anywhere, does it?"

He veered into the left lane and drove under the overpass, his right ear improving, beginning to pick up the guttural sounds of the engine and the whimpering of Cole.

A blur of city light, the Wells Fargo Building glowing green in the distance. They shot three miles through downtown and Old Town, past Tingley Park, and then across the Rio Grande into darkness again, the western edge of the city without power.

"You have blood coming out of your ear, Jack."

He wiped the side of his face.

Naomi said, "Are you hurt, Dad?"

"I'm fine. Comfort your brother."

They drove north along the river. Across the water, a great fire was consuming a neighborhood of affluent homes, their immense frames visible amid the flames.

Jack said under his breath, "Where the fuck is the military?"

Dee saw the lights first—a cluster of them a couple miles up the road.

"Jack."

He killed their headlights and braked, crossed the yellow line into the other lane, then dropped down off the shoulder onto the desert. The Discovery's corner lamps barely lit the way, showing only ten feet of the desert floor as Jack navigated between shrubs and sagebrush, finally skirting the edge of a serpentine arroyo.

The hardpan reached the broken pavement. Jack pulled back onto the highway and turned off the corner lamps. Some distance to the south, the roadblock they'd detoured at the intersection of 48 and 550 stood out in the dark—cones of light blazing into the night.

They rode north without headlights, cold desert air streaming in through the jagged glass. Jack's eyes were adjusting to the starlight, and he could just discern the white wisps of reflective paint that framed the highway. Their city fell away behind them, a mosaic of darkness and light and four distinct fires that burned visibly from a distance of twenty miles.

An hour north on the Zia Reservation, they met with a car heading south. Its taillights instantly fired, Jack watching in the rearview mirror as it spun around in the highway and started back after them. He accelerated, but the car quickly closed on their bumper, its light bar throwing shivers of blue and red through the fractured glass of the Discovery's windows.

— — —

The officer's boots scraped the pavement as he approached the Land Rover, his sidearm drawn and paired with a Maglite. He sidled up to Jack's lowered window and pointed a revolver at his head.

"You armed, sir?"

Jack had to turn his right ear to the man so he could hear. He blinked against the sharp light. "I have a Glock in my lap."

"Loaded?"

"Yes sir."

"Just keep your hands on the steering wheel." The state police officer shined his light into the backseat, saw Naomi and Cole, and holstered his gun. "You folks all right?"

"Not really," Jack said.

"Somebody shot your car up pretty good."

"Just a Thursday night in Albuquerque."

The cop laughed. "How are things there?"

"Terrible. What do you hear? We've been checking our car radio, but it's all static."

"I hear I've lost officers up on the northwest plateau, but I don't know that for certain. I've heard there are roadblocks, widespread home invasions, a National Guard unit getting slaughtered. But it's all rumors. Things came apart so fast, you know?" The officer pulled off his wool hat. He scratched his bald dome, tugged at the tufts of gray that flared out above his ears and ringed his skull. "Where you headed?"

"We don't know yet," Jack said.

"Well, I'd get off the highway. Least for the night. I been chased and shot at by several vehicles. They couldn't catch my Crown Vic, but they'd probably run you down no problem."

"We'll do that."

"You say you have a Glock?"

"Yes sir."

"Comfortable with it?"

"I used to deer hunt with my father, but it's been years since I've even shot a gun."

The officer's eyes cut to the backseat, his face brightening. He waved and Jack glanced back, saw Cole sit up and look through the glass. He lowered Cole's window.

"How you doing there, buddy? You look like a real brave boy to me. Is that right?"

Cole just stared.

"What's your name?"

Jack couldn't hear his son answer. The officer reached his gloved hand through the window.

"Good to meet you, Cole." He turned back to Jack. "Hunker down someplace safe for the night. You ain't a pretty sight."

"My wife's a doctor. She'll patch me up."

The officer lingered at his window, staring off into the emptiness all around them—starlit desert and the scabrous profile of a distant mountain range, pitch-black against the navy sky. "What do you make of it?" he said.

"Of what?"

"Whatever this is that's happening. What we're doing to ourselves."

"I don't know."

"You think this is the end?"

"Sort of feels that way tonight, doesn't it?"

The officer rapped his knuckles on the roof. "Stay safe, folks."

= = =

Ten miles on, Jack left the highway. He crossed a cattle guard and drove 2.8 miles over a wash-boarded, runoff-rutted wreck of a road until the outcropping of house-size rocks loomed straight ahead in the windshield. He pulled behind a boulder, so that even with the lights on their Land Rover would be completely hidden from the highway. Shifted into park. Killed the engine. Dead quiet in this high desert. He unbuckled his seatbelt and turned around in his seat so he could see his children.

"Know what we're going to do?" he said. "When this is all over?"

"What?" Cole asked.

"I'm taking you kids back to Los Barriles."

"Where?"

"You remember, buddy. That little town on the Sea of Cortez where we stayed over Christmas a couple years ago? When this is over, we're going back for a month. Maybe two."

The overhead dome light cut out. Jack could feel the car listing in the wind, bits of dust and dirt and sand slamming into the metal like microscopic ball bearings.

Cole said, "Remember that sandcastle we built?"

Jack smiled in the darkness. They'd opened presents and gone out to the white-sand beach and spent all day, the four of them, building a castle with three-foot walls and a deep moat, wet sand dribbled over the towers and spires to resemble eroded stone.

"That sucked," Naomi said. "Remember what happened?"

A storm had blown in that afternoon over Baja as the tide was coming in. When a rod of lightning touched the sea a quarter mile out, the Colcloughs had screamed and raced back to their bungalow as the rain poured down and the black clouds detonated. Jack had glanced back as they scrambled over the dunes, glimpsed their sandcastle rebuffing its first decent wave, the moat filling with saltwater.

"Do you think the waves knocked it down?" Cole said.

"No, it's still standing," Naomi said.

"Don't speak to your brother that way. No, Cole, it wouldn't have lasted the night."

"It was a big castle."

"I know, but the tide's a powerful force."

"We walked out there the next morning, Cole," Dee said. "Remember what we saw?"

"Smooth sand."

"Like we hadn't even been there," Naomi said.

"We were there," Jack said. "That was a great day."

"That was a stupid day," Naomi said. "What's the point of building a sandcastle if you can't watch it get destroyed?"

Jack could hear in her voice that she didn't mean it. She was just trying to push whatever button she thought he'd left unguarded. Under different circumstances, it would've pissed him off, but not tonight.

He said, "Well, it wasn't stupid to me, Nay. That was one of my favorite days. One of the best of my life."

Jack unlocked the shotgun. He found a good-size rock and smashed out the taillights and brake lights and reverse lights. Unloaded everything from the cargo area and picked the glass slivers out of the carpet and knocked the remaining glass out of the back window, the rear right panel, the front passenger window. The army-green paint of the front passenger door and the back hatch bore several bullet holes. A round had even punctured the leather of Jack's headrest—a white puff of stuffing mushroomed out of the exit hole.

Jack had folded the backseat down. Naomi and Cole slept in their down bags in the car. It was after 1:00 A.M., and he sat against a boulder. Dee's headlamp was shining in his eyes as she wiped the right side of his face with an iodine prep pad. She used plastic tweezers from the first-aid kit to dig the glass shrapnel out of his face.

"Here comes a big one," she said.

He winced.

"Sorry."

The shard clinked into the small aluminum tray, and when she'd removed all the glass she could see, she dabbed away the blood with a fresh iodine pad.

"Do I need stitches?" he asked.

"No. How's the left ear?"

"What?"

"How's the left ear?"

"What?"

"How's the—"

He smiled.

"Fuck you. Let's dress that hand."

= = =

They inflated the Therm-a-Rests, crawled into their sleeping bags, and lay on the desert floor under the stars.

Jack heard Dee crying.

"What is it?" he said.

"Nothing."

"No, what?"

"You don't want to hear it."

"Kiernan." Jack had known about him almost from the inception of their affair. She'd been honest with him from the beginning, and on some level he respected her for that. But this was the first time he'd spoken the man's name.

"That wasn't him," she said. "He's a decent man."

"You loved him."

A sob slipped out.

"I'm sorry, Dee."

The wind kicked up. They faced each other to escape the clouds of dust.

"I'm scared, Jack."

"We'll keep heading north. Maybe it's better in Colorado."

In the intermittent moments of stillness, when the wind died away, Jack stared up into the sky and watched the stars fall and the imperceptible migration of the Milky Way. He kept thinking how strange it felt to be lying beside his wife again. He'd slept in the guest room the last two months. They'd lied to the kids, told them it was because of his snoring, having promised each other they'd handle the dissolution of their marriage with grace and discretion.

Dee finally slept. He tried to close his eyes, but his mind wouldn't stop. His ear throbbed, and the scorched nerve endings flared under the barrel-shaped blister across the fingers of his left hand.

COYOTES woke him, a pack trotting across the desert half a mile away. Dee's head rested in the crook of his arm, and he managed to extricate himself without rousing her. He sat up. His sleeping bag was glazed with dew. The desert the color of blued steel in the predawn. He wondered how long he'd slept—an hour? Three? His hand no longer burned, but he still couldn't hear a thing out of his left ear except a lonely, hollow sound like wind blowing across an open bottle top. He unzipped his bag and got up. Slipped his socked feet into unlaced trail shoes and walked over to the Land Rover. Stood at the glassless back hatch watching his children sleep as the light strengthened all around him.

— — —

They were packed and on the road before the sun rose, pressing north, the morning air whipping through the broken windows. For breakfast, they passed around a bag of stale tortilla chips and a jug of water that had chilled almost to freezing in the night. Eighty miles through sagebrush and pinion and long vistas and deserted trading posts and buttes that flushed when first struck by sunlight and a casino at seven thousand feet in the middle of nothing on the Apache res. The two towns they blazed through on the northwest plateau stood perhaps too quiet for 8:30 on a Friday morning, like Christmas and everyone indoors. But nothing else seemed wrong.

— — —

They climbed through high desert as the road followed the course of a river. Dee turned on the radio, let it seek the AM dial. Nothing but static. FM landed just one station, an NPR affiliate out of southwest Colorado that had diverged markedly from its standard programming—a young man read names and addresses over the airwaves.

Jack slammed the palm of his hand into the radio.

The volume spiked, the station changed, the car filled with blaring static.

Twenty miles ahead, out of a valley tucked into the juniper-covered foothills, reams of smoke lifted into the blue October sky.

— — —

When the kids were younger, they had vacationed in this tourist town—ski trips after Christmas, autumn driving tours to see the aspen leaves, the long holiday weekends that framed their summers.

"Let's not go through there," Dee said.

A few miles ahead, everything appeared to be burning.

"I think we should try to get through," Jack said. "This is a good route. Not too many people live in these mountains."

— — —

Power lines had been cut down to block the business route, forcing Jack to detour up Main Avenue, and when they turned into the historic district, Dee said, "Jesus."

Everything smoking, getting ready to burn or burning or burned already. Broken glass on the street. Fire hydrants launching arcs of white spray. Tendrils of black smoke seething through the door and window frames of the hotel where they used to stay—a redbrick relic from the mining era.

Two blocks down, the smoke thickened enough to blot out the sky. Orange fire raged through the exploded third-floor windows of an apartment building, and the canopies of the red oaks that lined the sidewalks flamed like torches.

The kids stared out their windows, speechless.

Jack's eyes burned.

He said, "We're getting a lot of smoke in here."

The windows blew out of a car on the next block. Flames engulfed it.

"Go faster, Jack."

Cole started coughing.

Dee looked back between the front seats. "Pull your shirt over your mouth and breathe through it."

"Are you doing it too, Mama?"

"Yes."

"What about Daddy?"

"He will if he can. He needs his hands to drive right now."

They passed through a wall of smoke, the world outside the windows grayish white, all things obscured. Then rolled through an intersection under dark traffic signals.

"Look out, Jack."

"I see it."

He steered around a FedEx truck that had been abandoned in the middle of the street, its left turn signal still blinking at half speed, like a heart with barely any beat left in it. Cole coughed again.

They emerged from the smoke.

Jack slowed the car, said, "Close your eyes, kids."

Cole through his shirt: "Why?"

"Because I told you to."

"What is it?"

Jack brought the Land Rover to a stop. An ember blew in

through Dee's window and alighted upon the dash, smoldering into the plastic. Ash fell on the windshield like charcoal snow. He looked back at his children.

"I don't want you to see what's up ahead."

"Is it something bad?" Cole said.

"Yes."

"But you're going to see it."

"I have to see it because I'm driving. If I shut my eyes, we'll wreck. But I don't want to see it. Mama's going to close her eyes too."

"Just say what it is."

Jack could see Naomi already straining to peer around her mother's seat.

"Is it dead people?" Cole asked.

"Yes."

"I want to see them."

"No, you don't."

"It won't bother me. I promise."

"I can't make you shut your eyes, but I can give you fair warning. This is the kind of thing you'll dream about. So when you wake up tonight crying and scared, don't call out for me to comfort you, because I warned you not to look."

Thinking, Will there be a tonight to awake from?

Jack drove on. They had been shot down, ten or fifteen of them, some killed outright, brain matter slung into quivering gray-pink globules on the street. Others had managed to cover some ground before dying, the distance of their final crawl measured by swaths of purple-stained pavement, and in one instance, a long gray rope of gut, as if the woman had been tethered to the street. Jack glanced back, saw Naomi and Cole staring through the window, their faces pressed to the glass. His eyes filled up.

— — —

In the center of town, they crossed a river that sourced from the mountains. In the summertime, in direct sun, it shone luminescent

green and teemed with rafters and fly-fishers. Today, the water reflected the colorless, smoked-out sky. A body floated down the rap-
ids under the trestle bridge, jostled in the current, and Jack spotted
numerous others rounding the bend—a group of blindfolded children.

= = =

Main Avenue widened to four lanes. Burned, abandoned cars
clogged the street. Out of the valley rose a hundred unique trails of
smoke.

"It's like an army came through," Dee said.

They passed two fast-food restaurants, several gas stations, a
fairground, a high school, a string of motels.

Jack pointed to a grocery store. "We should get more food."

"No, Jack."

"Keep going, Dad," Naomi said. "I don't like it here. I'd rather be
hungry."

A woman stumbled out of the supermarket parking lot and ran
into the street, holding out her hands to the Land Rover as if will-
ing it to stop.

"No, Jack."

"She's hurt."

The Land Rover's bumper came to rest ten feet from the woman
in the road.

Jack turned off the engine and opened his door and stepped
down into the road. The door slam echoed against an unnerving
silence, disrupted only by a single sound Jack barely even registered with one unshattered eardrum—a baby wailing several blocks
away.

He could see in the way the woman watched him approach that
she'd witnessed pure horror in recent hours. He suddenly wished
he'd never stopped the car, that he'd stayed on the other side of the
windshield, because this was real, breathing agony standing before
him. She sat down in the road. The intensity of her weeping like
nothing Jack had ever heard, and he could feel the urge to dehu-

manize her, to shun sympathy. Too horrifying to identify with a human being who had reached this level of despair. There was something contagious in her grief and loss.

Her hair was dreadlocked with blood and her arms streaked red and her long-sleeved white T-shirt stained like a butcher's apron.

"Are you hurt?"

She looked up at him, eyes nearly swollen shut from crying. "How can this be happening?"

"Are they still here? The people who did this?"

She wiped her eyes. "We saw them coming with guns and axes. We hid in the closet. They came into the house, looking for us. I'd been in Mike's house before. He'd sung carols on our front porch. I'd taken his family Christmas cookies. He said if we came out they would do it quickly."

Jack squatted down before her in the road. "But you got out. You escaped."

"They shot at us as we ran out the back door. Katie got hit in the back. They were coming . . . and I left her."

"I'm so sorry."

"I left her and I don't even know if she was dead."

Dee opened her door. Jack glanced back, said, "You want to come take a look at—"

"That's a lie!" the woman said. "I'm a fucking liar. I know she wasn't dead because she was crying."

"We need to go, Jack."

"She was crying for me."

He touched the woman's shoulder. "Do you want to come with us?"

She stared back at him, her eyes glazing, mind drifting elsewhere.

"Jack, could we please leave this fucking town already?"

He stood.

"Katie was crying for me. I was so scared."

"Do you want to come with us?"

"I want to die."

Jack walked back to the Land Rover and opened the door as the woman screamed.

"What happened to her?" Naomi asked.

He started the engine.

Drove around the woman in the road and turned up a side street.

"Jack, where are you going?"

He pulled over to the curb and turned off the car and got out. The houses burned and smoking. A row of bodies in the street on the next block. Dee climbed out and walked around to the front of the car and stood facing him.

He said, "I heard a baby crying over here while I was talking to that woman."

"I don't hear a thing, Jack. Look at me. Please."

He looked down at her. As beautiful to him as she had ever been standing in this charred neighborhood in this murdered town. He saw the pulsing of her carotid artery in her long and slender neck. She seemed intensely alive.

Dee pointed to the Land Rover. "They're our charge. Do you understand that? Nobody else."

"You made me stop for the hospital patient last—"

"That was the doctor in me. I'm over it now. We don't have much food or water. We're so vulnerable."

"I know."

"Jack." She wouldn't go on until he'd met her eyes. "I am holding my shit together by a very thin thread. I need you to make smart decisions."

"Okay," he said, still straining to hear the cries of the baby.

— — —

North out of town. Out of the smoke and through a valley, its winding river marked by cottonwoods and the valley itself enclosed by red-banded cliffs and everything so purely lit under the lucid blue. Like a dream, Jack thought. Or a memory. The way he still saw

Montana that fall day all those years ago when he'd caught his first
glimpse of Dee.

   The highway paralleled a narrow-gauge railroad. They passed no
other cars. Pastured cows raised their oblong heads to watch them
speed by, and the air that filled the car carried the sweet, rich stink
of a dairy farm. In the backseat, Naomi leaned on the door, staring
out the window. Cole slept. For a second, it felt like one of those
weekend trips to Colorado, and Jack did everything in his power to
embrace the fantasy.

- - -

The road began to climb. Pressure building in Jack's ears. The sky
verging toward purple, and the air that rushed in through Dee's
window growing cooler and redolent of spruce trees. On the moun-
tainsides, the conifers were laced with aspen. The summits stood
treeless, all gray and broken rock patched with old snow. They
passed a deserted ski resort. A livery for tourists to purchase horse-
back rides. The road steepened. They climbed past ten thousand
feet through a stand of spruce and crested the first pass.

- - -

A few miles up the road, they came to a second, higher pass. Jack
pulled over into the empty parking lot and turned off the engine.
He and Dee got out and took a look around. It was late morning.
You could see for miles. The wind blew. Clouds amassing to the
north. He took out his phone and powered it up. No service.

   He said, "Silverton's down in that valley over there."

   Dee went to the car and came back with a pair of binoculars.
She glassed the road from the pass to where it disappeared into the
forest several miles north and a few hundred feet below.

   "Anything?" Jack asked.

   "Nothing."

- - -

They rode down from the pass, back into the forest, and then out of it again. The road had been gashed out of a cliff and the drop off the right shoulder was a thousand feet down to a river that snaked a canyon. The valley from which it flowed contained a small town dotted with brightly painted buildings and a railroad yard and a gold-domed courthouse at the north end.

"Well, it isn't on fire," Jack said. He glanced over, saw Dee massaging the back of her neck. "Headache?"

"Yeah, and it's getting worse."

"You know what it is, don't you?"

"The elevation?"

"Nope. I've got one too."

"Oh my God, you're right. We've missed our morning coffee."

They rounded a hairpin turn.

Three trucks were parked across the road, six men sprinting toward the Land Rover, guns pointed, screaming at them to stop the car.

"Jack, turn around."

"They're too close. They'll open fire."

"Won't they anyway?"

"What's happening?"

"Naomi, stay quiet. Don't wake Cole."

Jack still searched for a way out as the men closed in—a steep drop through trees over the right shoulder, an impossible climb up the mountainside off the left, and not enough room in this fast-diminishing increment of time to execute a three-point turn and haul ass back the way they'd come.

Jack shifted into park. "Put your hands up, Dee."

The first man arrived with a bolt-action Remington trained on Jack's head through the glass as the others surrounded the car.

"Roll it down," he said. Jack lowered the window. "Where the fuck are you going?"

"Just north."

The man was bearded but young. Not even twenty-five, Jack thought. He wore a camouflage hunting jacket and had a braided goatee tied off with black beads.

Someone standing behind the Rover said, "New Mexico tag."

"Why are you up here? Who are you with?"

"No one, it's just us."

Another man walked over and stood by Jack's window. A patchier beard. Long black hair flowing out of his corduroy bomber hat.

He said, "There's a kid sleeping in the backseat. Car's been shot to hell, Matt. They got supplies and shit in the back."

"We had to leave our home in Albuquerque last night," Jack said. "Barely made it out."

Matt lowered his .30-30. "You come through Durango this morning?"

"Yeah."

"We heard it got pretty fucked up."

"They burned it. Bodies everywhere." Jack watched the fear take up residence in the man's face—a sudden paling that made him look even younger than Jack had first suspected.

"It's bad, huh?"

"Biblical."

The others gathered around Jack's window.

Cole sat up and rubbed his eyes. "Are they bad guys, Daddy?"

"No, buddy, we're okay."

"Yeah, we're cool, little man."

The assembled men looked less like sentries than armed ski bums. Their weapons better suited to elk hunting than warfare— all toting high-powered rifles slung over their shoulders but not a pistol or shotgun to be seen.

"So you're guarding the road into town?" Jack asked.

"Yep, and there's another group stationed below Red Mountain Pass, trying to destroy the road."

"Why?"

"There've been reports of a convoy of trucks and cars heading south from Ridgeway."

"How many vehicles?"

"Don't know. Most of Silverton's already gone up into the mountains. Glad to see you driving a Land Rover, 'cause that's really the only route left."

"What route is that?"

"Cinnamon Pass to Lake City. And you should probably get going. It's a bitch of a road."

— — —

They rolled into the old mining town at midday. Jack pulled into a small grocery with two gas pumps out front. He sent Dee and the kids inside to scrounge for food while he flipped the lever and prayed there was something left. There was. He topped off the Rover's tank and walked into the store. The cash register stood unmanned, the shelves stripped bare, the store pillaged.

He called out, "You find anything?"

Dee said from the back, "Slim pickings, although I did get a road map. Any gas left?"

"I filled us up." Jack grabbed two five-gallon gas cans off a shelf in the automotive aisle and went outside to the pump and filled them up. He cleared out a spot amid the camping gear and lifted the red plastic cans through the open window of the back hatch. Inside the store again, it took him several minutes to find the plastic sheeting he was after. He carried two boxes of it, a roll of duct tape, and the single remaining quart of 10W-30 motor oil back outside with him. Dee and the kids were already in the car when he climbed in.

"How'd we do?" he said.

"Three strips of jerky. A can of diced tomatoes. Box of white rice. Bottle of seasoning."

"Sounds like a feast."

— — —

Up Greene Street for several blocks. Most of the shops closed. No one out. The sky sheeted over with gray clouds that had moved in so suddenly only a wedge of autumn blue lingered to the south, all the brighter for its dwindling existence. Jack turned into a parking space.

"I won't be long."

He left the car running and went into the sporting-goods store. It smelled of waterproofing grease and gunpowder. Everywhere, racks of bibs and jackets skinned in every conceivable pattern of camouflage. There were mounted deer and elk heads with their improbable racks and a stuffed brown bear standing on its hind legs, keeping watch over an aisle of nets and fly rods and hip waders. A burly man with the girth of a drink machine stood watching him from behind the counter. He wore a flannel shirt, a vest flecked with renegade feathers of down, and he was pushing rounds into a revolver.

"What are you lookin' for?"

"Shells for a twelve gauge and a—"

"Sorry."

"You're out?"

"I ain't sellin' any more ammo."

The gun cases behind the counter had been emptied.

"If you could just spare one box of twelve-gauge shells, I'd pay you twice their value."

"Tell you what." The man reached under the counter, brought out a sheathed hunting knife, and set it on the glass. "Take that. On the house. Best I can do."

Jack walked to the counter. "I already have a knife."

"What kind?"

"Swiss Army."

"Good luck killin' some son of a bitch with it."

Jack lifted the large bowie. "Thank you."

The store owner flipped the revolver's cylinder closed and set to work loading a pile of chunky, hollow-point rounds into another magazine.

"Are you staying?" Jack asked.

"You think I look like the type of hombre let some motherfuckers run me out of my own town?"

"You should think about leaving. They wiped Durango off the map."

"Under advisement."

Someone pounded the storefront glass. They both turned suddenly. Jack saw Dee waving frantically to come outside. He rushed to the door and, as he pushed it open, heard a distant growl—a symphony of engines growing louder with each passing second, like the opening mayhem of a speedway race.

Dee said, "They're here."

As he moved toward the Rover, gunshots broke out in the south end of town. Men were yelling and he glimpsed the lead trucks of the convoy already turning onto Greene Street.

He jumped in behind the wheel and reversed out of the parking space and shifted into drive. The hotels and restaurants and gift shops raced by, Jack running stop signs, doing seventy by the time he passed the courthouse.

The road turned sharply.

Jack braked, tires squealing.

Dee said, "You know where you're going?"

"Sort of."

The road left town and went to dirt, still smooth and wide enough for Jack to keep their speed above sixty. It ran for a couple of miles above the river before emerging into a higher valley.

They passed ruined mines.

Mountains swept up all around them, the craggy summits edging into the falling cloud deck. In the rearview mirror, Jack eyed the dust cloud a mile back. When he squinted, he saw the half dozen trucks contained within it.

They passed the remnants of another mine, another ghost town.

The road became rocky and narrow and steep.

"Can you go any faster?" Dee asked.

"Any faster, I'll bounce us off the mountain."

Naomi and Cole had unbuckled their seatbelts and they both sat up on their knees, facing the back hatch and watching the pursuing trucks.

"Get down, kids."

"Why?"

"Because I don't want you to get shot, Naomi."

"Are they going to shoot at me, Daddy?"

"They might, Cole."

"Why?"

Why indeed.

The road had gone completely to hell, the Rover's right tires passing inches from a nonexistent shoulder that plunged a hundred and fifty feet into a stream that boiled with whitewater.

Snow starred the windshield. A signpost appeared in the distance. Beside the words CINNAMON PASS, which had been engraved in the wood, an arrow pointed to a road that could hardly be called a road. It was nothing but a single lane of broken rocks that switchbacked up the flank of a mountain and disappeared into clouds.

Jack took the turnoff. Snow blew in through the open windows. They climbed several hundred feet above the main road, above timberline, and as Jack negotiated the first switchback, that squadron of trucks emerged out of the mist, cutting triangles of light through the falling snow.

Dee lifted the binoculars from the floorboard and leaned out the window and glassed the valley. Even without magnification, Jack could see five of the trucks veer onto the turnoff for Cinnamon Pass.

"Why's the one stopping?" he asked.

"I don't know," she said. "A man's getting out."

"What's he—"

"Everybody down!"

Something struck the Rover.

For a split second, Jack thought the tires had thrown a rock.

A rifle shot echoed off the mountains.

The Rover shook and pitched as Jack pushed their speed to ten miles per hour, maneuvering to avoid the largest, sharpest rocks that jutted out of the trail. The window at Naomi's seat exploded in a shower of glass and everyone screamed and Jack shouted his daughter's name and she said she was okay.

Another rifle shot.

They climbed into the base of a cloud, Jack thinking, *He's aiming for the tires* as a bullet punctured Dee's door and ripped through his seat, inches from his back.

The mist thickened. The rocks had just been wet. Now they were frosted. The snow melting and streaking the windshield and pouring into the car through the open windows. Jack thought he heard another shot over the engine, but when he glanced out Dee's window to where the valley should have been a few hundred feet below, there was only a blue-tinted mist cluttered with snowflakes that swirled and fell in disorienting profusion.

= − −

They climbed the mountainside, the road exposed, Dee and the kids still burrowed into the floorboards and Jack constantly checking the rearview mirror for headlights.

"Can we get up now?" Cole asked.

"Not yet."

The road leveled off and the Rover's headlights passed over another signpost: CINNAMON PASS ELEVATION 12,640 FEET.

Several inches of snow on everything in this tundra world.

No trees or shrubs but only rock and nothing visible beyond fifty feet through the fog and pouring snow. In some outpost of emotion, divorced from the horror of the moment, Jack found the isolated beauty of this pass heartbreaking. The kind of wild place his father had loved to take him when he was a boy.

He brought the Rover to a stop, turned off the car, threw open his door.

"You guys can sit up now."

He stepped down into the snow and shut his door. Straining to listen. At first, he heard only the whisper of snowflakes falling on his shoulders, the ticking of the cooling engine, the wind, the invisible shifting of rocks on some obscured peak.

Then he heard them—impossible to tell how far away, but the distant groan of engines became audible in the gloom below the pass, muffled by fog and snow.

He got back into the car and cranked the engine and they went on.

Jack shifted into four-wheel low.

The road descending, tires sliding on ice down the steeper grades.

After two miles, shrubs appeared again. Then tiny, crooked fir trees. They dropped into a forest and a stream fell in beside the road. It was still snowing here, but the snow had only begun to collect.

Jack turned off the Jeep trail.

They went across a meadow and forded a stream and climbed up the bank into a grove of fir trees. He turned off the car and got out and walked back to the stream and stared across the meadow toward the road. The mist had all but dissolved in the trees. He looked back at the Rover. To the road again. He scrambled down the bank to the edge of the stream and started to cross over to evaluate their hiding place from the meadow. The rumbling chorus of engines stopped him. He went back up the bank. Dee and Cole had gotten out of the Rover and were coming toward him. He waved them back.

"The trucks are coming."

"Can they see us from the road?"

"I don't know."

He glanced back at the meadow and could barely see the Rover's tire tracks in the dusting of snow. The tread had visibly bitten into the soft dirt of the bank—if the people in the trucks could see that far.

The engines got quiet and then loud again.

"Come on," he said.

The Rover reeked of hot brake fluid. Jack saw Naomi lying across the backseat. He knocked on the glass. She cut her eyes up at him and he held a finger to his lips and she nodded. They crouched behind the car.

Jack said, "I'm going to find a spot where I can watch the road."

"Can I come?"

"I need you to stay here and take care of Mama. I won't be far." He looked at Dee. "Be ready to run."

Jack jogged back toward the stream and stopped behind a rock that rose to his shoulders. The trees dripping. Snowing hard now.

He could smell the spruce. The wet rock. Already the ground was white. He poked his head around the boulder as the second truck emerged from the trees. It went alongside the meadow. He said, "There are no tracks to see, just keep moving," and it kept moving as the third and fourth and fifth trucks rolled into view—Dodge Rams, snow-blasted except for the engine-warmed hoods and heated cabs. He could see faces through the fogged glass of the passenger windows. He ducked back behind the rock and sat in the snow and studied the smooth motion of his watch's second hand. When it had made three revolutions, the engines had completely faded. Now the only sound was the dripping trees, the pounding of his heart.

— — —

They unloaded their camping equipment from the back of the Land Rover, and Jack unpacked the tent and read its instruction manual. Spent an hour trying to assemble the poles and unravel the mystery of how to thread them through the tent sleeves. The snow was ankle-deep and still falling when he finally raised the four-man dome. They carried their sleeping bags and air cushions over from the car and tossed them inside. Dee and the kids took off their wet shoes and climbed in.

Jack zipped them in and said, "Warm it up for me."

— — —

With the new hunting knife, he cut large squares out of the plastic sheeting. He wiped the snow off the window frames, dried the wet metal with the sleeves of his shirt, and duct-taped the plastic squares over three windows on the right side of the car, and a large rectangle over the back hatch. You couldn't see anything distinctly through the plastic. He liked this, so he taped a piece over the intact glass of Cole's window as well.

— — —

He spent what was left of the afternoon picking Naomi's window glass out of the backseat and the floor mats. Reorganizing everything in the cargo area. He checked the oil, washer fluid, tire pressure. When he finished, he looked for something else to do, needing his hands to be busy, his mind in the moment.

It still snowed. He thought the sky had imperceptibly darkened, the afternoon sliding toward dusk. He hacked some limbs off a dead spruce and snapped off a few clusters of brown needles toward the base of the tree that had been shielded from the weather.

— — —

The stream was freezing. He picked a dozen fist-size rocks out of the water and stretched out his T-shirt and loaded them all into the pouch it made. Inside the fire ring, he stacked wads of tissue paper and the browned spruce needles and a handful of twigs and enclosed them all in a framework of larger branches. Last fire he'd built had been at their home in Albuquerque the previous Christmas, and he'd cheated, used a fire-starter brick to get things going. His hands trembled in the cold as he held the lighter to the tissue paper and struck a flame.

— — —

Later, he heard the tent unzip. Dee crawled out, stepped into her wet shoes. She walked over and stood beside him.

"I guess it literally takes the end of the world to get a family camping trip."

"I'm just trying to get a fire going so we can dry some stuff out."

A wisp of smoke curled up from the pitiful pile of blackened twigs and half-burnt tissue paper.

"You're shivering," she said. "Come into the tent and get some sleep. I have your sleeping bag ready for you."

He stood, his legs cramping. He'd been squatting for over an hour.

"Are you hungry?" he asked.

"Let me worry about dinner. Go sleep."

— — —

Jack abandoned his wet clothes in a pile in the tent's vestibule and crawled into his sleeping bag. He could hear Dee moving around outside and he could hear the snow alighting on the rain fly. He didn't stop shivering for a long time.

His children slept. He reached over and held his hand to Cole's chest. Rise and fall. Rise and fall. Naomi lay on the other side of Cole against the tent wall. He leaned across, his hand searching out her sleeping bag in the mounting dark, then finally resting on her back. Rise and fall. Rise and fall.

— — —

When he woke it was pitch-black and he thought he was in his bed in the guest room in Albuquerque. He sat up and listened. He didn't hear his children breathing. He didn't hear anything but the pulsing in his left ear. He reached over in the dark. The sleeping bags empty. He almost called out for them, but then thought better of it. He dressed quickly in his cold, damp clothes and unzipped the vestibule and crawled outside. It had stopped snowing, and his footsteps squeaked in the half foot of powder. Inside the Rover, light flickered through the plastic windows. He went over and opened the driver's door and got in. Everyone sat in their respective seats eating out of paper bowls. A candle burned on the center .console.

"Smells good," he said.

Dee lifted a bowl off the dashboard and handed it to him.

"It's probably cooled off. I didn't want to waste fuel keeping it warm."

Tomatoes and rice, heavily seasoned, with pieces of jerky mixed in. He stirred it up and took a bite.

He glanced at his watch—a few hours later than he thought.

"This is good," he said. "Really good."

"I didn't like it," Cole said.

"Sorry, buddy. Beggars can't be choosers."

"What does that mean?"

"It means we don't have much food right now, so we have to be thankful for what we do have."

"I still don't like it."

Naomi said, "Another truck went by while you were sleeping."

"Was the light on in here?"

"No, Mom heard the engine coming in time to blow it out."

Jack finished off the bowl of rice and tomatoes. He was still hungry, figured everyone else was too. His head still pounded from caffeine deprivation.

"Can I have some water?" he asked.

Dee handed him a jug from the floorboard at her feet. He unscrewed the cap, tilted it back.

— · — —

They put Naomi and Cole to bed and went across the stream together and out into the meadow. The sky had cleared. Stars shone like flecks of ice and the serrated ridge of a distant peak glowed brighter and brighter as the moon came up behind it.

Dee said, "What's our plan, Jack?"

He looked at her. "Right now, I'm just grateful to be alive."

"But where are we going? How will we stay alive?"

They walked into the road, and it suddenly dawned on Jack what they'd done.

"Shit." He pointed at the meadow where their footprints led back into the trees, advertising the location of their camp.

Dee pushed him hard enough to make him stumble back. "Tell me how we're going to survive this, because I don't see it. It was pure luck we weren't all murdered today."

"I don't know, Dee. I couldn't start a fucking fire with matches and tissue paper this afternoon." As she stared at him, the moonrise lit her face. He said, "I just know we can't stay here after tonight. That's all I know right now."

"Because of food."

"Food and cold."

"That's not good enough."

"Then what are your brilliant ideas? What else do you want from me?"

"I want you to be a fucking man. Do what you *don't* do at home. Take care of your family. Be there. Physically. Emotionally—"

"I'm trying."

"I know. I know you are. I'm sorry." She sounded on the verge of tears. "I just can't believe this is happening."

— — —

Cole woke up crying in the night. Jack unzipped his sleeping bag, let the boy crawl inside with him.

"What's wrong, buddy?" he whispered.

"I had the dream."

"You're okay. It wasn't real."

"It felt real."

"You want to tell me about it? Sometimes, when you talk about them, nightmares don't seem so scary."

"You'll be mad at me."

"Why in the world would I be mad at you?"

"You told me not to look."

"Did you dream about those people we saw in the street today?" He felt Cole's head nodding.

"You said you wouldn't comfort me if I looked."

"I shouldn't have said that."

He wrapped his arms around his little boy. "You feel that?"

"Yes."

"I will always comfort you, Cole."

"Can I stay in your sleeping bag?"

"You promise to go right back to sleep?"

"I promise."

"Try not to think about all the bad stuff, all right? Think about a happy time."

"Like what?"

"I don't know. When's the last time you were really happy?"

The boy was quiet for a moment.

"When we went to see Grandpa."

"Last summer?"

"Yeah, and he let me run through the sprinkler."

"Then think about that, okay?"

"Okay."

Jack held his son as the pleasing weight of sleep settled back over him, and he was just beginning to dream again when Cole whispered something.

"What'd you say, buddy?"

The boy turned over, put his mouth to Jack's right ear. "I have to tell you something else."

"What?"

"I know why the bad people are doing it."

"Cole, quit thinking about that stuff. Good thoughts, remember?"

"Okay."

Jack closed his eyes.

Opened them again.

"Why, Cole?"

"What?"

"Why do you think the bad people are doing it?"

"'Cause of the lights."

"The lights?"

"Yeah."

"What lights? What are you talking about?"

"You know."

"Cole, I don't."

"The ones I saw the night I stayed at Alex's house, and we went outside real late with everyone."

Something like an electrical impulse shuddered through him. Jack shut his eyes and held his palm to the shallow concavity of his son's chest.

THEY slept long into the following day. Slept like people with no good reason to wake. As if the world to which they went to bed might become reconciled to itself, if they could only sleep a bit longer.

When Jack drove back across the stream, the water came halfway up the tires. It was early afternoon, and except for where the trees threw shade, the snow had disappeared from the meadow and the ground was supple. They turned onto the road and descended. It was muddy and crisscrossed with rivulets of water in the sunlight. Still snow-packed in the trees. They came down out of the snow and the pure stands of spruce into aspen.

In the late afternoon, the road widened and became smoother and ran along the shore of a large mountain lake. Up ahead, Jack spotted a car on the side of the road—a luxury SUV with all four doors flung open.

He sped past at fifty miles per hour.

A fleeting glimpse of—

Parents.

The man's head crushed in.

The woman naked, her thighs red.

Three children, all facedown, unmoving in the grass.

Jack glanced in the rearview mirror. Naomi and Cole hadn't noticed. He looked over at Dee—she dozed against the plastic window.

The road went to pavement at dusk. They entered a mountain hamlet. Everything had been burned, the streets lined with the charred skeletons of houses and cars and gift shops, Jack thinking it must have been razed several days ago because nothing smoked, and the air that streamed through the vents smelled like old, wet ash. His family slept. There was a field in the center of town near the school, browned and overgrown, with rusted, netless soccer goals at each end. Jack thought it was a mound of tires someone had torched in the middle of that field, until he saw a single black arm sticking up from the top of the heap.

They stabbed north into the night up a twisting, two-lane highway through the foothills of the San Juans, and they did not pass another car.

Jack pulled off the road into a picnic area beside a reservoir. They popped the back hatch of the Rover, and Dee fired up the propane-fueled camp stove and cooked a pot of chicken-noodle soup from two old cans. They sat near the shore watching the moonrise and passing the steaming pot between them. After a night in the mountains, it felt almost warm.

"I like this better than the tomatoes and rice," Cole said. "I could eat this every day."

"Careful what you wish for," Dee said.

Jack waved off his turn with the pot and stood. He walked down to the edge and dipped his fingers in the water.

"Cold, Dad?" Naomi asked.

"Not too bad actually."

"Why don't you go for a swim then?"

He glanced back, grinning. "Why don't you?"

She shook her head.

He cupped a handful and tossed it back at his daughter, the water like falling glass where the moonlight struck it.

Her screams echoed off the hills across the reservoir.

— — —

They drove west along the water.

"Where are we stopping tonight?" Dee asked.

"I wasn't planning to. I'm not tired, and I think it might be safer to travel at night."

"Look at you," she said.

"What?"

"Making a plan."

It was noisy in the car, the plastic windows flapping. In the backseat, Naomi slept and Cole played with a pair of Hot Wheels, racing them up the back of Jack's seat.

Jack said, "I was studying the road map you picked up in Silverton. I think we should head into northwest Colorado. It's a sparsely populated, middle-of-nowhere type of place. What do you think?"

"Okay. And then where?"

"Day at a time for now."

The road traversed a dam and climbed. They followed the rim of a deep canyon. Deer everywhere, Jack stopping frequently to let them cross the road.

He pulled over after a while, and the slowing of the car roused Dee from sleep.

"What's wrong?"

"Nothing. I have to pee."

He left the car running and got out and walked to the overlook. Stood pissing between the slats of a wooden fence, looking out across the canyon, which by his reckoning couldn't have spanned more than a couple thousand feet. Down in the black bottom of the gorge, invisible in shadow, he could hear a river rushing.

The road turned north away from the canyon. They rode through dark country, no points of house light anywhere, but the moon bright enough on the pavement for Jack to drive the long, open stretches without headlights. He watched the fuel gauge falling toward a quarter of a tank and thought about the phantom cries of that baby he'd heard the day before, wondering—if they were real—what had become of it.

Late in the night, Jack reached over and patted Dee's leg. She stirred from sleep, sat up, rubbed her eyes. He said nothing, not wanting to wake the kids, but he pointed through the windshield.

City lights in the distance.

Dee leaned over and whispered into his ear, her breath soured from sleep, "Can't we just go around?"

He shook his head.

"Why?"

"We're on fumes."

"We have ten gallons in the back."

"That's for emergencies."

"Jack, it's an emergency right now. Our life has become a fucking emergency."

The town was empty, but then it was almost three in the morning. The air that poured through the vents bore no trace of smoke and the houses seemed untouched, if vacant, a few even boasting porchlights.

At the intersection of highways, Jack pulled into a filling station. He stepped out and swiped his credit card and stood waiting for the machine to authorize the purchase.

The night air was pleasant at this lower elevation. While the super unleaded gasoline flowed into the tank, he went across the oil-stained concrete into the convenience store.

The lights were on. The empty coolers along the back wall hummed in the silence. He perused the four aisles, all heavily grazed, and emerged with a package of sunflower seeds and another quart of motor oil. The pump had gone quiet, the ticker frozen at a hair past eleven gallons. He squeezed the handle, but the lever was still depressed. The tank had run dry.

With the hearing in his left ear still impaired, it took him a few seconds to get a fix on the sound. A mote of light tore up the highway toward the filling station, accompanied by the watery growl of a V-twin, two pairs of headlights in tow a quarter mile back, and Dee already shouting inside the car as he yanked out the nozzle.

Dee had his door open and he jumped in, pressed the engine-start button.

Naomi sat up, blinking against the overhead dome light. "What's going on?"

The cycle roared up on them. He went straight at the black-and-chrome Harley, the rider cranking back on the throttle to avoid a collision, the bike popping up on one wheel as it surged out of the way.

Jack turned out into the highway, back tires dragging across the pavement as he straightened their bearing.

"Get the shotgun, Dee."

"Where is it?"

"Behind the backpacks."

She unbuckled her seatbelt and crawled over the console into the backseat.

"Mama?"

"Everything's okay, Cole. I just need to get something. Go back to sleep."

Jack forced the gas pedal to the floorboard. Above the din of engine noise and the plastic windows flapping like they might rip off, Jack registered the vibration of the cycle in his gut.

"Hurry, Dee."

"I'm trying. It's wedged under your pack."

He looked in the rearview mirror, saw darkness specked with the diminishing lights of town.

Punched off the headlights.

The pavement was silver under the moon and glowing just enough for him to stay between the white shoulder lines. As the speedometer crept past 110 mph, the entire car vibrated through the steering wheel.

Dee crawled back into her seat.

"Jesus, Jack, how fast are we going?"

"You don't want to know."

A piece of fire bloomed and faded in the side mirror, and the square of glass exploded.

"Get down!"

The gunshot was lost to the flapping windows, but the V-twin wasn't.

"Give me the gun." Dee hoisted it up from the floorboard, barrel first. "I need you to steer."

The cycle screamed just a few feet behind their bumper, only visible where its chrome caught glimmers of moonlight.

His foot still on the gas, Jack turned, vertebrae cracking, and aimed through the back hatch. He pulled the trigger. Nothing happened. Pumped the twelve-gauge, squeezed again. The thunder of its report sent a spike through his left eardrum and filled the Rover with the blinding, split-second brilliance of a muzzle flash. Through the shredded plastic of the back hatch, the cycle had disappeared.

Bullets pierced the left side of the Rover, glass spraying the backseat.

Jack spun into the driver seat, his right ear ringing.

He took control of the steering wheel, eased off the gas.

The cycle shot forward.

Its taillight blipped and vanished.

Cole screaming in the backseat.

"Naomi, is he hurt?"

"No."

"You sure?"

"He's just scared."

"Are you hurt?"

"No."

"Help him."

"Where's the motorcycle, Jack?"

"I don't see it. Steer again."

She grabbed the wheel and Jack pumped the shotgun. "I still can't hear too well," he said. "You have to tell me when you—"

"I hear it now."

He strained to listen, couldn't see for shit through the plastic window, but he did hear the cycle's engine, the throttle winding up, and then the guttural scream was practically inside the car.

"Hold on and stay down!"

He turned back into the driver seat, clutched the wheel, hit the brake pedal.

Something slammed into the back of the Rover, the sickening clatter of metal striking metal, Jack punching on the headlights just in time to see the cycle turning end over end as it somersaulted off the road into darkness, throwing sparks every time the metal met the pavement.

Thirty yards ahead, the rider had been deposited on the double yellow. The man sat dazed and staring at his left arm, which dangled fingerless and unhinged from his elbow, his unhelmeted head scalped to the bone.

Jack struck the man at 55 mph.

The Rover shook violently for several seconds, as if running a succession of speed bumps, and then the pavement flowed smoothly under the tires again.

He killed the lights and pushed the Rover past a hundred,

watching Dee's side mirror for tailing cars. When the road made a sharp turn, he slowed and eased off the shoulder down a gentle embankment.

He turned off the car.

Cole wept hysterically.

"It's okay, buddy," Jack said. "We're all right now."

"I want to go home."

Dee climbed into the back and swept the broken glass off the leather seat and took Cole up into her arms.

"I know," she whispered. "I want to go home too, but we can't just yet."

"Why?"

"Because it's not safe."

Jack glanced back and, before the overhead light cut out, saw Naomi's chin quivering too.

He opened his door, said, "I'll be right back."

He crawled through weeds up the embankment and lay on his stomach at the shoulder's edge, his heart beating against the ground, listening.

He could still hear Cole crying and Dee hushing him like she had when he was a baby. His hands shook. He was cold. The highway silent.

They came so suddenly he didn't have time to roll back down the hill—two cars tearing around the corner with no headlights and tires squealing, one of them passing within a foot of his head.

They raced on into darkness, invisible, the groan of their engines slowly fading.

Jack had dust in his eyes and grit between his teeth and the odor of burnt rubber was everywhere.

AT dawn, they entered the largest city they'd seen since Albuquerque. The lights were still on. Gas stations beckoned. They undercut an empty interstate and soon the city dwindled away behind them, Jack watching the image of it shrink in the only reflection left—the cracked side mirror on Dee's door.

– – –

They crested a low pass.

A small weather station stood beside the road.

Fragile light on this minor range of green foothills.

That city thirty miles back and to the south, its lights still glittering on the desert. A distant range to the west and Jack beyond exhaustion, shoulder aching from the twelve-gauge kick, his children awake, staring into the plastic of their respective windows. Catatonic.

Dee snoring softly.

– – –

They rode down from the pass and out of the pines into empty, arid country. As the sun edged up on the world, Jack saw a building in the distance. He took his foot off the accelerator.

The motel had been long abandoned, its name bleached out of the thirty-foot billboard that stood teetering beside the road. Dee stirred and sat up as Jack veered off the highway onto the fractured pavement.

"Why are we stopping?"

"I have to sleep."

"Want me to drive some?"

"No. Let's stay off the road today."

He pulled around to the back of the building, where their car wouldn't be seen from the road. Killed the engine.

Sudden stillness.

The cathedral quiet of the high desert.

Jack looked at the gas gauge—between a quarter and a half. He studied the odometer, said, "Five hundred fifty-two miles."

"What are you talking about?"

"That's how far we've come from home."

The room had two double beds. A dresser. An old television with a busted screen. Graffitied walls. Tied-off and shriveled condoms on the carpet and a bathtub full of shattered beer bottles. Jack carefully peeled back the rotting covers so as not to disturb the dust, and they laid their sleeping bags on the old sheets—Jack and Cole on one bed, Dee and Naomi on the other—and fell asleep as the sun climbed.

Jack sat up suddenly. His wife stood over him. Dust trembling off the ceiling. A glass ashtray rattling across the bedside table.

"Something's happening," she said.

They parted the curtains and climbed over the rusted AC wall unit through the open window frame. Noonday light beat down on the desert, and the ground was vibrating beneath their feet, the inconceivable noise shaking jags of glass out of other windows, doors quivering in their frames. They walked over to the motel office and Jack ventured a glance around the corner of the building.

On the road, a convoy was rolling by—SUVs, sedans, beater trucks with armed men riding in the beds, Jeeps, fuel trucks, school buses, a flatbed with a dozen hollow-eyed people crammed into a metal cage, all moving at a modest speed and raising a substantial cloud of dust in the wake of their collective passing.

Jack turned to Dee, said into her ear, "They can't see our car from the road."

Another five minutes crept by, Jack and Dee standing against the crumbling concrete of the motel until the last car in the convoy had passed, the drone of several hundred engines fading more slowly than Jack would have thought.

Dee said, "What if we'd been traveling south on this road?"

"We'd have seen them from miles away."

"With the binoculars."

"Yeah."

"What if the kids and I were sleeping and you weren't—"

"Don't do this, Dee. They didn't see us. We weren't on the road."

"But we could've been." She bit her bottom lip and stared east toward a range of low brown hills. "We have to be more careful," she said. "We have to always be thinking the worst. I can't watch my children—"

"Stop. Nothing bad happened."

Dee peered around the corner.

"Still see them?" Jack asked.

"Yeah. Sun's reflecting off all that chrome."

Jack couldn't hear the engines anymore.

"They're getting organized," Dee said.

– – –

Naomi and Cole slept in the motel room. Jack and Dee sat outside on the concrete walkway, watching the light slant across the desert.

Dee held her phone in her hand. "Still no signal."

"Who are you trying to call?"

"My sister."

She started to cry, and he didn't know what to say, so he just put his arm around her for the first time in months, thinking now about the last time he'd spoken to his father.

It had been a week ago. Sunday morning on the telephone. Sitting on the screened back porch and watching the lawn sprinklers water the fescue. They'd talked about the coming election and a movie they'd both seen and the World Series. When the time had come to hang up, he'd said, "I'll talk to you next weekend, Pop," and his father had said, "Well, all right then. You take care, son."

Same way they always ended their phone calls. What killed him was that it hadn't, in any way, felt like the last time they would ever speak.

— — —

They changed out of their three-day-old clothes, and Dee lit the camp stove and brought the last two cans of old vegetable soup to a simmer. Sat in the darkening motel room, passing around the cooling pot and their last jug of water.

— — —

At dusk, Jack stood in the middle of the road with the binoculars, glassing the high desert.

South: nothing.

North: no movement save a handful of pump jacks that dotted the landscape and ominous lines of black smoke ascending out of the far horizon.

He turned at the sound of approaching footfalls. Naomi stepped into the road and pushed her chin-length yellow hair out of her face. The dark eyeliner she always wore had faded, she'd taken the silver studs out of her ears, and he thought how she looked like his little girl again yet older, her features sharpening into the Germanic, Midwestern prettiness of her mother. He couldn't remember the last time she'd let him hold her or, if he was honest, the last time he'd wanted to. He'd lost sight of his daughter amid the teenage angst, and he saw, not for the first time, but for the first time with clarity, how in the last few years he'd become a stranger to the two most important women in his life.

"What are you doing?" Naomi asked.

"Just having a look around."

She stood beside him, kicking the soles of her black Chuck Taylors across the pavement.

"What do you think about all this?" he asked.

She shrugged.

"Worried about your friends?"

"Yeah. You think Grandpa's okay?"

"I hope so. No way to really know." He wanted to put his arm around her. Restrained himself. "I'm really proud of how you're taking care of your brother, Nay. As proud as I've ever been of you. Your being brave is helping Cole to be brave."

She nodded, and he could see tears shivering in her eyes. He drew her suddenly into him and she wrapped her arms around his waist and cried into his chest.

— — —

With the Rover packed, they climbed in and took their seats and Jack started the engine. The desert deepening from blue into purple as they pulled out of the motel parking lot and onto the highway. Stars fading in and the moon rising over the hills.

They went north without headlights and, within a half hour, had come upon a town. Everywhere—houses burned and the dead in the road and the side streets and front yards.

Jack made himself stop counting.

"Don't look out the windows," he warned, and this time his children listened.

The town had lost power.

Jack punched on the headlights so he could see.

Smoke streamed through the light beams and filled the car.

The highway became Main Street. They passed between old buildings and a couple of restaurants and a dark marquee advertising two movies.

A few blocks past the downtown, he turned off the highway into the parking lot of a grocery store and stopped the Rover in the fire lane by the entrance.

"Jack, please, let's just get the hell out of here."

"We're out of food. Almost out of water. I have to look."

He turned off the car and reached under his seat for the Glock. "Dee, you have the flashlight?"

She handed it to him.

"Don't leave, Daddy."

"I'll be right back, buddy." He touched Dee's leg. "Anything happens, you lay on this horn and I'll be here in five seconds."

===

The automatic doors stood a foot apart. He squeezed through, hesitating. Every part of him protesting against this. He flicked on the Maglite and made himself go on, thinking how it didn't smell anything like a grocery store should. A tinge of rust and rot in the air. He dislodged a cart from the brood of buggies and set the gun in the child's seat. Started forward, the wheels rattling, one squeaking, his light playing off the registers. He passed through the self-checkout aisle. No sound but the distant voltage in his left ear that still hummed like a substation.

He pushed the buggy toward produce. The shelves bare but still carrying the smell of vegetables and fruit. Ten feet ahead, a man lay beside empty wooden crates. The blood around him shimmering off the linoleum like black ice under the light. Jack stopped the cart. There were others behind this man, and though he wouldn't put his light directly on them, he stared at what the shadows didn't hide. The closest: a woman facing him with her eyes still open and her long, yellow hair matted to the gore that had been bludgeoned out of her head.

He picked a cluster of overripe bananas off the floor, the only offering of produce, and pushed the cart between the dead. The wheels went quiet, greased with blood. Dark shoeprints tracked through double doors into the back of the store. He took the gun and left the cart and pushed through them, swinging his light across pallets of stock that had already been scavenged of anything resembling food. He shined the light on the concrete floor and followed the bloody tracks to where they ended. There were over a hundred brass casings and spent shotgun shells in the vicinity of the freezer's big silver door. Massive quantities of blood had leaked out from underneath it. He started to pull it open. Stopped himself.

He walked back into the store. The rear of the supermarket stank of spoiled meat. As he rounded a corner into the first aisle, the cart bumped into a young child who had been hacked to pieces, a single neck tendon shy of a full decapitation. Jack turned and vomited into a naked shelf. Stood retching and spitting until his mouth quit watering. He'd seen a few frames of horror since Thursday night, but nothing like this. He tried to shove it into the back of his unconscious, but its shape wouldn't fit anywhere. Beyond all comprehension.

He went on, searching the shelves for anything, finding nothing but a gallon of water and more bodies to steer around. Rolled past empty glass cases that had held frozen meals and then turned into the last aisle of the store, the beam of his Maglite illuminating someone sitting up against a shelf lined with cartons of room-temperature milk. The teenage boy's eyes opened, milky and failing to dilate at the onslaught of light. He was holding his belly as if trying to keep something in.

Jack left the cart and walked over to the boundary of where the blood had pooled. He squatted down. The boy's respirations coming labored and sodden. He ran his tongue across his dried and cracking lips and said, "Water."

Jack went to the buggy and rolled it back over and set the flashlight beside the gun. He broke the seal and twisted off the cap, held the mouth of the jug to the boy's lips. He drank. A skinny, long-legged kid. Black denim jeans and a western shirt. He turned away from the water and drew a breath.

"You got to take me to Junction. I ain't going to make it through tonight." The boy looked off into the darkness. "Where's Mama?"

"I don't know."

Jack got up.

"Where you going?"

"My family's waiting outside."

"Don't leave me, mister."

"I'm sorry. There's nothing I can do for you."

"You got a gun?"

"What?"

"A gun."

"Yeah."

"You can shoot me."

"No, I couldn't."

"I can't just sit here in the dark. Please. Shoot me in the head. You can do that for me. I'd be in your debt. You got no concept how this hurts."

Jack lifted the jug of water.

"Don't leave me, mister."

He took the gun from the cart and jammed it down the back of his waistband. Tucked the bananas under his right arm and grabbed the flashlight and started walking up the aisle toward the front of the store.

"You son of a bitch," the boy called after him, his voice full of tears.

— — —

They stopped at a filling station on the outskirts, but the pumps had run dry. Jack checked the oil and washed the dirty windshield and they headed north out of town into the high desert. The night clear and cold and nothing else on the road save the occasional mule deer. They ate the bananas—too soft and reeking of that over-sweet candy stench of fruit that has just begun to turn. Jack let them split his share. The two hamlets they passed through barely warranted the black specks they'd been assigned on the map—tiny ranching communities, burned and vacated. The most substantive structure for miles was a grain mill, looming above the desert like some improbable skyline.

— — —

Jack pulled onto the side of the road to let Cole and Naomi have a bathroom break, and when the kids were out of the car, Dee said, "What's wrong?"

He looked at her, glad when the overhead light cut off.

"Nothing. I mean, you know, besides everything."

"What'd you see in that store?"

He shook his head.

"We together in this?"

"Of course. That doesn't mean you need to have me putting things in your head that you can't get rid of." As his eyes readjusted to the darkness, he looked through the windshield at a stretch of hills in the east. Heard a sudden shriek of laughter from Cole that almost made him smile.

Dee said, "Don't push me away. I need to share this experience with you. I want to know what you know, Jack. Every single thing, because there's comfort in it. I need that."

"Not this, you don't."

— — —

Five miles on, Jack pulled off the road again, said, "Give me the binoculars."

"What's wrong, Dad?"

"I saw something."

"What?"

"Lights. Everyone just sit still and don't open your doors."

"Why?"

"Because the interior lights will come on, and I don't want anyone to see where we are."

"What if they see us? What will happen?"

"Nothing good, Cole."

Dee handed him the binoculars and he brought them to his eyes. At first, he saw nothing but black, and he thought maybe the focus had been jarred, but then he picked them up again, stretched along the road like a stateless strand of Christmas lights.

"What is it?" Dee asked.

He moved the knob, pulled everything into focus. "The convoy."

"How far?"

"Maybe ten miles. I think they're moving away from us."

"Are you sure?"

He lowered the binoculars. "Let's wait here awhile. Track their movement. Make absolutely certain."

— — —

Jack glassed the convoy through the windshield, watching its slow progression away from them while the kids played Rock, Paper, Scissors.

Within the hour, the lights had vanished.

— — —

Heat blasted out of the vents to check the frigid air that streamed through rips in the plastic windows, Naomi and Cole bundled in their sleeping bags and huddled miserably together.

Just before midnight, Jack turned off the highway onto a dirt road and punched on the headlights.

They'd gone several miles when Dee leaned across the center

console, then back into her seat, pushing a discreet exhalation through her teeth that no one but her husband would have caught.

"What?"

"You see the light?" she said.

"I see it."

"Do you think there's going to be a gas station out here?" She gestured toward the windshield and the expanse of empty country beyond the glass, devoid of even a spore of man-made light.

"It just came on a minute ago."

"It means we're out of gas, darling-heart."

"No, it means we can still go another twenty or thirty miles. It's called a reserve tank."

He could feel the heat of her stare even in the dark.

She said, "We have ten gallons of gas sloshing around back there, and I don't understand why you won't—"

"Dee, it's—"

"Oh my God, if you say 'emergencies' one more . . ." She turned away from him. Stared into her window of plastic. Jack was on the brink of just pulling over, an act of appeasement he would never have considered under any other circumstance, when the head-lights grazed a dark house.

He turned into the gravel drive and parked beside a powder-blue Chevy pickup truck from another time, headlights firing across a brick ranch with white columns on the porch.

"Let's not stop here, Jack."

"I think we have to take a look."

———

Jack and Dee followed the stone path to the house and stepped onto the front porch and knocked on the door. They waited. Heard nothing on the other side.

"Nobody's home," Jack said.

"Or maybe they saw a man approaching with a shotgun and they're waiting on the other side with a fucking arsenal."

"Always the pessimist."

He knocked again and tried the door.

— — —

Jack pried a piece of sandstone out of the walkway and lobbed it through the dining-room window. They crouched in the bushes and listened. A stalactite of glass fell out of the framing. Silence followed.

"I'll go in," Jack said, "make sure it's safe."

"What if it's not?"

He reached into his pocket, handed her the keys. "Then you get the hell out of here."

— — —

Standing in the dining room, the first thing to strike him was the warmth. He walked into the kitchen. The refrigerator humming. He opened it. Jars of mayonnaise and other store-bought condiments and a mason jar of pickled beets and something wrapped in tin foil. He went to the sink and turned on the tap. Water flowed.

— — —

Dee sat in the Rover in the driver's seat, her hands on the steering wheel. Jack opened the door, said, "It's empty and they have power."

"Food?"

"There's some stuff in the cabinets." He looked into the back-seat. "Nay, Cole, I want you to bring all the empty jugs inside."

— — —

Jack went around to the side of the house. He unsheathed his bowie and sawed off the nozzle to the garden hose. He unwound it and cut a six-foot length of green tubing. The opening to the Chevy's gas tank was next to the driver's-side door, a silver cap speckled with rust that took some hard cranking to unscrew. He'd already poured the five-gallon cans into the Rover, and they sat open on the gravel drive while he threaded the hose through the hole. It touched the bottom of the tank, the smell already wafting out of the end of the tube as he brought it to his lips.

The gas was oily in his mouth—sharp, pungent, and filthy-tasting. He spit it out and jammed the hose into the first gas can, his eyes watering, throat burning from the fumes.

Jack walked past the eight jugs of water lined up on the kitchen island. He leaned down into the sink and held his mouth under the open tap for a long time, but there was no flushing of the gasoline, which lingered in the back of his throat like a persistent fog.

"How'd we do?" Dee asked.

He stood up, lightheaded. "Six gallons."

"You all right?"

"I just need about fifty breath mints."

Naomi said, "Come look what we found, Dad."

He followed them across the wood laminate floor to a sliding-glass door behind the breakfast nook. The vertical blinds had been swept back and he looked through the glass into a square of domes-ticated yard, moonlit and bordered by desert. He saw a dilapidated swing set, a pair of lawn chairs shaded by an umbrella, and closer to the house, a thirty-foot steel antenna mast.

Naomi flipped through channels on a hulking television set that looked like it had occupied the same patch of shag carpeting for thirty years. Every station was drowned in static.

Jack lifted a telephone, held the receiver to his ear. Silence.

They walked down the hallway, the hardwood groaning under their footsteps.

"Can we turn on the lights? I don't like it dark."

"Lights might attract someone, Cole."

"You mean someone bad?"

"Yes."

"Where do you think these people went?" Naomi asked.

"No telling. Probably just left their home like we left ours."

Jack shined his flashlight through the first doorway they passed. A bedroom with two trophy cases and a large photograph above the headboard—a teenage boy riding an enraged bull.

They went on.

Naomi said, "Something smells bad."

Jack stopped. He smelled it too. Sharp enough to overpower the gasoline overload in his nasal cavity.

Dee said, "Kids, let's go back to the kitchen."

Naomi said, "What's wrong?"

"Go with your mother."

"Come on, guys," Dee said. "Jack, be careful."

"Is it—"

"Nay, think about your brother before you say another word."

"What about me?" Cole asked.

"Come on, Cole, let's go with Mom."

Jack watched his family retreating and then turned back toward the closed door at the end of the hall, the smell intensifying with each step. He breathed through his mouth as he turned the door-knob and shined the light inside.

A man and woman lay in bed. White-haired. Seventysomething. Framed photographs of what he presumed were their grown sons rested on their stomachs. The woman had been shot through the forehead, and the man cradled her to himself, a hole in his right temple, his right arm outstretched and hanging off the bed, a re-volver on the floor below his hand. The white comforter darkened with blood.

Above the bed, Jack put his light on a series of fifty-one photo-graphs that, in the low light, looked almost identical. He moved closer. The last photograph of the montage was a recent portrait of the couple on the bed, the man wearing an oversize tuxedo that swallowed him whole, the woman squeezed into a ragged wedding

dress many sizes too small. As Jack ran his light back over the por-
traits, the couple grew younger and their wedding clothes fit better
and their smiles brightened toward something like hope.

— — —

Jack walked into the kitchen, found Dee and Naomi standing
around the island, drinking glasses of ice water. In the living room,
Cole flipped through channels of static on the television.

"Everything all right?" Dee said.

"They weren't murdered."

"Oh."

"Can I see?"

"Why would you want to, Nay?"

She shrugged. "You saw it."

"I had to make sure everything was safe for us. I wish I hadn't
seen it."

— — —

Jack found the radio setup in the den—a low-band rig, microphone, headphones, power meter. The room had no windows, so
he turned on the desk lamp and settled into a cracking leather
chair. The amateur radio license hanging on the wall above the
equipment had been issued to Ronald M. Schirard, call sign
KE5UTN.

"What's all this stuff?" Naomi said.

"It's a ham radio."

"What's it do?"

"Lets you talk to people all over the world."

"Isn't that what cellphones are for?"

Dee said, "You know how to use this?"

"I had a friend in high school whose dad was a ham," Jack said.
"We'd sneak down into the basement at night and use his radio. But
this equipment looks way more sophisticated."

He turned on the transceiver and the microphone and put on

the headset. The radio had been tuned to 146.840 MHz, and he didn't tinker with it, just keyed the microphone.

"This is KE5UTN listening on the 146.840 machine."

Thirty seconds of silence.

He restated the call sign and repeater identification, then glanced up at Dee. "This may take some time."

— — —

Dee came back after a half hour and set a cup of coffee on the desk. Jack didn't remove the headphones, just said, "Thanks, but I can't go through caffeine withdrawal again."

"Anything?"

"Not a word."

— — —

An hour later and still no response, Jack finally reached for the dial to change the receiver frequency.

A voice crackled over the airwaves. *"KE5UTN? This is EI1465."* Heavy Irish accent.

Jack keyed the mic. "This is KE5UTN. Who am I speaking with, please?"

"Ron? Thank God, I thought something had happened."

"No, this is Jack."

"Where's Ron Schirard? You're using his call sign."

"I'm in his house, on his station."

"Where's Ron?"

Jack heard the door open behind him. Glanced back, saw Dee walk in. He said, "You a friend of Ron's?"

"Never met him, but we've been talking on the radio going on nine years."

Jack hesitated.

"Jack? Is my modulation off?"

"I'm sorry to have to tell you this, but Ron and his wife are dead. Where are you, if I may ask?"

The silence in the headphones went on for a long while. The voice finally returned much softer.

"Belfast. What are you doing in Ron's house?"

"We fled our home in Albuquerque, New Mexico, three days ago, and just stopped here to look for food and water. Cellphones don't work. Or landlines. There's no internet. Do you have any information about what's happening? Has it spread worldwide?"

"No, it's only the lower forty-eight of America and northern Mexico. There aren't too many reports coming out of the affected region, but you've heard about New England?"

"We've heard nothing."

"Boston and New York have been devastated. Total chaos. Astronomical death tolls. There's a handful of videos circulating—movies shot on mobile phones. Streets clogged with bodies. People trying to get out of the cities. Real doomsday stuff. Are you and your family okay?"

"We're alive."

"You're lucky to be in a low-population-density area."

Jack glanced up at Dee, said to her, "You should be keeping a lookout in case someone comes."

"Naomi's on the front porch, watching the road."

Jack keyed the mic. "Has anyone figured out what's causing this?"

"There's been a lot of crazy theories, but over the last day or so, everyone's been focusing on this atmospheric phenomenon that happened over America about a month ago."

"The aurora?"

"Exactly. The talking heads have been blathering on about mass extinctions, that this is what wiped out the dinosaurs. Maybe it triggered a latent genetic defect in a percentage of the population. Mind you, I'm just regurgitating what I've heard on the telly. They're probably full of shite."

"Has everyone who witnessed the aurora become affected?"

"I don't know. Did you see it?"

"No. My family . . . we slept through it."

"Lucky for you, I guess."

"Do you know where the closest safe zone might be?"

"Southern Canada. They're setting up refugee camps there. How far away are you?"

Jack felt something in him deflate. "Almost a thousand miles. Anything else you can tell me about what's going on? We're blind here."

"Nothing that would cheer you up."

"I don't think I got your name."

"Paul Hewson."

"I'm sorry about your friend, Paul."

"Me too. How many souls in your family, Jack?"

"Four. I have a son and a daughter."

"When I go to mass tonight, I'll light a candle for each of you. I know it isn't much, but . . . maybe it is."

Jack opened the door and walked out onto the front porch. Naomi sat on the steps, and he eased down beside her. The night was cold. A lonely cricket chirping out in the yard and not another sound on the high desert. Not even wind.

"Mom told me we have to leave."

"Yeah. I just don't think we're safe here. This house is the only—"

"No, it's fine. I don't want to sleep in a house with dead people in it."

"Well, there's that."

"I went and looked at them."

"Why?"

She shrugged. "Why'd they do that, you think? 'Cause of what's happening?"

"Probably."

"That's weak."

"The Schirards had put together a good life for themselves, Nay. Been married a lot of years. They were old. Not capable of running. I'm not sure I'd call what they did weak."

"Would you do it?"

"Of course not. I have you and Cole and—"

"But if something happened to us and it was just you? Or just you and Mom?"

He stared at his daughter in the darkness. "That isn't something I ever want to think about."

Dee and the kids loaded water jugs into the Land Rover, and Jack poured the six gallons he'd siphoned out of the Chevy into their gas tank. They were under way a little after three in the morning. Traveling north with the high beams blazing like flamethrowers to ward off the riot of deer and antelope that continually shot across the road. It hadn't rained here in weeks, possibly a month, and their passage raised a trail of moonlit dust that never quite seemed to settle.

They climbed a series of plateaus and crossed into Wyoming at 4 A.M. The road went back to pavement and Dee cracked open the pickled beets, fed one to Jack, then handed the glass jar into the backseat.

"What is it?" Naomi asked.

"Beets. Try one."

She sniffed the open jar and winced. "That's disgusting, Mom."

"Aren't you hungry?"

"Yeah, but that's like, haven't-eaten-in-a-week, on-the-verge-of-death food."

"Cole?"

"He's asleep."

Jack kept watching the eastern sky, and when he saw the first hint of light, his stomach released a shimmer of heat.

Dee must have noticed, too, because she said, "Where are we going to stop?"

"Other side of Rock Springs."

"We have to go through another city?"

"Last one for a long time." Jack glanced into the backseat, said, "Look." Cole had slumped over into Naomi's lap, and his sister leaned against the door, also asleep, her fingers tangled up in his hair.

A tremor shook the Rover.

Jack studied the dash.

"We're losing oil," he said. "Engine's running hot."

"How many quarts do we have?"

"Two, but I don't want to use them yet."

"Right. Emergencies and such."

Dawn crept over a bleak waste of country. They could see for seventy miles to the east—a treeless, waterless, uninhabitable piece of ground.

Jack punched off the headlights.

THEY rolled into Rock Springs. The city had lost power. Streets empty. No one out. Jack eased to a stop at a vacant intersection, purely out of habit, and stared for a moment at the dark traffic signals. He lowered his window, listened to the harsh idle of the V8. Killed the engine.

Silence flooded in, and not just the dawn-quiet of a waking town.

"Everyone left," he said.

Across the street, the automated doors of a City Market grocery store had been leveled, like a truck had driven through them. Jack opened his door, stepped down onto the road, dropped to his knees, and stared up into the Rover's undercarriage.

Nothing to see in the poor light but a tiny pond of oil on the asphalt whose reflection of the morning sky trembled with each new drop.

= = =

The highway north out of Rock Springs was a straight shot into high desert. There were mountains to the northeast that after sev-

enty miles became mountains to the east. The sun appeared behind them and made the quartz in the pavement glimmer.

"We should find a place to stop," Dee said. "It's almost seven."

"Minute you see a tree, speak up."

They drove on, Jack thinking this was such a quintessential
highway of the American West. Long vistas. Emptiness. Desert in
the foreground, mountains beyond. Both sagebrush and snow
within eyeshot.

When Dee drew a sudden breath, Jack felt his stomach fall, on
the verge of asking for the binoculars, but he didn't even need them
now as the sun cleared that thirteen-thousand-foot wall of granite
twenty miles to the east and struck the oncoming procession of
chrome and glass.

Dee took the binoculars out of the glove box and glassed the
desert.

"How far?"

"Five, ten miles, I don't know."

Jack stepped on the brake, brought the Rover almost to a stop,
and veered off the highway into the desert.

"What are you doing, Jack?"

"Heading for that."

Several miles to the east, a butte rose two hundred feet above
the desert floor.

"Are you crazy?"

"We have less than a quarter of a tank. We'd never make it back
to Rock Springs on that."

"So you're going to hide us behind that butte."

"Exactly."

"Then go faster."

"Any faster, we'll raise a trail of dust they can follow."

Naomi lifted her head off the door. "Why's it so bumpy?"

"We're taking a detour," Jack said.

"Why?"

"Cars up ahead." Jack swerved to miss a sagebrush. "We making
a dust cloud?"

Dee opened her door, leaned out, glanced back. "Little one."

The butte grew bigger in the windshield—sunburnt strata of rock that rose to a flat-topped summit. The desert running like warped and shattered concrete under the tires and shaking the Rover all to hell.

"We're running really hot," Jack said. He kept searching for the road in his side mirror, kept forgetting the mirror had been shot out two nights ago.

"Where are the cars?" Naomi asked.

"We can't see them from here," Dee said. "Hopefully, they can't see us."

They rode into the shadow of the butte, Jack skirting the base until they reached the back side, the rock fired into pink by the early sun.

He slammed the Rover into park, turned off the engine.

"Binoculars."

Dee handed them over and he threw open the door and hopped down onto the hardpan. Ran up the lower slope of the butte, his quads burning after ten steps, perspiration beading on his forehead after twenty.

Where the slope went vertical for the last fifty feet, he traversed the edge of the cliff band and had just caught his breath when the highway came into view.

His knees hit the dirt. Jack lowered himself and propped his elbows on the ground, still cold from the previous night. Brought the binoculars to his eyes, pulled the highway into focus, and slowly traced it north.

Footfalls behind him.

He inhaled a severely faded waft of Dee's shampoo as she collapsed panting in the dirt beside him.

"You see them?" she asked.

He did. An eighteen-wheeler led the convoy, puffing gouts of black smoke into the air and followed by a train of cars and trucks that might have been a mile long. Five hundred engines sounded otherworldly carrying across the desert.

"Jack?"

"Yes, I see them."

"What about our trail?"

He lowered the binoculars and looked to where he thought they'd cut across the desert and lifted them to his eyes again. First thing he fixed upon were a pair of antelope standing motionless with their heads raised, staring toward the noise of what was coming.

He adjusted the focus knob, spotted their tire tracks.

"I see our path. I don't see any dust."

The convoy had begun to pass the point on the highway where they'd turned off.

Jack said, "They're not stopping."

He lowered the binoculars.

"What do we do when the gas runs out?" Dee asked.

"We can't let that happen."

"You said there aren't any other cities for a—"

"We'll have to get lucky."

"What if we don't get—"

"Dee. What do you want me to say? I can't predict what's going to—"

"Look." She grabbed the binoculars from him and turned his head toward the ribbon of dust that was unspooling across the desert behind two trucks.

Jack descended the butte at a full sprint, Dee calling after him, but he didn't stop until he reached the Rover.

Popped the cargo hatch, grabbed the shotgun, felt confident he'd replaced the spent shell yesterday afternoon at the motel. Wondered if that meant he had eight rounds, though he couldn't be sure.

"Dad?" Naomi said.

"Cole awake?"

"No."

"Wake him."

"Are people coming?"

"Yes."

Dee arrived breathless as he opened his door and took the Glock from underneath the driver's seat and a handful of twelve-gauge shells from the center console.

"Jack, let's just get in the car and go. Make them catch us."

He jammed the shells into his pocket.

Cole said, "I'm hungry."

Jack thinking this was one of those choices where, if you took the wrong road, there'd be no chance to undo it. They'd be dead. His son, his daughter, his wife, and him too if he was so lucky at that point.

"Jack."

He looked over Dee's head to where the desert sloped up to the base of the butte.

"Naomi, you see that large boulder fifty yards up the hill?"

"Where?"

Jack punched through the plastic window and tore it off the door. "There."

"Jack, no."

"Take your brother up there and hide behind the rock. No matter what happens, what you see or hear, don't move, don't make a sound, until we come get you."

"What if you don't?"

"We will."

"I'm hungry," Cole cried, eyes still half-closed, not fully awake.

"Go with your sister, buddy. We'll eat something later."

"No, now."

"Get him up that hill, Nay, and keep him with you."

He faced Dee, her eyes welling.

"You sure about this, Jack?"

"Yes." What a lie.

Naomi dragged Cole out of the car, but the boy fell crying to the ground, and he wouldn't get up.

Jack squatted down in the dirt.

"Look at me, son." He held the boy's face in his hands.

"I'm hungry!"

He slapped Cole.

The boy went clear-eyed and hushed, staring at his father, tears running down his face.

"Go with your sister right now, or you're going to get us all fucking killed!" He'd never sworn at his son, never laid a hand on him before.

Cole nodded.

Naomi helped her brother to his feet and Jack watched as they jogged up the slope together, hand in hand. Jack looked at Dee. "Let's go."

They ran south for sixty or seventy yards, and then Jack pulled Dee behind a piece of rock the size of a minivan that had calved off from the butte in another epoch.

Already Jack could hear the growl of an approaching engine.

Dee visibly trembling.

A Jeep appeared around the corner of the butte, kicking streamers of dust in its wake as the driver downshifted.

"Where's the other truck?" Dee asked.

He glanced back toward the Rover, didn't see it coming, but the Jeep was rolling toward them on a trajectory that would bring it within twenty or thirty feet of the boulder.

He stood, handed her the Glock. "Don't move from this spot."

Jack pumped the shotgun and stepped out from behind the boulder and ran.

Three men in the Jeep, and the one in back standing on the seat and holding on to the roll bar and a rifle, his long black hair blowing, and Jack slid to a stop in the dirt and pulled the stock into his shoulder and fired before they ever saw him. The driver started bleeding from holes in his face and the long-haired man fell backward out of the Jeep into a sagebrush. Jack pumped the shotgun and got off another round as the Jeep drew even with him, registered a muzzle flash from the front passenger seat at the same instant the buckshot punched the third man out of the doorless Jeep, which veered sharply away and accelerated into the desert, the driver's head bobbling off the steering wheel.

Dee shouted his name, and as he turned, fire blossomed in his left shoulder, coupled with a wave of nausea. A Ford F-150, beat to hell and coated in dust, rounded the north side of the butte. Jack ran back up the slope to Dee and crouched down beside her.

"How the hell did you just do that?" she asked.

"No idea."

He dug two cartridges out of his pocket and fed them into the magazine tube and jacked a shell into the chamber.

The F-150 skidded to a stop beside the Rover. Two women jumped down out of the bed. Two men climbed out of the cab.

"Take this." He gave her the shotgun and took back the Glock.

"You're bleeding."

"I know, I'm—"

"No, I mean you're *really* bleeding."

"Run like hell toward those mountains. When they follow, lay down in the dirt and let them get close and then open fire. Shoot, pump, shoot. Pump it hard. You won't break it."

"Jack." She was crying now.

"They are going to kill our children."

She stood and started down the slope into the desert.

He looked down at the Glock in his hand. It felt so small and held not a fraction of that devastating twelve-gauge reassurance.

Then he was running across the slope. Couldn't feel his legs or the bullet in his shoulder—nothing but the shudder of his heart banging against his chest plate. He saw Dee being chased by two people into the desert, and a man with a large revolver following a woman uphill toward the boulder where his children hid.

The man stopped and looked at Jack and raised his gun.

Between the two of them, they exchanged a dozen rounds that never came close to hitting anything.

The slide on Jack's Glock locked back, the man struggling to break open the cylinder of his revolver, and the woman had nearly reached the boulder.

She was thirtysomething, blond, and holding an ax under the blade. Naomi and Cole still huddled behind the rock, Jack twenty yards away and moving toward them at a dead run.

Shotgun reports erupted out of the desert.

The woman disappeared behind the far side of the boulder and

Jack screamed at his daughter to run over the roar of another shot-gun blast.

The woman emerged behind his children, hoisting the ax.

Jack crashed into her at full speed, driving her hard into the ground. Grabbed the first decent rock within reach and before he'd even thought about what he was doing, he'd broken the woman's skull with seven crushing blows.

Jack wiped her blood out of his eyes, picked up the Glock, and went to his children.

Naomi was in shock, holding her brother in her arms, shielding him.

The woman twitched in the dirt.

Down on the desert, someone groaned as they dragged them-selves across the ground.

Please. Not Dee.

Jack released the slide and stepped out from behind the boulder with the empty Glock. The man stood ten feet downslope, pushing rounds into the open cylinder of his revolver. When he looked up, his eyes went wide like he'd been caught stealing. Jack trained the Glock on him, a two-handed grip, but he couldn't stop his nerves from making it shake.

The man was roughly the same age as the woman, whom Jack could hear moaning behind the rock. He was sunburned and stink-ing. Lips chapped. Wore filthy hiking shorts and a pale-blue, long-sleeved T-shirt covered in rips and holes and dark sweat- and bloodstains.

"Drop it."

The revolver hit the dirt.

"Move that way," Jack said, directing him uphill, away from the gun. "Now, sit."

The man sat down against the boulder, squinting at the new sun.

"Naomi, you and Cole come here." He glanced over his shoul-der as he said it, glimpsed a small figure moving toward them on the desert.

It was Dee.

In the morning silence, he could still hear that Jeep heading toward the mountains, the noise of its engine on a steady decline.

The man glared at Jack. "Let me help Heather."

Naomi came around the boulder, struggling to carry Cole, who whimpered in his sister's arms.

"Put him in the car, Nay."

"Where's Mom?"

"Right down there."

"I want to see Heather," the man said.

Naomi looked at the man as she moved past. "Why? She's dead. Just like you're going to be."

The man called for her, and when Heather didn't answer, his face broke up and he buried it in the crook of his arm and wept.

Jack's left shoulder had established a pulse of its own. Lightheaded, he eased down onto a rock, keeping the Glock leveled at the man's chest.

"Look at me."

The man wouldn't.

"Look at me or I'll kill you right now."

The man looked up, wiped his face, tears cutting through the film of dirt and dust on his cheeks.

"What's your name?"

"Dave."

"Where you from, Dave?"

"Eden Prairie, Minnesota."

"What do you do for a living?"

It took Dave a moment to answer, as if he were having to sift back through several lifetimes.

"I was a financial advisor for a credit union."

"And this morning, out here in the desert, you were going to kill my children."

"You don't understand."

"You're fucking right I don't understand. But if you explain it to me right now, maybe you won't die."

"Can I see her first?"

"No."

Dave stared at Jack with a look of seething hatred.

"Heather and I came out several weeks ago with our friends on a backpacking trip near Sheridan. Up in the Big Horns. We camped at Solitude Lake. Little knoll a couple hundred feet above the water. Our first night there, we had this crazy supper: pasta, bread, cheese, several bottles of great wine. Smoked a joint before bed and crashed. The lights woke me in the middle of the night. I got Heather up, and we climbed out of our tent to see what was happening. Tried to wake Brad and Jen, but they wouldn't get up. We laid down in the grass, Heather and me, and just watched the sky."

"What did you see?" Jack asked. "That turned you into this?"

The man's eyes filled up. "You ever witnessed pure beauty? I saw perfection for fifty-four minutes, and it changed my life."

"What are you talking about?"

"God."

"You saw God."

"We all did."

"In the lights."

"He is the lights."

"Why do you hate me?"

"Because you didn't."

"Were those your friends in the Jeep?" Jack asked, though he already knew the answer. As Dave shook his head, Jack felt a molten-liquid mass coalescing in the pit of his stomach. "You murdered them."

Dave smiled, a strange and chilling postcard of glee, and he was suddenly on his feet and running, four steps covered before Jack had even thought to react.

The full load of double-aught buckshot slammed into Dave's chest and threw him back to the ground. Dee stood holding the shotgun, still trained on Dave, who was trying to sit up and making loud, gasping croaks like a distressed bird. After a minute, he fell back in the dirt and went into silent shock as he bled out.

Jack struggled onto his feet and walked over to Dee.

"You're hurting," she said.

He nodded as they started back down the slope toward the Rover and the F-150.

"I need to see your shoulder. Do you think the bullet's still in there or—"

"It's in there."

They approached the vehicles.

Dee said, "Wish we could take the truck. At least it has windows."

"We will take its gas."

"You kept the hose from the Schirards' house?"

"Yeah."

In the backseat of the Rover, Naomi cradled her brother in her arms, rocking him and whispering in his ear.

"Get the gas cans out of the back," Jack said.

The F-150 was black and silver under the layers of dust. Jack pulled open the passenger door with his right arm and stepped up into the cab. It smelled of suntan lotion. Trash cluttered the floorboards—empty boxes of ammunition, empty milk jugs, hundreds of brass shell casings.

He tugged the keys out of the ignition.

Back outside, he unlocked the gas cap.

"How much is in there?" Dee asked.

"I didn't look at the gauge." He took the hose from her and worked it through the hole. "Where's the can?"

"Right here."

He could feel a cool trickle meandering down the inner thigh of his left leg, wondered how much blood he'd lost.

"You okay, Jack?"

"Yeah, I just . . . a little lightheaded."

"Let me help with that."

"I've got it. Just unscrew the cap."

"It is."

"Oh."

As Jack brought the hose to his lips, a voice from the truck disrupted the fog in his head.

"Eighty-five, come back."

Jack found the walkie-talkie inside the glove compartment.

"Eighty-five and Eighty-four, we've got Sixty-eight through Seventy-one headed back your way to check on things. If you're already en route, please advise, over."

Jack pressed talk. "We're en route."

Another voice cut in, strained with pain, barely a whisper. *"This is Eighty-four . . . oh, God . . . send help . . . please."*

"I didn't copy that, over."

Jack dropped the radio and climbed out. "That was the driver of the Jeep. We're leaving."

"Without the gas?"

"There isn't time."

He staggered to the Rover, pulled open the door, slid in behind the wheel.

"We need gas, Jack. We're under a quarter of a—"

"They're sending four vehicles. Gas won't help us when we're dead."

She ran back to the Ford and grabbed the tubing and the empty cans, tossed everything into the back of the Rover, and slammed the hatch.

"I'm driving," she said. "You're in no shape."

She had a point—his left shoe was filling up with blood. He crawled into the front passenger seat, and Dee climbed in and shut the door and started the engine.

"Nay, get yourself and Cole buckled in—"

"Just fucking go," Jack said.

They started back across the desert, and Jack leaned against the door and tried to focus on the passing landscape instead of the fire in his shoulder. The pain was becoming unmanageable, sickening. He must have let slip a moan because Naomi said, "Dad?"

"I'm fine, honey."

He closed his eyes. So dizzy. Gone for a while and then Dee's voice pulled him back. He sat up. Microscopic dots pulsating everywhere like black stars.

"Binoculars," she was saying. "Can you look down the highway?"

She'd set them in his lap, and he lifted the binocs to his eyes. Took him a moment to bring the road into focus through the driver's side window.

The glint of sun off the distant windshields was unmistakable.

"They're coming," he said. "Still a ways off. Couple miles, maybe."

The awful jarring of the desert disappeared as Dee turned onto the highway.

"Don't do your safe, gas-mileage conserving acceleration," he said. "Floor it."

The motor sounded harsh and clattery as they sped north, Jack fighting the impulse to lean over and see the fuel gauge since the concept of unnecessary movement ran a bolt of nausea through him.

"What's the gas situation?" he asked.

"Little under a quarter."

"How fast you going?"

"Eighty-five."

Jack opened his eyes and stared through the windshield— empty desert to the west, jagged mountains to the east. He was overcome with the feeling that they'd reached the end of their four days of running. They were going to use up the last of their gas on this highway in the middle of nowhere and then those four trucks would show up and that would be the end of his family. Jack's eyes filled with tears and he turned away from Dee so she wouldn't see.

= = =

The smell of smoke roused Jack off the door.

"Where are we?"

"Pinedale."

The tiny western community had been cremated, its honky-tonk Main Street littered with burned-out trucks and debris from looted stores. Near the center of town, a line of corpses in cowboy hats sat along the sidewalk like gargoyles, charred black and still smoking.

"Reserve light came on a minute ago," Dee said.

"That was bound to happen."

"How you holding up?"

"I'm holding."

"You need to keep pressure on your shoulder, Jack, or it's going to keep bleeding."

They broke out of the smoke and Dee accelerated. The morning sky burned blue overhead, oblivious to all.

Jack straightened and glanced back between the seats—nothing to see through the plastic sheeting that hyperventilated over the back hatch.

He said, "I don't like that we can't see the road behind us. Pull over."

Three miles out of Pinedale, Dee veered onto the shoulder and Jack stumbled out of the Rover. He heard the incoming engines before he'd even raised the binoculars to his face—a dive-bomber wail like they were being pushed to the limits of their performance capabilities.

He jumped back into the front seat, said, "Go," and Dee shifted into drive, hit forty before Jack had managed to shut his door.

"How far?" she asked.

"Not very. Where'd you put the shotgun?"

"Backseat floorboard."

"Hand it up, Nay?"

Jack took the Mossberg from his daughter, had to yell over the straining engine. "How many times did you shoot it, Dee?"

"I don't know. Four or five? I wasn't keeping count."

Jack flipped open the center console, grabbed a few shells, started feeding them in. The pain was brilliant with every twitch of the deltoid in his left shoulder.

"Nay, climb into the back and peek through those holes. See if you can spot whatever's coming."

He reached under his seat and grabbed the map. Opened it across his lap to the Wyoming page and traced their route north out of Rock Springs through Pinedale.

"There's a turnoff coming up. Highway 352. Take it."

"Where's it go?"

"Into the Wind River Mountains. It dead-ends after twenty miles or so."

"I see the trucks!" Naomi shouted.

"How far?"

"I don't know. They're small, but I can see them. Getting closer for sure."

"Why would we take a dead-end road, Jack?"

"Because they can see us and run us down on these long, open stretches. Go faster."

"We're doing ninety."

"Well, do a hundred. If they catch us before the turnoff, it's over."

"I think I see it."

They screamed toward a sign.

"You're about to miss it," Jack said.

She stepped on the brake and took the turn at thirty-five, swinging wide into the oncoming lane, the Rover briefly on two wheels.

"Nice," Jack said.

Through the fist-size hole in his plastic window, he stared back down the highway, saw four vehicles streaking toward them. Inside a half mile, he would've guessed.

"See them?" Dee asked.

"Yeah. Get us up into those mountains as fast as you can."

The road shot through the last bit of desert before the mountains, and Jack could smell the heat of the engine and the sagebrush screaming by.

At a hundred miles per hour, they ripped through a ghost town—three buildings, two of them listing, a derelict post office.

The foothills lifted out of the desert less than a mile away, and already they were climbing.

"How's the fuel gauge, Dee?"

"We're on the empty slash."

The road cut a gentle turn away from the foothills and passed through a grove of cottonwoods. They sped alongside a river and into a canyon, the colder, pine-sweetened air streaming through the plastic windows.

Jack said, "Start looking for a place to pull over."

"Trees are too tight here."

"Naomi, get in the back again. When we make our move, we need to be certain they can't see us."

The sun blinked through the trees in shards of blinding light.

Jack leaned against the door again, felt Dee take hold of his hand.

"Talk to me, Jack."

"I don't feel like talking."

"Because of the pain?"

"Yeah."

"I don't see them yet!" Naomi yelled.

"Cole all right?" he asked.

"Sleeping, if you can believe it."

Into a meadow, the frosted grasses sparkling under the sun, the road straight for a quarter mile.

As they reentered the woods on the other side, Naomi said, "They're just now coming into the meadow."

"How many?"

"Four."

"You feel that, Jack?"

"What?"

"Engine just sputtered."

He struggled to sit up.

Leaned back over.

Vomited into the floorboard.

"Is there blood in it?" Dee asked.

"I don't know."

He sat up, focused on the passing trees instead of the acid burn in the back of his throat.

When they rounded the next hairpin curve, Jack saw a corridor through the pines—not a road or a path, just a little space between the trees.

"There, Dee. See it?"

"Where?"

He pointed. "There. Slow down. Just left of that boulder. Drive off the road right there."

Dee steered into the trees.

The violent jarring launched Jack into the dashboard, something struck the undercarriage, and by the time he was back in his seat, nose pouring blood, Dee had pulled the Rover into a shady spot between several giant ponderosa pines.

She killed the engine and Jack opened his door and stumbled out.

It was easy to see the path they'd blazed through the forest—saplings severed, pale tire tracks in the trampled grass.

A couple hundred yards through the trees, four trucks raced by. Jack stood listening to the roar of the engines, which, after ten seconds, quieted down to a distant idling that went on and on, Jack listening, inadvertently holding his breath while his shoulder throbbed like a second heartbeat.

Dee walked over.

"They're wondering if we've gotten ahead of them, or pulled a fast one," he said. "If they're smart, they'll send two trucks up the canyon and two trucks back to the meadow to wait."

"But they don't know we're out of gas," Dee said. "If they think we doubled back, maybe they'll keep going all the way to the highway."

The engines went silent.

Naomi called out to Jack.

He spun around. "Shhh."

"You think they've moved on?" Dee whispered.

"No. They're listening for the sound of our engine. Go get the guns."

$- - -$

They walked as far back into the woods as Jack could manage—barely fifty yards—and lay down in a bed of pine needles.

"Dee," Jack whispered.

"What?"

"You've got to listen for what's coming, okay? I have to rest now."

She ran her fingers through his hair. "Just close your eyes."

Jack turned over onto his right side, and he tried to listen for approaching footsteps but kept passing in and out of consciousness as the sun moved over the pines and made a play of light and shadow on his face.

The next time he woke the sun was straight overhead and he could hear Dee telling Cole a story. He sat up. His head swirled. Looked down at the pine needles, some of which had become glued together with blood. He felt feverish and cold, and soon Dee was there, easing him back onto the forest floor.

He opened his eyes, tried to sit up, then thought better of it. Dee sat beside him and the sun was gone. Through the pines, the pieces of sky held the rich blue of late afternoon.

"What time is it?" he asked.

"Four-fifteen. You've been sleeping all day."

"Where are the kids?"

"Playing by a stream."

"Nobody came?"

"Nobody came." She unscrewed the cap from a milk jug and held it to his mouth. The coldness of the water stung his throat and ignited a fierce and sudden thirst. When he finished drinking, he looked up at his wife.

"How am I doing, Doc?"

She shook her head. "I stopped the bleeding, but you're not so hot, Mr. Colclough." She reached into the first-aid kit, cracked open a bottle of Tylenol. "Here." She dumped a handful of pills onto Jack's tongue, helped him wash them down. "I have to get that bullet out, and I need to do it before we run out of daylight."

"Fuck."

"There's worse people you could be stuck with in this situation."

"Than Wifey, MD?"

"Fuck you."

"You're a GP," he said. "When's the last time you even held a scalpel? Med school? I mean, do you even have the tools to—"

"Really, Jack? You want me to tell you the gory details of what I'm about to do, or you want to turn your head away and let me work?"

"You can do this?"

She squeezed his hand. "I can. And I have to or you'll get an infection and die."

= = =

Jack lay flat on his back, his head turned away from his left shoulder, wishing for unconsciousness.

"I need you to be as still as you possibly can."

Dee cut away his shirt.

"Using my Swiss Army knife?"

"Yep."

"You're going to sterilize it?"

"I'm afraid your health insurance plan doesn't cover sterilizations."

"That's hilarious. Seriously—"

"It's already done."

"What with?"

"A match and an iodine pad. I'm going to wipe down your shoulder now."

It felt like ice on a flaming wound as she cleaned the dried blood from the entry hole.

"How's it look?" he asked.

"Like somebody shot you."

"Can you tell how far in it went?"

"Please let me focus."

Something moved inside his shoulder. There was pain, but nothing like he'd feared.

Dee said, "Shit."

"First-rate bedside manner. What's wrong?"

"I thought maybe I could do this easily. Just pull the bullet out with these plastic tweezers."

"That sounds like a super plan. Why can't you do it?"

"I can't get at it."

"Fuck, you're going to cut me." Jack heard the snap of a blade locking into place. "Big blade? Small blade?"

"Think about something else."

"Like what?"

"Like what we're going to have for dinner."

And he did think about it. For four seconds. Pictured the jar of pickled beets in the Rover and it made him want to cry, all of it— lying here in the woods in extraordinary pain without food and the day leaving them and nowhere to go and no way to get there—and then the knife entered his shoulder in a revelation of searing pain.

"Holy motherfuck—"

"Hold still."

She was really going after it, and Jack made a crushing fist, fighting back a surge of nausea as he tried to ask if she saw the bullet yet, if she could get at it now, desperate for some indication that this would be ending soon please God, and then his eyes rolled back in his head and he descended into a merciful darkness.

When he came to, Dee was crouched over him, headlamp blazing and Cole and Naomi beside her looking on. She was lifting a piece of string attached to a needle, and she looked exhausted.

"You passed out, you big baby."

"Thank God for that. Please tell me you got it."

Naomi held up a squashed mushroom of lead between her fingers.

She said, "I'm going to make you a necklace so you can wear it."

"You must have read my mind."

He groaned as Dee ran the needle through his shoulder again and tightened the knot.

"I know it hurts, but I have to finish." She started another stitch. "I really had to cut you to get it out. You lost two, maybe three pints of blood, which is right on the verge of not being okay."

He woke often during the night, freezing even inside his sleeping bag. Stars shone through the pines, and he was caught up in a fever dream—crawling toward a stream and dying of thirst, but every time he reached the water and cupped a handful to his mouth, it turned to ash and the wind took it.

Once, he woke and it was Naomi's voice that came to him in the dark.

"It's okay, Daddy. You're just having a bad dream."

And she brought the jug of water to his lips and helped him drink and she was still there, her hand against his burning forehead, when he sank back down into sleep.

HE registered the sun on his eyelids. Pulled the sleeping bag over his head, let his right hand graze his left arm.

The sickening heat had gone out of it.

Cole's laughter erupted some distance away in the forest.

Jack opened his eyes and pushed away the sleeping bag and slowly sat up.

Midday light.

The smell of sun-warmed pine needles everywhere.

Wind rushing through the tops of the trees.

— — —

Dee inspected his left shoulder. "Looking good."

"What about all that blood I lost?"

"Your body's making it back, but you need to be drinking constantly. More water than we have. And you need food. Particularly iron so you can remake those red blood cells."

"How are the kids?"

"Hungry. Nay's been amazing with Cole, but I'm not sure how much longer she can keep it up."

"How are you?"

She looked back at the Rover. "Think it'll start?"

"Even if it does, we might have a gallon of gas left."

"We can't just sit here and wait."

"We could head back toward the highway or keep going up the canyon. See how far we get."

"Jack, we're not going to find anything, and you know it."

"Yeah."

"We need more gas."

"We need a new car."

She looked at him. "If we don't find something, if we're still in these mountains tonight and we have no way to travel except on foot, which you don't have the strength for, it's going to get very bad very fast."

— — —

The engine cranked on the first attempt, though when Dee shifted into reverse an awful racket jangled under the hood. She backed them out of the grove and took it slow through the trees toward the road.

"Which way, Jack?"

"Upcanyon."

"You sure?"

"Well, we know what's back toward the highway—nothing."

She turned onto the road and eased through a gentle acceleration. They'd torn the plastic windows out, and the noise of the engine precluded any communication softer than shouting. Jack glanced into the backseat, saw Naomi and Cole sharing the jar of beets. Winked at his son, thinking he looked thinner in the face, his cheekbones more pronounced.

"We're completely below the empty slash," Dee said.

They did forty up the road, Jack constantly looking back through the glassless hatch for anything in pursuit.

After four miles, the pavement went to gravel.

They came out of the canyon.

The road had been cut into a mountainside and the pines exchanged for hardier, more alpine-looking evergreens and aspen in full color.

At 2:48 P.M., the engine sputtered, and at 2:49, on a level stretch of road on the side of a mountain, it died.

They rolled to a stop and Jack looked over at Dee and back at his children.

"That's all, folks."

"We're out of gas?" Cole asked.

"Bone-dry."

Dee set the parking brake.

Jack opened his door, stepped down onto the road. "Come on."

"Jack." Dee climbed out and shut her door. "What are you doing?"

He adjusted the sling that Dee had fashioned out of a spare T-shirt for his left arm, said, "I'm going to walk up this road until I find something that helps us or until I can't walk anymore. You coming?"

"There's not going to be anything up this road, Jack. We're in the middle of a fucking wilderness."

"Should we just lay down in the road right here then? Wait to die? Or maybe I should get the Glock and put us all—"

"Don't you ever—"

"Hey, guys?" Naomi got out and walked around to the front of the Rover and stood between her parents. "Look."

She pointed toward the side of the mountain, perhaps fifty feet up from where they'd stopped, at an overgrown one-lane road that climbed into the trees.

Jack said, "It's probably just some old wagon trail. There used to be mining around here, I think."

"You don't see it."

"See what?"

"There's a mailbox."

= = =

The mailbox was black and unmarked, and the Colcloughs walked past it up the narrow road into the trees. Jack was winded before the first hairpin turn, but keeping far enough ahead of Dee and the kids that he could gasp for air in private.

At 4:30 in the afternoon, he stopped at an overlook—dizzy, heartbeat rattling his entire body, pounding through his left shoulder. He collapsed breathless on the rock, still sucking down gulps of air when the rest of his family arrived.

"This is too much for you," Dee said, out of breath herself.

They could see a slice of the road several hundred feet below, where it briefly emerged from the forest. A square-topped dome of a mountain loomed ten miles away, its summit dusted with snow. Even bigger peaks beyond.

Jack struggled to his feet and went on.

— — —

The road wound through an aspen grove that was peaking—pale yellows and deep yellows and the occasional orange. When the wind blew through the trees, the leaves fluttered like weightless coins.

The sun was falling through the western sky. Already a cool edge to the air in advance of another clear and freezing night. They hadn't brought their sleeping bags from the car. Hadn't brought water. Nothing but the shotgun and the Glock, and it occurred to Jack that they might very well be sleeping under the stars on the side of this mountain tonight.

— — —

Several switchbacks later, the road curved and Jack walked out of the aspen into a meadow.

He stopped.

Took the Glock out of his waistband and tugged back the slide.

Dee gasped.

Cole said, "What is it, Mama?"

Jack turned around and shushed them and led them back into the woods.

"Is anyone there?" Dee whispered.

"I couldn't tell. Let me go check things out."

"I should go, Jack. You're too weak."

"Don't move from this spot, any of you, until I come back."

He jogged into the meadow. Now he could see the desert in the west, the sun bleeding out across it and the distant gray thread of Highway 191. It was getting cold. He slowed to a walk, his shoulder pulsing again. The wind had died away and the trees stood motionless. Somewhere, he heard the murmur of a stream.

A covered porch ran the length of it, loaded with firewood. Solar panels clung to the steep pitch of the roof. Dormers on the second floor. A chimney rising up through the center. The windows were dark, reflecting the sunset off the glass so he couldn't see inside, even as he walked up the steps.

The wooden porch bowed and creaked under his weight. He leaned in toward a window, touched his nose to the glass, framed his face in his hands to block the natural light.

Darkness inside. The shape of furniture. High ceilings. No movement.

He tried the front door. Locked. Turned away, shielded his eyes, and swung the Glock through the window.

Dee shouted something from the woods.

"I'm okay!" he yelled. "Just breaking in!"

He straddled the window frame and stepped down into the cabin. Through the skylight above the entrance, a column of late sun slanted through the glass and struck the stone of a freestanding fireplace with a medallion of orange light. It didn't smell like anyone had been here in some time. The mustiness of infrequent habitation.

From what he could see in the fading light, the floor plan was spacious and open. A staircase corkscrewed up to the second level, where the banistered hallway and three open doors were visible from Jack's vantage.

He moved across the hardwood floor toward the kitchen.

A deep sink and granite countertops lined the back wall of windows, which looked out over the deck into brilliant aspen.

He walked over to the pantry, pulled open the door.

– – –

Jack led his family up the front porch steps into the cabin.

"There's food here, Jack?"

"Just come on."

The last trickle of daylight was just sufficient to illuminate the kitchen. Jack had thrown open every cabinet so they could see the treasure he'd found.

Dee sat down, put her head between her knees, and wept.

– – –

They spread out on the floor as the world went black out the kitchen windows, each with their own cold can and sharing a big bag of sourdough pretzels torn open and spilled across the floor beside a sixer of warm Sierra Mist.

"Oh my God, this is the best thing I've ever tasted," Naomi said, halfway through her clam chowder. Grunts of agreement all around—Jack had gone for the chili, Dee the beef vegetable soup, Cole the Chef Boyardee cheese ravioli.

– – –

A half hour later, Naomi slept on a leather couch near the fireplace while Jack covered her with two quilts he'd found in a game closet. He went up the spiral staircase, holding one of the kerosene lamps they'd taken from the coffee table downstairs, Dee in tow, carrying Cole.

In the first bedroom, Jack pulled back the quilt, blanket, sheet, and Dee laid their son on the mattress and kissed his forehead and covered him up.

"It'll get cold in here tonight," she said.

"Not as cold as last night."

"If he wakes up and no one's here, he's going to be scared."

"You think so? After these last few days? He's done in, Dee. I don't think he'll wake for hours."

— — —

They lay in bed downstairs in the dark under a pile of blankets. Somewhere, the tick of a clock's second hand. Naomi's deep respirations in the living room. No other sound.

"Do you think we're safe here?" Dee whispered.

"Safer than starving and freezing to death on the side of a mountain."

"But long-term, I mean."

"I don't know. I can't think about it right now. I have nothing left."

Dee snuggled up to him and stretched a leg across his, her skin cool and like fine-grit sandpaper after days without shaving. She ran her fingers through the hair on his chest. First time in months that she'd put her hands on him, and it felt, in the best kind of way, like a stranger was touching him.

"Nothing, Jack?" She slipped her hand inside the waistband of his boxers. "'Cause this doesn't feel like nothing."

"Our daughter is twenty feet away," he whispered.

Dee climbed out of bed, crept across the floor, and closed them in behind the French doors and their panes of opaque glass. He heard the lock click in. She pushed the straps off her shoulders. Her undershirt puddled around her feet, and Jack watched her come back to him, naked and pale, wishing for some moonlight for her to move through as she crawled across the bed.

N the morning, Jack hiked down to the road with a gallon of the gasoline he'd found in the shed. There was plenty more where it came from—a row of five-gallon containers that he figured were meant for the backup generator in case the solar power system failed.

The Rover managed to crank, and he put it into four-wheel high.

A hundred yards up the mountain, he stopped and grabbed the chainsaw he'd also found and came out of his sling. Took him thirty minutes just to hack through the dense lower branches so he could get at the base, going slow so he didn't rip the stitches in his shoulder. Another twenty to carve a wedge into the trunk, and when the spruce finally fell across the road, it perfumed the air with sap and splintered wood.

Naomi and Cole were still sleeping when Jack returned to find Dee in the kitchen, pulling down all the food from the cabinets and the pantry to see what they had to work with.

"Doesn't look like much," he said by way of greeting.

Dee looked up from where she sat on the kitchen floor, surrounded by cans and glass jars and packages. "How'd the car do?"

"Rough as hell, but I got it to the shed. Maybe I'll play mechanic in a few days, see if I can fix whatever's wrong."

They spent the morning dividing out the food and trying to see what they might make from the staples like flour and sugar, assuming Jack could fire up the solar power system and get the stove working. In the end, rationing as frugally as they could stomach, they calculated enough meals to feed their family for thirteen days.

"That's not good enough," Jack said. "And we're going to be hungry all the time before we actually begin to starve to death."

Dee said, "It's more food than we had yesterday. I saw some fly-fishing gear in the shed, and there's a stream out back."

"I took one class. Two years ago. None of my flies at home ever touched water, and you think I'm going to go out there and catch enough fish for us—"

"In the last week, I've seen you do some pretty incredible shit to protect your family. I have total faith."

= = =

He assembled a six-weight fly rod in the shed, stocked his vest with an assortment of flies, and carried a small cooler into the woods toward the sound of moving water. Found it fifty yards in—a lovely stream that flowed through the aspen. He sat down on the grassy bank. The sun as high as it would be all day. Light coming down through the trees in clear, bright splashes. The sky cloudless. Almost purple.

He filled the cooler in the stream. Got the tippet tied on and chose a fly at random. Took him five attempts to cinch the knot, and then he walked downslope until he came to a shaded pool several feet deep and out of the ruckus of the main current.

His first cast overshot the stream, and the fly snagged on a spruce sapling. He waded across, the water knee-deep and freezing, and clambered out onto the warm grass on the opposite bank.

An hour later, he felt his first tap.

Midafternoon, he hooked a fish, Jack tugging the green line and backing away from the stream. It flopped in the grass, and he carefully lifted its body, which torqued violently and then went still, gills pulsing in his hand. It was silver and spotted with brown dots. He unhooked the fly. It was just a fingerling—two or three bites at most if he didn't completely destroy the thing when he tried to clean it.

— — —

They dined at the kitchen table as the light ran out—two cans of cold navy beans split among the four of them, three pretzels apiece, and water from one of the plastic jugs Dee had brought in from the Rover.

"How many fish did you catch?" Cole asked.

"Just one," Jack said.

"How big?"

Jack held his pointer fingers five inches apart.

"Oh."

"I let it go. But I saw some big ones."

"Can I come fishing with you tomorrow?"

"Absolutely."

— — —

Middle of the night, Jack sat up in bed.

"What's wrong?" Dee asked, still half-asleep.

"I should've cut down the mailbox."

"What are you talking about?"

"The mailbox by the road. The one Naomi saw that led us here."

"Do it first thing in the morning."

"No, I'm going now. I won't be able to sleep."

— — —

He hiked down with the chainsaw in the dark, reached the road at four in the morning. Cold. Below freezing he would've guessed.

That distant, square-topped mountain shone silver under the moon. He walked out into the road and stood listening in the great, vast stillness.

The chainsaw motor seemed inappropriate at this hour. Like screams in a church. He decapitated the mailbox and carried it across the road and launched it down the mountainside.

— — —

Walking back up to the cabin, he rounded a hairpin curve and froze. Heart accelerating at what loomed just twenty feet up the road. It raised its enormous head, the giant rack pale and sharp in the predawn. He'd almost brought the shotgun, decided against it, fearing his left arm couldn't bear the weight. And so he watched the seven-hundred-pound elk saunter off the road and vanish into the trees, wondering how long it might have fed his family.

B Y midmorning, he had the off-grid power system up and running, water pumping in through the tap from the underground cisterns, and the water heater beginning to warm. They filled five plastic grocery bags under the faucet and tied them off and stowed them in the chest freezer. Tried not to acknowledge the fact that they were all skipping lunch.

— — —

Jack left Dee and Naomi to scour *The Joy of Cooking* for efficient bread recipes that worked with their ingredient list, and took his son with him into the woods.

Since there wasn't any spinning tackle in the shed, he surprised the boy with a provisional pole he'd fashioned that morning—an aspen sapling skinned of bark and fitted with an eight-foot length of nylon string and a ceiling screw hook.

The knot-tying went faster and the casting smoother, Jack sticking the fly in the vicinity of his intent almost every time.

He'd caught two fingerlings by 3 P.M. and his first grown-up fish by 4 on a dry fly—a twelve-inch rainbow that had been loitering in a pool beside a cascade. Cole screamed with delight as Jack brought the fish ashore, both of them squatting in that pure fall light to inspect the reddish band and the black spots and the micaceous skin that faded into white at the edges.

"It's really something, isn't it?" Jack said.

He set his rod in the grass and worked the hook out and carried the trout back across the stream toward the cooler with as much care as he'd handled Naomi and Cole when they were squirming newborns.

— — —

When they returned to the cabin, the sun had just slipped below the desert, and Dee and Naomi were hanging blankets over the windows and the whole place smelled of sweet baking bread.

The women had carried in several armloads of firewood from the porch and stacked it around the hearth, and while Cole regaled everyone with the story of catching the fish, Jack built a base of kindling using a dozen pinecones stored in a wicker basket and an issue of *USA Today*.

The front-page headlines stopped him as he ripped out a sheet—six-month-old bits of news about two distant wars, savage political infighting, Wall Street, the death of a young celebrity.

"What's with the blankets over the windows?" he asked as he balled up the sports page and hoisted the first log onto the grate.

"To keep the heat in," Dee said, "and so our fire won't be visible."

Two more logs and then he struck a match, held it to the newsprint.

— — —

Jack lay in bed watching fire shadows move across the walls of the living room. He was warm under the blanket. Hungry but content.

"We can't have fires like this anymore," he said.

"What do you mean?"

"When we don't need them. The winter here is going to be awful. We should save the firewood for blizzards. Nights when it drops below zero. I'm going to have to cut a hell of a lot more wood."

"So you want to stay?"

"If we can get the food situation under control."

"I don't know, Jack."

"You'd rather go back out into what we just escaped?"

"No, but we'll starve here."

"Not with a seasoned outdoorsman like me taking care of things. I might even grow a beard."

A tremor of laughter moved through her.

"You noticed any changes in Cole?" he asked.

"No. Why? What makes you ask that?"

"That man in the desert—the one you shot when he lunged for me? He and his wife had been camping with another couple. They saw the aurora. The other couple slept through it. Afterward, they murdered their friends."

"What does this have to do with Cole?"

"You, me, and Naomi, we all slept through the aurora. Cole spent the night with Alex. Their family went out to the baseball field with most of the neighborhood and watched. Remember him telling us about it the next day?"

Dee was quiet for a long time.

Jack could see the embers in the fireplace, and he could hear his daughter snoring out there.

"It doesn't mean anything, Jack, what that man told you. He's our son, for chrissake. You think he wants to hurt us?"

"I don't know. Today, I caught him staring at himself in the mirror. For a long time. It was weird. I don't know what that was about, but—"

"We don't know that any of what's happening is connected to the lights. Not for sure."

"I agree, but what if Cole changes? What if he becomes violent?"

"Jack, I'm just telling you, if it turns out . . . just fucking shoot me."

"Dee—"

"I'm not kidding, not exaggerating, just telling you that I do not have it in me to handle that."

"We have a daughter too. We don't have the luxury not to handle our shit."

"'Should we kill our son if he becomes a threat?' Is that the question you're dancing around?"

"We have to talk about it, Dee."

"I think I already answered your question."

"What?"

"I would rather die."

"Me too," Jack said.

"So what are we saying?"

"We're saying . . . we're saying he's our boy. And we stay together. No matter what."

AT dawn, Jack crept out of bed and dressed in the dark, grabbed the shotgun leaning against the bedside table, and took it with him out into the living room.

He unlocked the front door and stepped outside.

It was freezing. A heavy frost on the grass.

He walked across the meadow into the trees and sat down against the base of an aspen. Everything still. Everything he loved in that dark house across the way.

His breath steamed and he thought about his father and he thought about Reid, his best friend in the humanities department, and the pints they'd put down Thursday nights at Two Fools Tavern. The remembrance touched something so raw he disavowed it all, on the spot. Focused instead on the coming hours, and all the things he had to do, and the order in which he might do them. Nothing before this cabin mattered anymore, only the given day, and with this thought he cleared his mind and scanned the trees that rimmed the meadow, praying for an elk to emerge.

— — —

He took the chainsaw and felled aspen trees until lunch. His stitches held, so he fished the rest of the day, taking three cutthroats and a brook trout out of a stretch of water a quarter mile upslope that boasted an abundance of deep pools.

— — —

In the late afternoon, Jack stood across the stream from Cole, watching the boy float aspen leaves into a cascade. He reeled in and set his rod down and waded across. Climbed up onto the bank and sat down dripping in the leaves beside his son.

"How you doing, buddy?"

"Good."

Cole pushed another leaf into the water. They watched the current take it.

"You like being here?" Jack asked.

"Yeah."

"Me too."

"These are my little boats, and they're crashing in the waterfall."

"Can I sail one?"

Cole offered a leaf, and Jack sent another golden ship to its death.

"Remember the aurora you watched with Alex?" Jack said.

Cole nodded.

"I want to ask you something about it."

Cole looked up at his father.

"Did you feel different after you saw it?"

"A little bit."

"Like how?"

"I don't know."

"Did you have any strange thoughts toward your mom and your sister and me?"

The boy shrugged.

"You can tell me. You can always tell me anything. No matter what it is. No matter how bad you think it is."

"I just wish you saw the lights too," Cole said.

"Why's that?"

"They were very pretty. More than anything I ever saw."

— — —

Jack and Dee sat in rocking chairs on the front porch drinking ice-cold bottles of Miller High Life from a case that had been left behind. They were watching great spirals of smoke swirl up into the sky sixty miles to the northwest near the base of Grand Teton.

"I wonder what's burning out there," Dee said.

"I think that's Jackson Hole."

They ate dinner and put the kids to bed. When they came back out onto the porch, the sun had finally crashed, leaving the flames of that distant, burning city to stand out in the darkness like some abandoned campfire.

Jack cracked open more beers, handed one to Dee. He was tired and strangely satisfied with the soreness in his body.

He'd been rehearsing how he would say it all day, the last two days even. Figured he might as well get on with it, though the phrasing had completely escaped him.

"Does it feel to you," Jack said, "like we're starting a new life?"

She looked at him. "Yeah. A little bit. How many days have we been here?"

He had to think about it. "Three."

"Feels longer."

"Yeah."

He could feel the good beer buzz beginning to swarm in his head. Didn't know if it was the altitude or malnourishment, but he couldn't think of the last time two beers had gotten him this close to drunk.

"I need to tell you something," he said.

"What?" She laughed. "*You're* seeing someone?"

None of the permutations of this conversation, as he'd imagined it, had involved Dee asking that question straightaway. His head cleared so fast it left him with a subtle throbbing at the base of his skull.

"Two years ago. It's over now."

Dee's face emptied of the lightness of the moment and her bottle hit the porch and the beer fizzed out and drained through a crack between the floorboards.

"Lasted a month," he said. "It was the only time I ever did that, and I ended it because I couldn't stand—"

"One of your fucking TAs?"

"We met in—"

"No, no, no, I don't want to hear a single detail. I don't ever want to know her name. Nothing about her. Just why you're telling me this now. In this moment. I could've died never knowing and you took that from me."

"When we left Albuquerque, our marriage was on life support. I mean, the other night was the first time we'd been together in . . . I don't even know—"

"Seven months."

"Dee, I know I've been checked out on our family. For a long time. Because of guilt, depression, I don't know. These last eight days have been the worst, hardest of our life, but in some ways, the best too. Now it feels like we're starting something new here, and I don't want to start it with any lies. Nothing between us."

"Well, there is now. Why the *fuck* would you tell me this? At least I was honest with you about Kiernan."

"Yeah, that was such a comfort as our marriage imploded."

Dee got up from the rocking chair and walked off the porch and vanished into the meadow.

Jack finished his beer and sat watching the horizon burn to the soundtrack of his wife crying out there in the dark.

A T 5:15 A.M., Jack rose up slowly, shouldered the shotgun, and took aim on the neck of the same giant bull he'd seen two mornings before on the hike up from the road. The recoil drove a splinter of pain through his left shoulder, and a thundering blast ripped across the clearing.

The elk's head dipped. It staggered.

Jack on his feet, bolting through the frosted grass as he pumped the Mossberg and fired again.

When he reached it, the animal lay on its side, eyes open, breathing fast and raggedly. Jack knelt beside it and held one of the spurs on the enormous rack as the blood rushed out across the ground.

— — —

He hadn't field dressed an animal in over twenty years, since the last time he'd hunted with his father in Montana when he was in college. But the anatomy and the method slowly returned to him.

Naomi and Cole looked on in semi-horror as he tied off the

hooves, heaved the animal onto its back, and with the bowie knife he'd been given in Silverton, Colorado, slit the elk from anus to throat.

He worked hard. He tried to work fast. As the first rays of sunlight streamed through the aspen onto the meadow, he severed the muscle tissue that held the entrails and let the steaming gut pile roll out of the carcass into the grass. He excavated the colon and bladder, liver and heart, and sent Cole back to the cabin in search of several blankets.

He was three hours skinning the elk, two more separating the shoulder from the rib cage. All afternoon removing the backstrap, boning out the meat from between the ribs, peeling off the tenderloins from underneath, everything laid out to drain and cool on a large blanket. He cut the hindquarters from the pelvic bone as the sun slid down over the desert, trying not to slice the meat itself but still doing a fair amount of damage.

Naomi brought him a can of tomato soup for supper, which he drank down in less than a minute. When he asked about her mother, she told him Dee was sleeping. Had been all day.

In the chilling dusk, thirteen hours after the kill, Jack carried, in five trips, what he estimated to be two hundred pounds of meat to the front porch of the cabin.

= = =

The bags of water had frozen solid in the chest freezer, and Jack stowed the meat inside, still wrapped in blankets. He was sunburned and weak and covered in blood—the elk's and his. Several stitches had ripped, the wound in his shoulder opening again.

He took his first shower since arriving at the cabin. Twenty minutes under near-scalding water scrubbing the blood out of his hair and skin and watching the filth swirl down the drain between his feet. Crawled into a double bed on an aspen frame a little before 10:00 P.M. in the second upstairs bedroom. Cole snored softly next door. Through the window he could hear the sound of the stream in the woods.

A footstep snapped him awake. He opened his eyes to the silhou-ette of Dee standing in the doorway. She came over and climbed into bed, their faces inches apart in the dark.

"I hear we have an elk," she whispered.

"In the freezer. As we speak."

"You're your kids' superhero, I hope you know. I've never heard Naomi talk about you like she did today."

"I'm going to miss being a constant source of embarrassment."

She put her hand on his face. "You don't stink," she said.

"Showers will do that."

"Why are you up here and not in my bed?"

"Figured you still needed some space."

She kissed him. "Come with me."

S NOW, just a dusting, lay upon the meadow the following morning, but it was gone before lunch. Dee replaced the stitches in Jack's shoulder, and he spent an hour butchering steaks out of the tenderloins, then made a dry rub from the available spices in the kitchen, which he worked into the meat.

He found a wiffle ball set in the shed. They used empty milk jugs for bases and weeded a pitcher's mound and held a series, boys versus girls, that concluded in game seven when Cole knocked a line drive over third base that brought Jack home.

The afternoon Jack spent sitting on the porch drinking beer and watching Dee and the kids playing in the meadow. He wouldn't allow himself to think back or forward, but only to register the moment—the wind moving through gold aspen leaves, his skin warm in the sun, the sound of Cole's laughter, the shape of Dee when, every so often, she turned to look back toward the porch. Her shoulders were brown and the details of her face obscured by distance, but he could still pick out the white brushstroke of her smile.

As another day set sail, Jack grilled the elk steaks and a rainbow trout and surprised everyone with a bottle of 1994 Silver Oak he'd found hidden away in a cabinet over the sink. They gathered at the kitchen table and ate by candlelight, even Cole getting his own small pour of wine in a shot glass. Toward the end of supper, Jack stood and raised his glass and toasted his son, his daughter, and his wife. Then he said to everyone, his voice breaking only once, that of all the days of his life, this had been the finest.

ANOTHER fall day in the mountains, Jack fishing alone with his thoughts and the sound of moving water that never seemed to leave him now, even in dreams. Imagining what winter might be like in this place. An entire season spent indoors.

He caught two brookies before lunch and stowed them in the cooler. The exhaustion from taking the elk still lingered. He found a bed of moss downstream and took off his disintegrating trail shoes and eased back onto the natural carpet. There weren't as many leaves on the aspen as there had been when they'd arrived, and the woods were brighter for it. He could feel the moisture from the moss seeping through his shirt—cool and pleasant—and the sunlight in his face a perfect offset. He dozed.

— — —

Walked home in the early evening with four fish in the cooler.

Called out, "I'm home!" as he climbed the steps to the porch.

Set the cooler down, kicked off his shoes.

Inside, Dee and the kids were playing Monopoly on the living-room floor.

"Who's winning?" he asked.

"Cole," Dee said. "Nay and I are broke. He's bought every property on the board. Owns Community Chest and Chance. I just sold him Free Parking."

"Can you even do that?"

"I think he's paying us not to quit at this point. It's all very ridiculous."

He bent down, kissed his wife.

"You smell fishy," she said. "How'd we do?"

"Four."

"Big ones?"

"Decent size."

"We can eat whenever you're ready."

Jack showered and dressed in a plaid shirt and blue jeans that were perhaps a size too small and still smelled strongly of their prior owner—tinged with the remnants of cigar smoke. Something crinkled in the back pocket as Jack walked from the bedroom to the kitchen. He dug out a receipt for a box of tippet from the Great Outdoor Shop in Pinedale, purchased four months ago with a credit card by Douglas Walker.

A three-course meal: freshly baked bread, one can of broccoli-cheddar soup, and rainbow trout, seasoned and grilled. They had learned to eat slowly, to stretch out each course with conversation or some other diversion. That afternoon, Dee had perused a shelf of old paperbacks in the game closet, found a David Morrell thriller, and now she read to them the first chapter during the soup course.

After supper, she boiled a pot of chamomile tea.

"That soup was excellent," Jack said as she carried four steaming mugs over to the table, two in each hand. "You really outdid yourself."

"Old family recipe, you know. The Campbells."

"Who's that?" Cole asked.

"Mom's joking."

"But seriously, Jack, the fish was incredible."

He sipped his tea. Could've been stronger, but it felt so good just to hold the warm mug in his hands, which were still raw from long hours of casting.

"Busy boy today," Dee said. "Four fish and how much wood did you cut?"

"I didn't cut any wood."

"Of course you did."

He flashed a perplexed smile. "Um, I didn't."

"Are you joking?"

"About what?"

"Cutting firewood."

"No, I only fished today."

"But I heard a chainsaw."

Jack set his mug on the table and stared at Dee.

"When?" he asked.

"Late afternoon."

"Where was the sound of the chainsaw coming from?"

"The driveway. I thought you were taking down more trees."

Cole said, "What's wrong?"

"Jack, you're playing around, and considering what we've all been through, this isn't funny at—"

"I fished. All. Day. Naomi, did you take the chainsaw out?" He knew the answer before she spoke, because her mug was rattling against the table in her trembling hands.

Dee started to rise.

"No, don't get up."

"We have to—"

"Listen." Jack lowered his voice. "If people have found the cabin, then they're probably watching us right now through that window at your back, waiting until we go to bed."

"Waiting for what?" Naomi asked.

"Everyone drink your tea and act like we're wrapping up a nice family evening."

Jack's mouth had run dry. He sipped his tea and let his eyes move briefly past Dee's shoulder to the window behind the kitchen table. It was the only one in the house they hadn't shielded with a blanket, since it backed right up against the woods. Nothing to see at this hour, the sun long since set. He wondered—*was someone crouching out there in the dark, watching his family?*

"You're sure you heard it?" he said quietly. "The chainsaw?"

"Yes."

"I heard it too." Tears rolled down Naomi's face. "I thought it was you, Dad."

Before supper, Jack had switched off the solar power system to recharge overnight. They'd eaten by firelight. Several candles glowed in the living room, too, and one in each of the upstairs bedrooms.

"The shotgun and the Glock are under our bed," Jack said. "I think we have a box of ammo for the Glock that's mostly full, but there's only a half dozen twelve-gauge shells." He looked at Naomi, then Dee, then Cole. Hating the fear he saw. "We're going to act like it's just another normal night. I'll put Cole to bed. Naomi, you head up to your room. Dee, clear the table and get all the cans of food and whatever bread's left into a plastic bag. Some silverware, too, and a can opener. We don't know how close they are to the cabin, if they can see inside, see us in the other rooms, so don't hurry, but don't take too much time either."

"What about all our meat?"

"Leave it. I'll come back downstairs, and then your mom and I will blow out the living-room and kitchen and bedroom candles. We'll dress in the dark, all of us, all the clothes we can wear, and then we'll meet in the other downstairs bedroom—the one near the shed. Naomi, you stay upstairs with your brother after I've left and listen for me to call you down. Got it?"

She was crying. "I don't want to leave."

"Me either, but can you do this? What I'm asking?"

She nodded.

"Look, maybe there's nobody out there. But we have to make sure, and we aren't safe in here until we know."

"Are we taking the car?" Dee asked.

"No. They probably have us blocked in. I'm sure they were using the chainsaw to cut that tree I brought down across the driveway. So they could drive up. We just need to get into the woods and hide until we can figure out what's going on."

Jack carried his son through the kitchen, up the spiral staircase, and into the bedroom. Threw back the covers and laid Cole on the mattress.

"Naomi's right next door," Jack said. "You listen to your sister, okay?"

"Don't blow out the candle."

"I have to, buddy."

"I don't like it dark."

"Cole, I need you to be brave." He kissed the boy's forehead. "I'll see you in a minute."

Jack extinguished the candle on the dresser and tried not to rush down the steps. The kitchen was already dark, the plastic bag of food tied off and sitting on the hearth. He blew out the candles on the coffee table and moved blindly toward his and Dee's bedroom, his eyes slowly adjusting to the darkness.

Dee stood by the blanketed window.

"What are you doing?" he whispered.

"Just looking out at the meadow. Haven't seen anything yet."

"Let's get going."

Jack donned two more cigar-scented shirts, his fingers struggling with the buttons in the dark, heart slamming in his chest. When he'd dressed, he slid two shells into the Mossberg to replace the two he'd used on the elk. Then he crammed the four remaining shells into the side pocket of his jeans, grabbed the Maglite from the bedside table drawer, and handed Dee the Glock.

In the living room, Jack called up to his children. Laced his trail shoes while Naomi and Cole descended the stairs, and they all went together past the fireplace into the second bedroom.

Jack crawled across the bed and tugged down the blanket Dee had tacked over the glass and unlatched the hasp.

The window slid up. The night cold rushed in.

Jack climbed over the sill, stepped down into the grass.

"All right, Cole, come on."

He grabbed his son under his arms and hoisted him out of the cabin. "Stay right beside me, and don't say a word."

He helped Naomi through and then Dee. Lowered the window back and pulled his wife in close to whisper in her ear.

"We can't leave without our packs. They're in the back of the Rover, right?"

"Yeah."

"Wait for me to call you over."

Jack crept across the grass and peered around the corner of the cabin.

The meadow stretched into darkness.

No wind.

No moon.

No movement.

He sprinted twenty yards to the shed and crouched down behind it, straining to listen and hearing nothing but the internal combustion of his heart.

Jack blew a sharp, stifled whistle, then watched as Dee and the kids emerged from the shadows behind the cabin, running toward him, their pants swishing in the grass for eight agonizing seconds before they reached him.

"Did I do good?" Cole asked.

"You did great. Dee, I'm going around to the front of the shed to get our packs. If something goes wrong, if you hear gunshots, yelling, whatever, take the kids into the woods, all the way back to the stream. I'll find you there."

He came to his feet, moved along the backside of the shed, the shotgun in one hand, flashlight in the other. Rounded the corner, the driveway looming just ahead. The single lane descended out of meager starlight into the darkness of the aspen grove, and he followed it down until he came around the first hairpin turn.

A Suburban blocked the way, its color indeterminate in the low light. A pickup truck behind it. He put a light through the glass and checked the ignitions of both vehicles. No keys. No idea how to hotwire a car.

He ran back up the driveway. The clearing appeared almost bright. Stood there for a moment scanning the meadow and the trees around the periphery, but the shadows kept their secrets so well, he couldn't even see his family in the darkness behind the shed.

Twenty strides brought him to the side of it.

He swung around the corner and got his hand on the doorknob and the hinges ground together with a rusty shriek as he slipped inside.

A wave of disorientation accompanied the absolute, unflinching darkness.

Jack knelt down, laid the shotgun in the dirt, and fumbled with the head of the Maglite, trying to turn it on.

Several feet away—a shuffle in the dirt.

Jack froze, bracing against a shot of liquid fear, thinking it could be a rodent or some tool that had shifted.

Or someone pointing a gun at him.

Two choices. See it or shoot it.

He lowered the flashlight back onto the dirt floor. As he felt around for the shotgun, a motor coughed ten feet away, like someone had pulled a start rope. Then it sputtered again and the shed filled with the reek of gas and the banshee-wail of a two-stroke. A small LED light cut on—affixed to the handle with black electrical tape. It sent out a schizophrenic beam that hit the Rover, the shed walls, and the large, bearded man who came at Jack with the screaming chainsaw, gripped like a bat, spring-loaded to swing.

Jack grabbed the shotgun and jacked a shell as the man reached him, no time to stand or brace.

The blast knocked Jack onto his back in the dirt, and at point-blank range, cut the ski-jacketed man in half at the waist.

Jack clambered back onto his feet, pumped the shotgun again, lifted the Maglite, and screwed the bulb to life.

The man still clutched the idling chainsaw.

Jack leaned down and flipped the kill switch.

In the renewed silence, the man emitted desperate, drowning noises. Over them, Jack could hear Dee calling his name through the back wall of the shed. He went to it and put his mouth to the wood and said, "I'm okay. Go to where we talked about."

He hurried over to the Rover and lifted his pack out of the cargo area, trying to recall what all it held, if it might be worth rifling through Dee's pack or bringing it too, but there wasn't time.

He shouldered his pack and clipped the hip belt and chest strap and went back over to the man in the ski jacket who'd turned sheet white and already bled a black lake across the dirt.

"How many of you?" Jack asked. But the man just stared up at him with a kind of glassy-eyed amazement and would not, or could not, speak.

Jack killed the Maglite and eased open the door to the shed.

Already, they were halfway across the meadow—four shadows running toward him and two smaller, faster ones out ahead of the others.

He leveled the shotgun, squeezed off three blinding reports.

Four points of light answered, flashing in the dark like high-octane lightning bugs, and bullets struck the wood beside him and punched through the door above his head.

He sprinted to the back of the shed.

His family was gone.

Quick footfalls approached, the jingle of a chain, and snarling.

He turned back to see the pit bull tear around the corner, skidding sidelong across the grass, trying to right its forward motion.

Jack raised the shotgun, the animal accelerating toward him, and fired as it leapt for his throat, the buckshot instantly arresting its momentum. He pumped the slide and took aim on the second dog—a hulking rottweiler—which ripped around the corner with greater efficiency. He dropped it whimpering and tumbling through the grass.

Jack ran ten feet into the woods and slid out of his pack. He prostrated himself behind a log. Couldn't hear a thing over his own panting, and he closed his eyes and buried his face in the leaves until the pounding in his chest decelerated.

When he looked up again, four figures stood behind the shed, where his family had been just moments ago. Three others joined them.

Someone said, "Where's Frank?"

"In the field. He caught some pellets in his neck."

A woman walked over, the helve of an ax resting on her shoulder.

She said, "Someone ran into the woods a minute ago."

A beam of light struck the ground. "Let's head in. It's only four of them, and two are children."

Another light.

Another.

Someone shot their beam through the woods. Jack ducked behind the log, the light slanting past him, firing the fringes of the bark. They were still talking, but he'd lost their voices with his face jammed up under the log and straining to fish the twelve-gauge shells out of his pocket. Jack was on the brink of shifting to another position when the footsteps stopped him.

They were approaching now—must have been all eight of them—filling the woods with the dry rasp of crushed leaves. Someone stepped over the log, and the heel of a boot came down inches from Jack's left arm. He caught the scent of rancid body odor and then watched them all move by, eight distinct fields of light sweeping the woods. He wondered how far in his family had made it, if Dee had any concept of what was coming her way.

After a while, he rolled out from under the log and sat up. Glanced back toward the shed. Into the woods again. He could hear the footfalls growing softer, indistinguishable and collective like steady rain, glimpsed the bulbs of distant light and occasionally a full beam where it swung through mist.

Jack dug into his pocket for the shells and fed in the last four.

Six rounds. Eight people.

He stood up and got his pack on.

Jacked a shell, started toward the lights.

After forty yards, the stream murmur filtered in, and soon there was nothing but the sound of it and the cool, sweet smell of the moving water.

He eased down onto the bank. The lights had moved on. Blackness everywhere. Thinking he'd told Dee to get to the stream, but she may have seen the group of flashlights coming, been forced to go elsewhere. The urge to call out for her was overwhelming.

He got up, started hiking again.

Sometimes the starlight would find a way down through the trees and he would catch a glimpse of the stream like black glass, warped and fissured, but mainly it was impossible to see anything. He didn't dare use the Maglite.

Fifteen minutes of blind groping brought him a quarter mile uphill.

He collapsed in a patch of cold, damp sand and stared back the way he'd come, trying to catch his breath, but the longer he sat there, the more the panic festered inside of him. Finally, he rose to his feet. He was running uphill now, running until his heart felt like it was going to swell out of his chest, and he went on like this for what seemed ages, and every time he stopped it was still just him alone in the woods and the dark.

T HE violence of his own shivering woke him.

Jack lifted his head out of the leaves.

Dawn. A moment before. Frail blue light upon everything in the brutal cold.

He had dreamed, but they were too sweet and vivid to linger on.

- - -

Worked his way up the mountain for thirty minutes before stopping streamside by a boulder covered in frosted moss. He looked around. Wiped his eyes. Considered all the ways they could have fucked this up—he might have gone upstream when he should've hiked down, or Dee and the kids had pushed hard all night and gotten too far ahead of him, or he'd unknowingly passed them in the dark, or maybe they hadn't even stayed with the stream and become lost elsewhere on this endless mountain.

Another two hundred yards and he came around a large boulder and saw three people lying huddled together in the leaves on the opposite bank.

He stopped. Looked down at his shoes. Looked up again. They

were still there, and he didn't quite believe it, even as he rock-hopped to the other side of the stream.

Dee stirred at the sound of his footsteps, then bolted upright with the Glock trained on his chest. He smiled and his eyes burned and then he was holding her as she shook with sobs.

"I heard all those gunshots. I thought you had—"

"I'm here. I'm safe."

"I didn't know if we should wait or keep going, and then I saw all those lights in the woods, and we just—"

"You did exactly what you should have."

Naomi sat up and rubbed her eyes. She looked at her father.

"Hey," she said.

"Morning, sunshine."

- - -

"We can't go back," Jack said. He was staring down at the bag of soup cans Dee had brought and the contents of his backpack, which he'd spread out in the leaves. A tent. Two sleeping bags. Water filter. Camp stove. Map. Not much else.

"But what if they leave?"

"Why would they? I saw their cars, Dee. They have no provisions, haven't fallen in with a big group, so they're facing the same problems we were—no gas, no water, no food. And they just stumbled across all of those things at the cabin, plus shelter, plus two hundred pounds of meat in the freezer."

"That place was perfect. We could have—"

"There's eight of them. Eight armed adults. We'd be slaughtered."

"Well, I don't much feel like wandering aimlessly through the wilderness."

"Not aimlessly." He knelt down and opened the Wyoming road map. "We're here," he said, "northern edge of the Wind Rivers. We're actually not that far from the east side of the mountains." He traced a black line north. "Let's shoot for this highway."

"How far is it?"

"Fifteen, twenty miles tops."

"Okay." He could hear the panic rising in her voice. "So **we** reach this road in the middle of nowhere, and then what?"

"I don't know. We'll need a miracle, I guess."

"That's right. That's how we're going to stay alive from here **on** out. Big fucking miracles. And you want us to hike across these—" Her voice broke and she turned away and walked off into **the** woods.

"Mom." Naomi started after her, but Jack caught his **daughter's** arm.

"Just give her a minute."

— — —

They were all day hiking the mountainside. The aspen giving **way to** evergreens the higher they climbed. The stream shrinking **toward** headwaters, burbling softer and softer, until at last it **disappeared** into a rocky hole in the mountain, never to be heard from **again**.

— — —

They stopped while there was still plenty of light at a small **lake at** nine thousand feet. It backed up against a two-hundred-foot **cliff,** which had calved a rock glacier into the water—giant **boulders** half-submerged on the far side.

Jack raised the tent and collected fir cones and browned **nee-**dles and more wood than they could burn in three nights.

He walked to the edge of the lake as the sun fell. The **water** looked black, and so still as to suggest ice or obsidian, except **for** the slow concentric circles that eddied out when a trout **surfaced.** He kept reminding himself what a beautiful place this was, **that** they could be suffering on the East Coast, or in Albuquerque, **or be** dead like so many others. But somehow the bright side of **things** had burned out tonight, and the light draining from the sky **and the** lake's reflection of it just felt tragic.

He glanced back at his family. The kids were sitting outside **the** tent, watching Dee build a fire. He started toward them. A day's worth of walking in his swollen knees and lots more of that to come.

His children looked up at his approach.

He forced himself to smile.

— — —

In the middle of the night, Cole said, "What's that sound?"

Jack lay beside him. The noise had woken him, too, and he whispered, "Just that rockfall across the lake."

"Is someone throwing rocks?"

"No, they're shifting."

"What are those splashes?"

"Fish jumping out of the water."

"I don't like it."

"Want me to go out there and tell them to cut it out?"

"Yes."

"It's okay. I promise. Go back to sleep."

"No one's coming after us?"

"We're safe up here, Cole."

"I'm hungry."

"We'll eat something in the morning."

"First thing?"

"First thing."

The boy fell back asleep almost instantly, but Jack lay awake, trying to ignore the rock jutting up through the bottom of the sleeping bag into his side. The moon was bright through the tent walls. He listened to everyone's heavy breathing, thinking how, in his lifetime, he'd lain awake at night worrying over so much pointless shit—money, his job, a fight he'd had with Dee—and now that he had real life-and-death stuff to obsess about, all he wanted to do was sleep.

A FILM of ice rimmed the lake. Steam lifting off the surface in the early morning sun. Jack knelt on the grassy bank, pumping water through the filter into a stainless steel pot. He boiled the water, added three packets of oatmeal from his emergency kit, and they sat around the smoking remnants of the campfire, passing the pot and trying to wake up.

After breakfast, they broke down the tent and packed up and headed out while there was still frost on the dying grasses.

They followed no trail.

With his compass, Jack marked a cirque of forbidding granite spires ten miles away as their definitive eastern goal.

$$- - -$$

They climbed all morning through a spruce forest, emerging at midday onto a broad, ascending ridge of meadows.

Herds of unattended cattle grazed the open range.

Mountains in every direction and the warm, adobe glow of desert to the east.

In the early afternoon, Cole began to complain that his legs hurt.

Dee took over Jack's pack, and Jack put his son on his shoulders.

They'd all had plenty of water with breakfast but had sweated it out under the high-altitude sun. Jack could feel a dehydration headache coming on. He feared they'd all be suffering soon.

They pushed on in silence, everyone too tired and thirsty to talk.

In the evening they came down into a valley that framed another lake. Naomi crying as she shuffled along on the sides of her blistered feet, telling everyone she was okay, that she could make it to the water.

Jack assembled the filter and pumped while his family drank straight from the plastic tube. Fifteen minutes to satisfy their thirst, and then Dee pumped for him, Jack lying in the cool grass and letting the freezing lake water run down his throat and over his sunburned face.

He felt delirious, his head undergoing a slow implosion, and it was all he could do to construct the tent. A fire was out of the question, and he didn't want to eat—no one did—but Dee opened a can for each of them and handed out three tablets of maximum-strength Tylenol apiece.

"I'll just throw up," Jack said.

"No, you won't. You'll keep it down. We're all severely dehydrated and suffering from altitude sickness." She handed him a can of pork and beans. "Get that in you, and drink some more water, and go to bed."

His family slept, but the agony in Jack's head would not relent. He crawled outside a little after midnight and staggered to the edge of the lake. Bitter cold. Moon shadows everywhere. He lowered himself onto his hands and knees and dipped his head through a crust of ice into the water.

I N the morning, his pain had eased. Jack could hear his family up and about outside. It was almost hot inside the tent with the sun beating down. He didn't remember coming to bed. Couldn't recall much of the preceding night. His head felt mushy, like he was coming off a bender.

They were eating down by the lake when he joined them. The sun already higher than he would've liked. They'd be getting a late start.

"How we doing?" he asked.

"Aces," Naomi said.

He sat beside his daughter, and she passed him her can.

He sipped the cold corn chowder. "How are your feet?"

"They don't look too pretty anymore. Mom wrapped them up."

"We need to start sleeping with our food," Dee said. "There's ice crystals in my cream of mushroom."

"I personally love ice in my soup," Jack said.

Cole laughed.

"I wouldn't exactly call this rationing," Jack said, handing the can back to Naomi.

"We have to eat," Dee said. "We're expending so much energy in these mountains."

"What are we down to?"

"Eight cans."

"Jesus."

The climb up the east slope of the valley took them into the early afternoon. They finally broke out above the timberline onto the top of a knoll. Those granite spires loomed several miles to the east, their summits puncturing the low cloud deck. Not a tree in sight, rock everywhere, and four lakes visible from where they stood.

They hiked east as the clouds lowered.

It grew dark early and a fine, cold mist began to fall. They pushed on to the farthest lake at the foot of the cirque, everyone wet and shivering as they raised the tent on one of the few patches of level grass.

Stripped out of their wet clothes. Climbed in. Jack zipped them up, and they huddled under the sleeping bags and listened to rain patter on the tent and watched the light fade.

"Can I say something?" Naomi said. "Something not very nice, but it'll make me feel better?"

"You can say whatever you want," Jack said.

"This sucks."

"No," Dee said. Everyone looked at her. "This. Fucking. Sucks." Naomi smiled.

After supper, Jack dressed in dry clothes and dug the water filter and pot out of his pack.

"Back in a bit," he said.

He slipped on his wet trail shoes and crawled outside.

Down to the lakeshore, crouched by the water. His breath pluming in the blue dusk. He strained to pick out the voices of his family, wanted to hear them talking, but nothing broke the awesome silence.

Across the lake, he made out the faintest impression of the cirque. No texture, no detail. Just a charcoal silhouette of a jagged ridgeline several thousand feet above. The ghost of a mountain.

He filled the pot and carried it to the tent.

"This one's for Naomi," he said.

She gulped it down in two long, ravenous sips.

He pumped a pot for Cole, then another for Dee, and went back outside one last time to drink his fill.

The cirque had vanished, the dusk deepened, and flakes of snow were mixing in with the rain. He stopped halfway through filling the pot. His hands were trembling with cold and fear.

Get it over with. If you have to lose it, lose it here.

He buried his face in the bend of his arm and cried until there was nothing left.

— — —

They nestled together in the cold and the dark, Jack and Dee on the outside, the kids between them. No one had spoken in a long time, and Jack said finally, "Everyone all right?"

"Yeah."

"I guess."

"Yes."

"Wow, that was so convincing."

"This the worst thing you ever been through, Dad?"

"Yeah, Nay. By miles."

Cole said, "Are we going to die?"

"No."

"How do you know?"

"Because that isn't going to happen to our family. I'm not going to let it happen. Okay?"

"Okay."

"Do you believe me?"

"Yes."

"Good night, all."

"Night."

"Night."

"Night."

"You know I love you all very much. Right? Do I say it enough?"

"Yes, Dad, you do."

For a split second, a flash of the Naomi of old—sassy, sarcastic, acerbic.

It elicited his sole smile of the day.

A FRAGILE inch of snow clung to the tent and glazed the rocks. Jack stared at the sky and the lake, which reflected the sky. Deep cobalt. He was hungry. Starving actually. But the purity of the morning light moved him with a fleeting weightlessness that broke his heart to see it go.

The cirque loomed. There was simply no avoiding it. He stood in the cold trying to see a route, but it all looked steep as hell. Like a stupid fucking thing to even consider, fact aside that he needed to get his seven-year-old son up and over it.

He woke his family, and while Naomi and Cole launched snow-balls at each other, Dee pulled the stitches out of Jack's shoulder.

Then they packed up, rebandaged their blistered feet, drank as much water as their stomachs could hold, and struck out before the sun had cleared the ridge.

= = =

They walked around the perimeter of the lake and into a field of car-size boulders. Didn't even begin to climb until after lunchtime, which passed unacknowledged. By midafternoon the snow had vanished except for in the shadows, and they were a thousand feet above the lake, which shone like a diamond in the valley's hand.

Cole had already arrived at the threshold of his endurance with Naomi not far behind, but they kept climbing, even as they cried, the rocks getting smaller and the slope steeper and the sun plunging toward night.

They would climb in increments of fifty feet and stop while Cole fell apart and Dee and Jack calmed and primed him to go just a little farther. Big, bold lies that they were almost there.

At 4:30, Jack gave his pack to Dee and lifted his son onto his shoulders. Climbed another hundred feet, and when he stopped this time the sun was perched on the western horizon and he knew they'd gone as far as they were going to make it for the day, that they'd be spending the night on the side of this mountain. He looked up, his head swimming, the rock turning pink and the summit spires glowing far above them in the late sun.

"Let's stop," he said.

"Stop?"

"We should find a place to hunker down."

"For the night?" Naomi said.

"Yeah."

"Where's the tent going to go?"

"No tent tonight."

Naomi eased down onto the loose rock, and the sound of her crying swept down into the basin.

Jack let Cole off his shoulders and crawled over to her.

"I'm so sorry, Nay. I know this is hard."

"I hate it."

"Me too, but we're going to find the best spot on this mountain. Think about the view we'll have."

"I don't give a shit about the view."

"Yeah, me neither."

"I hate this fucking mountain."

— — —

Jack collapsed in the dirt on the downslope side of the largest stable boulder he could find, his hands raw from eight hours of climbing. They reclined against the mountain using their spare clothes for pillows and blanketed under the two sleeping bags. Not a cloud in the sky and everything still and Jack praying it would stay that way.

Already it was freezing. The sun had retreated below the horizon, and Jack could see seven lakes on that treeless tableland below.

Somewhere down there, a band of coyotes yapped.

Jack cracked open the last four cans of food and they ate in silence, watching the last bit of light drain away.

The planets faded in and then the stars and soon the sky was swarming with pinpricks of ancient light, and they slept, dug into the side of the mountain.

JACK woke cold and stiff and thirsty. His family slept, Cole burrowed into his side completely under the sleeping bag, and Jack let them sleep, a temporary escape from the diamond-cut hardness of this place. The panic was certainly there. He felt it creeping toward him. He'd gotten them into a terrible bind, it whispered—out of food, out of water, twelve thousand feet up a mountain they had no business climbing. He'd failed them, and now they were going to die.

Naomi said, "A box of Froot Loops, and I don't mean one of those little ones."

"Family-size."

"Exactly. I'd pour the whole thing into one of our glass mixing bowls and open a carton of cold whole milk. Oh my God, I can almost taste it."

"Lucky Charms," Cole said. "Except just the marshmallows, and chocolate milk."

"I would kill for one of those southwest breakfast burritos from that place near campus," Dee said. "Filled with scrambled eggs and chorizo sausage and green chiles. Steaming cup of dark roast. Jack?"

"Bacon, short stack, two eggs over easy, biscuits smothered in sausage gravy. Everything, and I mean everything, drowned in maple syrup and hot sauce."

"No coffee?"

"Of course coffee. Goes without saying. Might even splash some bourbon in it. Start the day off right."

--- --- ---

They got under way, climbing in shadow, the rock still freezing. Logged another two hundred feet and then emerged from the loose talus onto solid granite. It was the steepest pitch they'd seen, Dee leading now and Jack climbing under the kids, all four appendages on the mountain.

He was reaching for the next handhold when Dee said, "Holy shit."

"What?"

"Have you looked down?"

He looked down. The sweep of the mountain falling away beneath them was nothing short of a total mindfuck.

"That looks way worse than it is," Jack said, though he felt like he was going to be sick. He shut his eyes and leaned into the mountain, clutching it, his chest heaving against the rock. "Just keep climbing," he said. "Don't look down if it bothers you."

"It doesn't bother me," Cole said.

"I'm fucking freaked out," Naomi said.

"I can't do this, Jack. There's no way."

"Dee, you want to know something?"

"What?"

"We're kicking ass. Think of everything we've been through since—"

"This is the worst."

"Worse than getting shot at? Than some of the things we've seen?"

"For me it is. I've had nightmares about being stuck on a cliff."

"Well, we aren't stuck, and we have to get over this mountain. That's all there is to it."

"My legs are shaking," Dee said.

"You can do this. You have to do this."

They started to climb again, Jack hanging back, watching their progression, monitoring how comfortable Naomi and Cole looked on the rock, telling them how good they were doing. Struggling to hide his own fear.

It was almost worse looking up the mountain. He couldn't see the spires anymore, had no idea how far they were from the summit ridge. It was just cold, fissured rock and the deep blue sky above it all and a blinding cornice of sunshine.

As he worked his way up a series of ledges in a wide dihedral, it occurred to him that even if they wanted to, going back down would be impossible.

"We taking a rest?" Jack asked.

His family stood just above him on a grassy ledge.

"This is bad, Jack."

"What?"

"This." Dee patted the vertical rock. "It just got steeper."

He climbed the last few feet to them.

"There's another way up," he said. "Has to be." He stepped around Naomi and followed the ledge along the rockface. After twenty feet, it slimmed down to a lip that was barely sufficient to support the toes of his shoes.

He sidestepped back over to them. "That way's no good," he said, staring up the rock that Dee leaned against. It was certainly steeper than anything they'd been on thus far, but the handholds and footholds were prominent, and twelve feet above, a wide crack opened up.

"I think we can climb this," he said.

"Are you crazy?"

"Watch."

He reached up, slid his fingers into a crack, and pulled himself up, jamming his foot into a ledge.

"There's no way, Jack."

"This really isn't bad," he said, though he could feel the threat of a tremor in his right leg, which, at the moment, held all of his weight. He lifted his left foot onto a bulging rock and reached for another handhold—seven feet above the grassy ledge now and the world tilting, an ocean of open air beneath him.

Nothing to do but keep climbing.

The next move brought him to the crack, where he squeezed into a space no larger than a coffin.

"Send the kids up!"

"Jack, come on."

"Just do it, Dee. Cole, can you climb to me, buddy?"

"If they slip—"

"No one's going to slip."

"I can do it, Mom."

Cole reached up and pulled himself onto the rock. "Spot him, Dee."

"No, Cole."

"You have to let him go."

She raised her arms, said, "Cole, you be so careful, baby."

The boy moved up the rock as if he had no concept of the price for falling. Jack on his knees in the nook, stretching his right arm down as the boy came within range.

"Grab my hand. I'll pull you up."

Cole reached for him.

Jack got a solid grasp on his wrist and heaved his boy up the rest of the way.

With the cumbersome pack and the shotgun tied to it, the two of them took up every square inch of the recess in the cliff.

"Dee, you still have the Glock?"

"Yeah, why?"

"I have to get rid of this pack."

"It has our tent, our sleeping bags, our—"

"It's the last thing I want to do, but I can't move in this crack with the pack on."

He unhooked the hip belt.

"Jack, please. We have to have a tent."

Then the chest strap.

"We'll make do."

"How?"

"I don't know. Look out." He slid out of the shoulder straps and launched the pack hard enough to clear the ledge.

It fell uninterrupted for two hundred feet, struck rock, then bounced through a series of echoing ricochets for another four hundred feet until it vanished in the upper realm of the boulder field, the delayed sounds of its ongoing fall still audible.

"All right, Naomi," Jack said, "it's all you."

She began to climb, far less sure of herself than Cole.

Halfway to the crack, she froze.

"I'm stuck," she said.

"You're not stuck. There's a great handhold a couple feet higher."

"I can't hold on any longer. My fingers are—"

"Listen to me, Nay. Reach above you and pull yourself up. If you get to that point, I can grab you."

She looked up at him, tears streaming from the corners of her eyes and so much fear, her entire body trembling, knuckles blanching from the strain of clutching the rock.

"I'm slipping, Dad."

"Naomi. Reach up right now or you're going to fall."

She lunged for the handhold, and Jack saw her miss it, fingers dancing across smooth rock. He reached so far down he nearly fell out of the nook, catching her wrist as she came off the mountain, her feet dangling over the ledge, one hundred and five pounds slowly tugging Jack's shoulder out of its socket and dragging him toward the edge.

"I've got you! Get your feet on the rock, Nay!"

"I'm trying."

"Don't try. Do it." She found purchase and Jack pulled with everything he had, walking her up the rock and then over the ledge, all three of them now crammed into the nook.

"Have a nice life, guys," Dee said, "because there is no fucking way."

"Come on, sweetheart. Get up here. It's cake from here on out."

"Honestly?"

"Maybe 'cake' is too strong a word. It's shortbread. How's that?"

"I hate you so much."

But she started to climb.

— — —

Moving up the crack proved easier, if only because of the illusion of safety—boxed in on three sides and plenty of handholds. They climbed all morning, blisters forming on Jack's fingertips, and he kept wondering how close it was to midday, the adrenaline rush having skewed his perception of time. Doubted their morale could withstand another night on this mountain.

— — —

Thirty feet above, Cole yelled.

Jack's heart stopped. He looked up, the sun burning down, couldn't see a thing through its cutting-torch glare.

"Everyone okay?"

Dee yelled back, "We're at the top!"

— — —

Jack stood on the ridge, bracing against the wind and staring east. The mountain fell away beneath them toward pine-covered foothills that sloped down into high desert. Several miles out and one vertical mile below, a highway ran north to south.

"There it is," Jack said. "I don't see any cars."

"Backside of this mountain doesn't look too awful," Dee said.

"No, just long as hell."

Dee lowered herself off the ridge.

"Ready to get off this rock, huh?" Jack said.

"Like you can't even imagine."

— — —

They descended the east slope—a steep boulder field streaked with last year's snow, which was hard as asphalt. Evening was coming on by the time they stumbled into the trees. After two full days on nothing but rock, the moist dirt floor felt like sponge under Jack's feet. He was too tired and sore to register hunger, but his thirst verged on desperation.

"Should we stop?" Dee asked as they hiked through the darkening woods. "I mean, it's not like we need to find the perfect spot for our tent or anything. Any old piece of ground will do."

"A stream would be nice," he said.

— — —

Jack stopped four times so they could listen for the sound of running water. They never heard it, and exhaustion finally won out.

— — —

Jack climbed under a huge spruce tree and broke off as many lower limbs as his strength would allow. His family joined him under the overhanging branches, and they all lay huddled together on the forest floor.

Dee reached over, held Jack's hand.

Cole was already asleep.

Hardly any light left in the sky, and what little there was struggled to pass through the spiderweb of branches. Jack wanted to say something to Dee and Naomi before they drifted off, something about how proud he was of them, but he made the mistake of closing his eyes while he tried to think of what he should say.

$$- - -$$

He woke once in the middle of the night. Pitch-black and the patter of rainfall all around them. The branches thick enough over
where they slept to keep them dry. Jack's body was cold, but he
could still feel the glow of the sunburn in his face. Brightness when
he shut his eyes. Thinking, water is falling out there. Water. But
thirsty as he was, he couldn't bring himself to move.

THE woods smelled of last night's rainfall and everything still dripped. They could've lain there all day under the tree, watching the light spill through the branches, but he made them get up. Two full days since their last sip of water at that high lake on the other side of the mountain. He fought a raging headache.

– – –

They left while it was still early. No trail to follow but the path of least resistance, slowly winding their way down through the spruce. Cole wouldn't walk, so Jack carried him on his shoulders. He felt dizzy, his legs cramping, thinking he should have dragged them all out from under the tree last night and made a catchment for the rain. They were dying of thirst, and he'd let a shot at water pass them by.

– – –

Midafternoon and stumbling half-mad through the woods. Back down into pine trees, descending toward desert and the heat of it and the tang of dry sage in the upslope wind.

They would've missed it but for Cole.

The boy said, "Look." Pointed toward a boulder a little ways off in the trees with a dark streak running down its face that glistened where the sun struck it.

Jack lifted his son off his shoulders and set him down and ran for it, hurdling two logs and sliding to a stop on his knees in the wet mud.

A steady trickle the width of a string ran off the lip of the rock. He bent down and took a sip, just one to make sure it tasted safe, the water down his throat so cold and sweet he had to physically tear himself away from it.

"How is it?" Dee said. "Safe to drink?"

"Like nothing you ever tasted." Jack stood, traced the stream to where it disappeared into rock. "It's a spring," he said. "Come here, Cole." He helped his son down onto the wet mud and held his mouth under the stream for thirty seconds.

"All right, buddy, it's your sister's turn."

They each got a half minute under the trickle, and then, beginning with Cole, took turns, each as long as they wanted, drinking their fill.

It was torture watching his children gulp down mouthful after mouthful, so Jack wandered away from the boulder to look for a place for them to sleep. Came upon it almost instantly—a stretch of dirt underneath an overhang that would probably keep them dry unless a wild storm blew in. He picked all of the rocks from the dirt and found some patches of moss nearby, which he peeled off the ground and spread out like plush, moist carpeting. He sat down on the moss in the shade of the overhang and stared at the sky through the tops of the trees. Didn't have his watch, but he bet it was four or five in the afternoon. The light was getting long and the clouds dissipating. The chill coming.

= = =

While his family slept, Jack lay under the trickle of water. It took fourteen seconds for his mouth to fill, and then he'd swallow and open again. He lay there forty minutes, watching the sky darken, drinking until his stomach bloated and sloshed.

— — —

Their wet clothes froze during the night, and they lay shivering under the overhang while the moon lifted above the desert. Jack got up and wandered out into the woods and broke off as many limbs as he could find—all pine, the needles densely clustered. Carried an armful back to their pitiful camp and laid the branches over the tangle of bodies that comprised his family.

He stood watching them, then looked back toward the west.

The mountain they'd scaled loomed in the dark.

Broken granite shining in the moonlight.

And he felt something like a drug enter his bloodstream—several heartbeats of pride coursing through him, only it wasn't really pride. Just knowledge. Clarity. A brief window passing through his field of vision. He saw himself objectively, what he'd done, how with his hands and his mind and his handling of fear, he'd kept his family alive this far, a realization surfacing, and it was this: a part of him needed this, loved this, loved being strong for them, going hungry and thirsty for them, even killing for them. He knew he would do it again and without a moment's hesitation. Hell, a part of him might even welcome it. There was simply nothing in his experience that even compared with the thrill of killing to protect his family. In this moment, it was the purpose of his existence.

He felt, possibly for the first time in his life, like a fucking man.

At last, he crawled under the branches and wrapped his arms around his son.

Cole's teeth chattered. "I'm cold," the boy said.

"You'll warm up."

"When?"

"In a minute."

"Can you die of cold?"

"Yes, but that's not going to happen to you."

"I'm still not warm."

"Be patient. It's coming."

JACK woke at dawn and laid his hands upon his children.

"They're breathing," Dee whispered. "I just checked myself."

"You sleep?"

"Not much."

"We stink," he said.

"Speak for yourself."

"No, I think I can safely speak for you too."

He looked at his wife just to look at her. First time he'd done that in . . . ages.

Her cheeks were smeared with dirt. Lips cracked. Sunburned all to hell.

"You've got a few dreadlocks starting," he said.

"I'm hideous, aren't I?"

"Just a tad."

"You smooth talker." She reached across the kids, touched his hand. "We can't keep doing this," she said.

"We're almost out of these mountains. It's going to get better then."

"You think?"

"We're going to find someplace safe, where we can survive.

Where we can get back what we lost. I need you to believe that's
what's going to happen."

"I'm just so tired. And hungry. I look at them and know they're
suffering even more."

"We could be dead, Dee. All of us or some of us. But we're not.
We're together. You have to hold on to that. Let it carry you."

— — —

They came out of the woods in the late morning onto a bare hill
that sloped down to a river, and several hundred yards past, a paved
road. Beyond it all, to the east, lay miles of badlands. It was a pale,
dry country. Rippled and treeless.

They worked their way down through the sage to the riverbank
and stopped for a drink.

Jack lifted Cole onto his shoulders and waded across, Dee and
Naomi trailing behind, his daughter gasping at the icy shock of the
water, which was low in advance of winter, coming only to their
knees at the deepest point.

On the other side, at the top of a small rise, they rested in the
weeds and watched the road.

Nothing passed.

There was no sound but the river and the wind blowing through
the grass.

— — —

Early afternoon and low gray clouds streaming across the sky from
the west.

Jack stepped into the road.

He could see a quarter mile of it from where he stood.

Looking back, that rampart of mountains they'd crossed two
days ago soared above everything, powdered with snow.

"What if a car comes?" Dee said. "There's no way to know if
they're affected."

"We'll have to make a split-second decision. If it's only one car, with one or two people inside, maybe we chance it. Otherwise, we hide."

They walked north along the shoulder.

"Let me have the gun, Dee."

She handed him the Glock, and he ejected the magazine, thumbed out the rounds to count them—nine—and loaded them back.

"Do you know what road this is?" Dee asked.

"I think it's Highway 287."

"Where does it go?"

"To the Tetons, then north up to Yellowstone and into Montana."

"We want to go to Montana?" Naomi asked.

"That's right."

"Why?"

"Because after Montana comes Canada, and we might be safe there."

— — —

They walked for several hours. No cars passed. The road seemed to be some kind of geographic dividing line—badlands to the east, foothills rising toward mountains in the west.

The clouds thickened, and by late afternoon the first raindrops had begun to strike the pavement. They had walked about two miles, Jack figured, and hadn't seen a glimmer of civilization beyond the telephone poles that ran alongside the west shoulder of the road.

"We have to get out of this rain," he said.

They went across the road and up into the trees—tall, straight pines that offered little in the way of shelter.

It was getting dark and the sound of the rainfall filled the woods.

They sat down against one of the pines, and Jack could instantly feel the difference in his legs from just a few hours of walking on pavement. His knees were swollen. Shins riddled with pain like a million tiny fractures. He grimaced as he stood back up.

"I'm going to look for something to keep us dry."

"Please don't go far, Jack."

He wandered away from them up the hillside through the old-growth forest.

After a quarter mile, he came out of the trees.

Stopped, smiled.

= − =

He led them up through the woods into the clearing, gestured proudly toward their accommodations for the evening—the ruins of a stable.

"It ain't the Hilton," he said, "but it'll keep us dry."

The logs were weathered and sun-bleached. The tin roof, deep brown with rust, covered only half of the shelter, and they settled in the far-right corner on the only patch of dry dirt.

The rain drummed on the roof.

"We're lucky to be out of the mountains," Jack said. "Probably snowing up there."

Through the doorway, they could see the rain falling and watch the world getting dark—a grayness deepening toward blue.

Cole crawled into Jack's lap, said, "My stomach hurts."

"I know, buddy, we're all hungry."

"When can we eat?"

"We'll find something tomorrow."

"You promise?"

"He can't promise, Cole," Naomi said. "He doesn't know for sure if we'll find anything to eat tomorrow. All we can do is try."

Cole began to cry.

= − =

It was still raining. They hadn't moved from their corner and they weren't going to be moving anytime soon with it so black out there they couldn't see their hands in front of their faces.

"Wish we had a fire," Naomi said.

"That would be nice."

"I know how," Cole said suddenly, just a voice in the dark.

"How to have a fire?" Dee asked.

"How to tell if they're good or bad."

"Who are you talking about, honey?"

"If we hear a car coming."

"You've been thinking about that?"

"If they have the light around them, we'll know they're bad."

Jack said, "What light, buddy?"

"The light around their head."

"What's he talking about, Jack?"

"I have no idea. Cole, what light do you mean? Do we have it around any of us? Me or your mom or sister?"

"No."

"Do you have it around you?"

The boy was quiet for a moment. "Yes."

"What does it look like?"

"Like white light around my head and my shoulders."

"Why is it around you and not us?"

"Because you didn't see the lights. They didn't fall on you."

"Remember when I asked if you felt different after the aurora?"

"Yes."

"Do you have any bad feelings toward any of us right now?"

"No, Daddy."

"You're sure?"

"I'm sure."

"I don't want to sleep in here with him."

"Stop it, Naomi. He's your brother."

"He's affected. He saw the lights like the rest of those crazy—"

"He's a child."

"So what?"

"Has he tried to hurt you or any of us?" Jack asked.

"No."

"So maybe it doesn't affect children the same way."

"Why would that be?" Dee asked.

"I don't know. Because they're innocent?"

Cole began to cry again. "I don't want to hurt anybody."

"I know you don't," Jack said, and he pulled the boy into his arms.

$$- - -$$

Jack woke several hours later to Cole moaning.

"Dee?"

"What?"

Still couldn't see a thing in the dark.

"Something's wrong with Cole. He's shivering."

Dee's hand slid over his and onto the boy's face.

"Jesus, he's burning up."

"Why's he shaking?"

"He has the chills. Let me have him."

She took Cole into her arms and rocked him and hushed him and Jack lay in the dirt as the sound of rain striking the tin roof tried to carry him off.

COLE looked pale in the gray dawn light that filtered into the ruins of the stable.

Jack said, "What's wrong with him?"

"I can't tell if it's viral or bacterial, but it's getting worse."

"We'll stay here for the day. Let him rest."

"A fever is very dehydrating. He needs water."

"You want to keep moving?"

"I think we have to."

"What else can we do for him?"

Tears welling, Dee shook her head. "Let's try to find some water, then get him someplace warm and dry. That's all we can do."

— — —

Dark, swollen clouds.

Cold.

Everything wet and dripping.

Jack carried Cole in his arms.

The boy had woken but his eyes were milky and unfocused. Not present.

They went down through the pine forest to the road.

The first mile was a straight and steady climb. Then the road curved through a series of switchbacks, and when Jack looked down again, Cole was sleeping.

In the bend of the next turn, he stopped and squatted down in the road, keeping Cole's head supported so he wouldn't wake.

"There's just no way," Jack said. "I could carry him on my shoulders for a little while longer, but not like this."

"We can rest," Dee said.

"Resting isn't going to make my arms stronger. He weighs fifty-four pounds. I just can't physically hold him."

He looked around. They had hiked up into snow—a sloppy inch of it upon everything except the asphalt, the evergreen branches dipping and bouncing back as the snow sloughed off.

"Jack, what do you—"

"Just let me rest for a minute. He's sleeping, and I don't want to wake him."

— — —

They sat in the road. Everything was still except the melting snow and the wind in the spruce trees. Cole shivered in his sleep and Jack wrapped his own jacket around him. Every five minutes, Dee would lay her hand against the boy's forehead.

Naomi asked, "Is he going to die?"

"Of course not," Jack said.

They ate enough snow to quench their thirst and make them all much colder, and Jack fed Cole handfuls of slush. After an hour, they struggled onto their feet and went on. The road kept climbing. Soon there was slush on the pavement. Then snow. Instead of cradling him, Jack found he could manage the weight better by carrying Cole draped over his left shoulder. They would walk a ways and stop and start up again, the periods of walking getting shorter, the rests longer.

It snowed off and on through the day, the road leading them back up into high country. Toward late afternoon, they came across a deserted construction site, Jack's heart lifting at the prospect of finding a pickup truck or even a forklift, but the only motorized equipment left behind had been a small crane, its snow-dusted framework looming over stockpiles of corrugated steel drainage pipe.

— — —

They spent the night inside one of the sixty-foot lengths of pipe, Jack sitting by the opening watching the snow come down until the light was gone. Listening to Dee whisper to Cole, the boy crying, mumbling gibberish, delirious with fever. Considering the state of their distressed little nation, he had no intention of falling asleep, but he shut his eyes just for a moment and

WHEN he opened them again, it was light out and the sky bright blue through the spruce trees and a half foot of fresh snow on the ground.

Naomi's snoring echoed through the pipe.

He looked over at Dee, who was awake and still holding Cole.

She said, "His fever broke about an hour ago."

Had he been standing, the relief would have knocked Jack over.

"Did you even sleep?" he asked.

She shook her head. "But I can feel it coming now."

Jack looked outside. Snow glittered in the early sunlight. "I'm going to have a look around."

"Food today," she said.

"What?"

"One way or another, we have to find some food. It'll have been five days tonight since we last ate, and at some point very soon, we won't have the strength to keep moving. Our bodies just cannot continue to perform like this."

He looked past Dee toward his daughter, sleeping in the shadows. "Nay's okay?"

"Yeah. For now."

"You?"

Dee broke a smile. "I've probably lost twenty, twenty-five pounds these last three weeks. I can't stop thinking how hot I'd look in a little bikini."

— — —

Jack crossed the construction site and climbed up onto the track of the crane. The door had been left unlocked. He scoured the cab. Found three balled-up potato-chip bags and a paper cup filled a quarter of the way with what appeared to be frozen cola.

He set the cup in the sun and moved back between the rows of stacked pipe.

The road was covered in snow.

He went up the hill, inhaling deep shots of frigid, snow-cleansed air. His stomach rumbled. It felt good to be up early and walking in the woods with the sun streaming through the trees.

Someone shouted.

Jack stopped in the road, glanced back, but the sound hadn't come from the construction site.

More voices spilled down through the trees.

He deliberated for three seconds, then started up the road, fighting for traction as he sprinted through powder.

The voices getting louder.

When he came around the next curve, there was a green sign that read TOGWOTEE PASS, ELEV 9658.

In the distance, a lodge. Gas station. Tiny cabins off in the spruce trees.

The parking lot was crowded with an array of vehicles—dozens of civilian cars and SUVs, three Humvees, two armored personnel carriers, one Stryker, a Bradley Fighting Vehicle, and a big rig with two Red Cross insignias emblazoned on the trailer that framed the words "Refugee Relief."

Jack headed toward a group of men in woodland camo BDUs standing by the gas pumps. One of them spotted him, and without a word to the others, shouldered his M16, which had been fitted with a nightscope. The rest of the men saw his reaction, drew their own weapons, and turned to face Jack.

He stopped, staring at five men pointing a variety of firearms in his direction, and the first thing to cross his mind was that it had been nine days since they'd fled the cabin, and how strange it felt to see people again who weren't his family.

"Where'd you come from?"

Jack bent over to catch his breath, pointed back down the road. The man closest to him was the one who'd spoken. A redhead. Very pale. Freckled. Looked to be his age, his height, but with thirty added pounds of muscle and only a two-day beard. He pointed a Sig Sauer at Jack's face.

Said, "You're on foot?"

"Yes."

"Carrying any weapons?" Jack had to think, realized he'd left the Glock back at the pipe with Dee, and, considering the firepower on hand, decided that was probably a good thing.

"No, nothing."

The man waved a hand toward the others and they lowered their machine guns.

"Where you from?"

Jack straightened. "Albuquerque. Been hiking through the mountains last week and a half. Haven't had food in five days."

The man holstered his pistol and smiled, said, "Well, by God, somebody get this man an MRE," but no one moved.

He had blue eyes the color of a washed-out summer sky and he was squinting a little in the sun. "Good thing you caught us. We were about to move out."

"I'm Jack Colclough." Jack stepped forward and extended his hand, which the man accepted.

"Good to meet you, Jack. My name . . ." The elbow caught Jack on the chin. He sat down in the snow as the reinforced steel toe of a black leather combat boot slammed into his face. "Is not really important." Jack opened his eyes. He lay on his back, the redhead's face inches from his own and the blue sky distorted by tears that streamed out of his eyes from his crushed nose. "Who else is with you?"

"No one."

The man's hand wrapped around his ring finger and twisted until Jack felt the bone snap. As he howled, the man stood on his arm and unsheathed a knife.

— — —

When Jack came to, the man was holding his ring finger in front of his face and sliding the gold wedding band up and down the free-range digit.

"Where is the person who put this ring on your finger?"

The pain reached up through Jack's entire left arm like a molten rod he couldn't shake free.

The man unholstered his Sig Sauer, pushed the barrel into Jack's left eye. "Sir, I will put a bullet through your cornea."

"They're dead," Jack said. "You crazy fuckers killed them."

— — —

Dee opened her eyes, the sound of cranking engines having stirred her from sleep. She eased Cole down onto the floor of the pipe and crawled outside.

The sun-glare blinding off the snow.

She called for Jack.

Scanned the construction site but didn't see him.

Hurried through the snow into the road as other engines roared to life.

They weren't far—just a short distance through the trees—and she was running up the road now toward a clearing.

She rounded a turn. There was a gas station at the top of the pass. Military vehicles rumbled in the parking lot, and for a moment her heart lightened and she thought they were saved. Her eyes fell upon two soldiers a hundred feet away, dragging a bloody-faced man by his arms toward the open doors of an eighteen-wheeler.

It was Jack.

She started toward him, got three steps before the mother inside her screamed louder than the wife. Out in the open now. The noise of two dozen engines deafening and the air filling with exhaust. The men were pulling her husband up the ramp into the back of the truck while two other soldiers aimed their weapons into the darkness of the semitrailer. She held the Glock, but in the face of all this, it felt like a bad joke. That voice inside her begging to run. Someone was going to see her and chase her into the woods, kill her or take her away, and then her children would be alone out here, and she couldn't imagine anything worse than that.

She backpedaled off the road into the woods and crouched down in a thicket as a Bradley Fighting Vehicle lurched out of the parking lot into the road, leading the convoy down the west side of the pass. Other cars and SUVs fell in behind as Jack's legs disappeared into the trailer. Soon after, the two soldiers emerged and lowered the rear door. They latched it, hopped down onto the pavement, lifted the metal ramp, and walked it underneath the bed of the truck. Then they ran to the Stryker, one of them ducking into the back while the other climbed up onto the roof and manned the 50-cal.

The big rig lumbered out of the parking lot, tailed by the Stryker, and it felt like her heart was being ripped from her chest as she watched the convoy slip away, rolling down the other side of the mountain.

In an instant, it was gone. All she could hear was the transfer truck downshifting on a steep grade. Then the top of the pass stood silent. No wind. No birds. Just the sun pouring down onto the snow.

Dee leaned over into the ice and came apart.

— — —

She staggered back into the road and followed it down the east side of the pass, her throat raw from crying. Desperate to do something

to fix this but she couldn't, and that helplessness felt like loose
electricity under her skin—wild and frantic but with no outlet. The
urge to put the gun to her own head bordered on irresistible.

She reached the construction site and walked over to the pipe.
Her children still slept. She crawled inside and sat with her knees
drawn into her chest, trying not to cry again so they might sleep a
little longer. Jack was slipping farther away with every passing second. She could feel the expanding distance and it tore her guts out.

Naomi was stirring. Dee turned and stared into the shadow of the
pipe, watched her daughter sit up and rub her eyes.

She looked around.

"Where's Dad?"

Dee whispered, "Come outside. I don't want to wake Cole."

"What's wrong?"

"Just come with me."

When Dee told her daughter what had happened, Naomi cupped
her hands to her mouth and ran to a far stack of pipes and crawled
into one on the bottom row. Dee stood in the snow, her eyes welling
up again, listening to the pipe distort Naomi's sobs like some tragic
flute.

Cole stared at her, as grave as she had ever seen him, but he didn't
cry. They were sitting on a patch of dry pavement in the road in the
warmth of high-altitude sunlight.

"Where did they take him?" the boy asked.

"I don't know."

"Why did they?"

"I don't know."

"Are they going to kill him?"

The questions came like little stabs, shoring up the horror of it all.

"I don't know."

Cole looked back toward the construction site. "When's Naomi going to come out?"

"In a little while. She's upset."

"Are you upset?"

"Yeah."

"When can we see Daddy again?"

She shook her head. "I don't know, Cole."

The boy stared at a trickle of snowmelt gliding down the pavement. "This is one of the worst things that ever happened, isn't it?"

"Yeah." She could tell he was mulling something over, sorting out the ramifications.

"If we don't find Daddy, does that mean you're my wife and I get to be in charge of Naomi?"

Dee wiped her face.

"No, sweetheart, it doesn't mean that."

In the afternoon, Dee walked over to the pipe where Naomi had holed herself up for hours and crouched down by the opening. Inside, her daughter lay unmoving. She reached out, touched her ankle.

"Nay? You asleep?"

Naomi's head shook.

"There are some buildings just up the road. I thought we could check them out, see if there's food. Warm beds to sleep in."

No movement. No answer.

"You can't lay here forever, wishing things aren't the way they are."

"I know that, Mom. Can you just give me thirty minutes, please?"

"Okay. But then we have to leave."

= = =

The shadows stretched as they walked through slush to the top of the pass.

The lodge had been vandalized.

The restaurant raided.

Refrigerators contained nothing but rotting vegetables and fruit. Spoiled jars of condiments that she almost considered eating.

Dee had to break glass to gain entry to one of the tiny cabins. They climbed through the window frame. Just as cold on the inside, but at least there were two bunkbeds along the wall.

The kids crawled into bed and Dee unlocked the door and went back outside. She walked down to the road, stood at the crest of the pass. Thirty-five miles away, Grand Teton punctured the lower curve of the sun. The nearer peaks were catching alpenglow, the snow and the rock the color of peach skin.

She watched the sun drop, wondering where Jack was in all that darkness.

Closing her eyes, she spoke aloud. "Jack, do you hear me? Wherever you are, whatever's happening to you in this moment, know that I love you. And I'm with you. Always."

She'd never said anything with such desperation. It was the closest she'd ever come to prayer, and she wondered if the intensity of what raged inside her could carry the words to him on some secret frequency.

Beneath the stars, she started back toward her children, the snow crunching under her footsteps. A part of her still thinking that when she walked into that little cabin, Jack would be there, her sensory memory still operating on the default of his proximity.

In the total darkness of the cabin, she could hear Cole and Naomi breathing deeply. She pulled off her crumbling shoes and took a bottom bunk—sheeted mattress, no blanket. Hoped her children dreamed of something other than what their life had become.

I N the morning, Naomi had barely the strength to rise out of bed, and the prodding it took rivaled the difficulty Dee had experienced trying to rouse her two months ago on the first school day of the year.

They wandered outside, having slept through most of the morning, and now it was almost warm and the sun was high and there were only patches of snow in the shadows and the forest. They ate as much of it as they could get down.

The pavement was mostly dry. They started down the other side of the pass, Dee cold and more lightheaded than when she donated blood. The spruce trees and the sky had lost their vibrancy, almost sepia-toned, and the sounds of the forest and their footsteps on the road came muffled.

She wondered if they were dying.

— — —

In the midafternoon, Dee glanced up and saw that Naomi was sitting in the road, swaying over the double yellow.

Dee eased down beside her.

"Are we stopping?" Cole asked.

"Just for a minute."

The boy walked over to the shoulder to investigate a brown sign riddled with buckshot that warned, YOU ARE NOW IN GRIZZLY BEAR COUNTRY.

"I think a rest is a good idea," Dee said.

"I'm not resting."

"Then what is this?"

"I'm so hungry and tired and Dad's probably dead. I just want to die now too."

"Don't say that."

Naomi turned slowly and stared at her mother. "Don't you? Be honest."

"We have to keep going, Nay."

"Why do you say that? We don't have to do anything. We can stay right here and waste away or you can put us all out of our misery right now."

Her eyes flickered to the Glock tucked into Dee's waistband.

It surprised Dee as much as it did Naomi when she slapped her daughter hard across the face.

She whispered, "You get the fuck up right now, young lady, or I will drag your little ass down this mountain, so help me God. I didn't raise you to quit."

Dee struggled back onto her feet as Naomi slumped across the road and wept with what little energy she still had.

"Come on, Cole, let's go."

"What's wrong with Naomi?"

"She'll be okay. Just needs a minute."

"Are we leaving her?"

"Nope, she'll be right along."

They had covered barely a mile by evening when they left the road for a boulder-strewn meadow. No snow or running water anywhere. As the thirst stalked them, all Dee could think about was all the snow they'd passed up earlier in the day, how she should have taken a container from the restaurant at the pass, packed it with ice for later.

The ground was soft and moist from the recent snowfall, and they curled up on the far side of a boulder, hidden from the road, everyone asleep before the stars came out.

DEE woke with the sun in her face and a dehydration headache. Her children slept and she let them go on sleeping. Lethargic and hopeless. Nothing more unappealing than rising from the cool, soft grass to trudge on down that road.

— — —

She lay there, gliding in and out of consciousness, always returning to the question—where are you? And—are you? It seemed impossible that he could be gone and she not know. Not feel it in the pit of her soul.

— — —

She lay facing her daughter, Naomi's eyes half-open, blades of dead-yellow grass trembling between them that Dee had been giving serious thought to eating.

"I hurt everywhere," Naomi said.

"I know."

"Are we dying, Mom?"

"We're in rough shape, baby."

"Is it going to hurt a lot worse than this? Toward the end, I mean."

"I don't know."

"How much longer?"

"Naomi, I don't know."

Dee had completely lost time, and whether the sun's position in the sky indicated late morning or early afternoon, she couldn't tell. She reached over and put her hand to Cole's back. Confirmed the rise and the fall. The boy slept against the boulder and she could feel the cold radiating from the rock.

When Dee rolled back over toward her daughter, Naomi was sitting up in the grass, Dee thinking her zygomatic bones seemed extraordinarily pronounced, like crescent moons forming the lower boundary of her hollowed-out eye sockets.

"You hear that?" Naomi said.

Dee did. It was a sound like sustained thunder.

She looked up, said, "It's above us, Nay."

A jet was crossing the sky, its contrail iridescent in the brilliant blue.

Night and freezing cold. Dee lying with her back against the boulder, Cole shivering in her arms. The children slept, but she'd been awake for an hour, fighting black thoughts. She hadn't intended to lie in this meadow all day. Between the weakness and exhaustion, it had just happened. But tomorrow would involve a choice, and knowing they'd only be more exhausted, thirstier, and in greater agony, she was already making excuses for why they shouldn't push on. Basking in the increasingly soothing presence of what lay a few inches away in the grass, always within arm's reach.

Naomi shook her awake.

"Mom, get up."

Dee opened her eyes to her daughter silhouetted against the sweep of stars.

"What's wrong, Nay?" It hurt to speak, her throat swollen.

"Someone's coming."

"Give me a hand?"

She extricated herself from Cole's embrace and grabbed onto Naomi's arm and tugged herself upright.

Sat listening.

At first, nothing. Then she discerned the sound of an engine still a long ways off, had to strain to tell if it was fading away or approaching.

"It's coming toward us, Mom."

Dee used the boulder to pull herself onto her feet. She picked up the Glock, the metal glazed with frost. They walked through the alpine meadow to the shoulder of the road. The double yellow glowing in the starlight and the noise of the approaching car getting louder, like a wave coming ashore.

Dee's leg muscles burned. The warmth of her hand had melted some of the frost off the Glock, and she used her shirt to clear off the rest of the condensation and ice.

"Go back to the boulder, Nay."

"What are you going to do?"

Dee slipped the Glock into a side pocket of her rain jacket. "When you hear me call out, wake Cole and bring him over, but not until. And if something happens, you hide, and take care of your brother."

"Mom—"

"We don't have time. Go."

Naomi ran back into the meadow and Dee stepped out into the road, searching for the glint of headlights through the trees, but there was nothing save for the noise of the approaching engine, riding down from the pass.

A shadow blitzed around the corner.

A car with no headlights barreled toward her in the dark of night and she stood straddling the double yellow, waving her arms like a madwoman.

Inside of a hundred yards, the RPMs fell off and the glow of brake lights fired the asphalt red and the tires screeched against the pavement. Dee shielded her eyes from the imminent collision but did not yield an inch.

The engine idled two feet away from her and the smell of scorched rubber filled the air. She lowered her arm from her face as the driver's door squeaked open. It was an old Jeep Cherokee, dark green or brown—impossible to tell in this light—with four fuel containers strapped to the roof.

"You trying to commit suicide?" a man growled.

Dee took out the Glock and lined it up in the center of his chest. By the glow that emanated from the Jeep's interior lights, she could see that he was older—short, brown hair on top, a great white beard, salt-and-pepper mustache that struggled to merge the two. He held something in his left hand.

"Drop it," she said.

When he hesitated, she sighted down his face, and something in her eyes must have persuaded him, because a gun clattered onto the pavement.

"You're ambushing me?"

Dee shouted for the kids, heard them come running in the dark.

"Grab the top of the door," Dee said.

The man complied as Naomi and Cole hustled across the road.

On the door below the window, Dee noticed a National Park Service emblem.

"Do you see him, Cole?" Dee said as he sidled up next to her.

"Yes."

She wouldn't take her eyes off the man.

"Does he have light around his head?"

"Lady, what are you—"

"Be quiet."

"No, Mom."

"You're sure."

"Yes."

Still, she didn't lower the gun. "What's your name, sir?"

"Ed."

"Ed what?"

"Abernathy."

"What are you doing out here, Mr. Abernathy?"

"What are *you* doing out here?"

"Girl with the gun gets the answers."

"Trying to survive."

"We aren't affected," she said.

"Neither am I."

"I know."

"How exactly do you know?"

"You have water and food?"

He nodded, and it was just a flash of a thought—considering their present state, what the world had become, Dee should kill him right now and take his Jeep and whatever provisions it contained. Not fuck around for one more second, because there was too much at stake. Pulling the trigger, though, was another thing. Maybe he was a good guy, maybe not, but she couldn't shoot him in cold blood, not even for her children, and maybe because of them.

"There were four of us." Tears coming. "My husband was taken two days ago by some sort of military unit. Do you know where he might be?"

"I'm sorry, I don't."

"We haven't eaten in a week." Dee felt unstable, eased her right leg back to brace herself against falling. "I don't want to keep pointing this gun at your face."

"That'd be all right with me too."

She lowered the Glock, slid it into the back of her waistband.

Ed started to bend down. Stopped midway. "I'm picking up my gun, but there's no threat intended."

"Okay."

He ducked behind the door, lifted the revolver off the pavement, and came toward them. Squatted down to Cole's eye level.

"I'm Ed," he said. "What's your name?"

Cole didn't reply.

"Tell him your name," Naomi said.

"Cole."

"Do you like Snickers candy bars?"

Dee's stomach fluttered with a new pang of hunger.

"Yes."

"Well, you're in luck."

"Are you a nice person?"

"I am. Are you?"

Cole nodded and Ed pushed against his knees and stood to face Naomi.

"I'm Naomi," she said.

"Glad to meet you, Naomi."

Dee extended her hand. "Ed, I'm Dee."

"Very nice to meet you."

The upwelling came so fast and unexpectedly that she fell toward Ed and wrapped her arms around his neck. She was sobbing. Felt him patting her back, couldn't pick out the words, but the deep tone of his voice, which seemed to move through her like thunder, was the closest she'd come to comfort in days.

= = =

Ed pulled the Cherokee into the meadow and got out and popped the hatch. Dee and the kids gathered around as he rifled through a banker's box of packaged food. Three more plastic gas containers crowded the backseats, and there were jugs of water on the floorboards.

Dee sat in the back with Naomi and Cole, her fingers overanxious and shaking as she ripped open Cole's wrapper. At the smell of chocolate and peanuts, her hunger swelled into an ache.

They had two candy bars each and several apples and shared a gallon of water from a glass jug. So ravenous it felt less like eating and drinking, more like finally breathing again after being held underwater. When they'd finished, it was all Dee could do not to beg for more, but from the look of things, Ed was light on provisions.

"Where you coming from?" she asked.

He sat in the grass near the bumper, just inside the field of illumination thrown from the Jeep's rear dome light. "Arches National Park over in Utah."

"You a park ranger?"

"Yep."

"We left Albuquerque . . . I don't know, three weeks ago, I guess? What day is it?"

"Friday. Well, early Saturday now."

"We were trying to get to Canada. Heard there might be refugee camps across the border."

"I heard the same."

"Have you run into much trouble?"

He shook his head. "I left three days ago. Been traveling mainly at night. In fact, I need to get going."

As he rose to his feet, Dee noticed he wore green pants and a long-sleeved gray button-down, wondered if this was his ranger uniform.

She said, "Would you let us come with you?"

"I can't fit you all inside."

"Then take my children."

"Mom, no."

"Shut up, Nay. Would you? Please?"

Ed took out his revolver.

"I need you out of my Jeep right now. I've given you some of my food, my water. I'll even leave a jug with you, but I cannot take you."

Dee looked down at her filthy, stinking shoes.

"We'll die out here."

"And we may all die if you come with me. Now, get out of there. I have to go."

— — —

Dee stood watching the Jeep move across the meadow and into the road, heard the engine rev, saw its taillights wink out, listening as it sped away from them into darkness.

Naomi was crying. "You should've shot him, Mom. You had him back there with his gun on the ground and you just let him—"

"He's not a bad man, Nay."

"We're going to die now."

"He wasn't trying to hurt us. You want to live in a world where we have to kill innocent people to survive? I won't do that. Not even for you and Cole. There's things worse than dying, and for me, that's one of them."

Cole said, "Listen."

An engine was approaching. The shadow of that Jeep reappeared and shot out a triangle of light as it reentered the meadow.

The engine cut off.

Ed climbed out.

"I'm not happy about this," he said, walking around to the back, popping the hatch. "Not one goddamn bit. So don't say anything, and for God's sake don't thank me. Just get over here and help me make some room."

Ed loaded what would fit into the cargo area and made just enough room for Naomi and Cole in the backseat. Dee climbed in up front, buckled herself in, and Ed cranked the engine. Heat rushed out of the vents. The digital clock read 2:59 A.M. He put the car into gear and eased across the meadow, over the shoulder, back onto the road.

Turned on the stereo as he accelerated.

Dirty blues blasted from the speakers: *She's a kindhearted woman, she studies evil all the time. You well's to kill me, as to have it on your mind.*

Dee leaned against the window, watching the trees rush by. Felt so strange to be moving this fast again, the pavement streaming under the tires.

The road snaked down through the spruce forest on a **steep** descent from the pass and her ears kept popping and clogging, **the** world loud, then muffled, then loud again when she swallowed. With the moon full and high, it struck the road like sunlight and made shadows of the trees. The view to the west was long, and through the windshield she could see the massive skyline of the Tetons.

Dee glanced back between the front seats, saw Cole and Naomi sleeping sprawled across each other. She reached over, touched Ed's shoulder.

"You saved our lives."

"What'd I say about thanking me?"

"I'm not thanking you, just stating a fact."

"Yeah, but I didn't want to. I'm a supremely selfish fuck."

Dee tilted her seat back. "Let me know if you want me to **drive**."

He grunted, his hands tapping time to the blues, Dee wondering if he'd have sung along if they weren't in the car with him.

"You can sing if you want," she said. "Won't bother us."

"Might want to be more careful about what you offer in the future," he said, and started to sing.

His voice was awful.

= = =

She dozed against the window, dipping in and out of dream fragments that she couldn't quite commit herself to before settling finally into a hard and dreamless sleep.

Next time she woke, it was 5:02 A.M.

Still dark out the windows except where the faintest purple had begun to tint the eastern sky. Naomi and Cole slept. The music had stopped.

"Want me to drive for a bit so you can sleep?"

"Nah, I was going to stop in a few miles anyway. Get us off the road for the daylight hours."

THE Old Faithful Inn towered like a mountain against the pre-dawn sky. They pulled under the front portico. The kids were stirring, woken by the cessation of movement. Ed turned off the engine and stepped out and opened the back hatch. Took a flashlight from one of the supply boxes.

The red double doors stood ajar.

They pushed through them.

Ed flicked on the flashlight.

"Hello?" His voice echoed through the immense lobby as the beam of his light passed across the hearth and moved up four stories of framework supported by a forest of burnished tree trunks.

No response.

"Ever been here?" Ed asked.

"Once," Dee said.

They climbed the stairs to a row of rooms that overlooked the upper porch. Dee and the kids took one with two queen beds. The walls were cedar-paneled. A cast-iron radiator occupied the space beneath the window, and they didn't need a flashlight anymore with dawn fading up through the dormer.

Ed said, "I sort of feel like one of us should keep watch. Case someone comes."

"You drove all night," Dee said. "I'll do it."

"Five or six hours, I'll be good as new. Wake me at noon."

— — —

Dee strolled the corridors in near darkness. The silence of the place imposing. She'd been here before with Jack. Sixteen years ago. A summer day, the lobby bustling and filled with light. They were passing through on a move from Montana to New Mexico, Jack having just been hired by UNM, Dee en route to begin a residency at the university hospital. They'd only stopped for a few hours to have lunch in the dining room, but she still recalled the feel of that day—a lightness in her being and with the two of them married just four months, the sense that they were really beginning a life together, that everything lay open and accessible before them.

— — —

She walked down to the lobby and went outside, following the paved path to the observation point. The day had dawned clear. Across the basin, a herd of elk grazed the edge of a lodgepole pine forest still recovering from a recent fire and interspersed with dead trees.

A column of water launched out of the earth, steaming in the cold. There had been five hundred tourists here the last time Dee had watched it blow. She listened to the superheated water rain down on the mineralized field, a light wind in her face, the mist lukewarm by the time it reached her.

— — —

In the early afternoon, she and Ed made the climb to the widow's walk, stood on top of the lodge looking out over the basin and the hills, no sound but the flags flapping on the grounds below. Seemed

like if she stared hard and long and far enough, she might catch a
glimpse of him somewhere out there.

"You're missing your husband."

She wiped her eyes. "Did you leave anyone behind when you
left Arches?"

Ed shook his head.

"I was married once. I've been thinking about her. You know,
wondering."

"Any kids?"

"Haven't been in touch with them in a long time." He looked at
her as if he might offer some further explanation, then moved on to
something else instead. "I'm concerned the Canadian border is
going to be tough to cross. I've been considering other possibili-
ties."

"Like what?"

"We're only a few hours south of Bozeman. That's the nearest
airport. Maybe we get our hands on a plane."

"You're a pilot?"

"Used to fly commercial jets."

"How long since you've been in a cockpit?"

"You really want to know?"

"Can you still fly? I mean, doesn't the technology change?"

"We'd just be looking for a twin-prop. Nothing too complicated.
We could be in Canada in an hour."

— — —

Dee slept through the afternoon, and in the evening, she took
Naomi and Cole down to the observation point. When it finally
blew, the last rays of sunlight shot horizontally through the scalding
mist and turned the water into fire.

— — —

Ed gassed up the Jeep and added a few quarts of oil, employed
Cole to clean the dust and grime off the windows. They set out

with the moon high enough to obviate the need for headlights, speeding north through the park to the blues of Muddy Waters.

An hour and a half brought them to the Montana border. They roared across and up through the isolated towns of Gardiner, Miner, and Emigrant, all vacated and so thoroughly burned there wasn't even the temptation to stop and search for food.

A little before midnight, Ed pulled onto the shoulder.

"We're close to Bozeman," he said, "but if we stay on this road, we're going to have to get on the interstate." He opened the glove compartment, pulled out a map, and unfolded it across the steering wheel.

Dee leaned over and touched a light gray line that branched off from the bold one that denoted the highway they'd been driving all night.

"Here?" she said.

"Yeah, that's the one we need to find. See how it cuts right across? Once we hit it, we're only twenty miles from the Bozeman airfield."

$$- - -$$

Dee spotted the road as they raced past, and Ed turned around in the empty highway and headed back. It was an unmarked dirt road that exploited the Jeep's decrepit shocks, rocking them along for several miles on a gentle climb through a pine forest. Just dark enough when passing through the corridor of trees to persuade Ed to punch on the headlights.

"Could we actually fly out tonight?" Dee said.

"Assuming we find a plane with sufficient fuel, I'll probably want to wait until first light. Really don't want my first flight in over two decades to be by instrumentation."

"Decades?"

"Can I help fly?" Cole asked.

"Absolutely, copilot."

Dee stared out the window, thinking how flying out of all this madness, of finally getting her kids someplace safe, felt so far beyond the realm of possibility that she couldn't even imagine it happening.

Ed slammed the brakes.

She shot forward, painfully restrained by the seatbelt, looked up when she'd recoiled back into the leather seat, her first thought her children who were picking themselves up out of the backseat floorboards and her second the numerous points of light that were moving toward the Jeep.

"Back up, Ed!"

The windshield splintered and something warm sprayed the side of Dee's face as Ed fell into the steering wheel, the horn blaring, other rounds piercing the glass, the night filling with gunshots. Dee unbuckled her seatbelt and shoved the gearshift into park and crawled over the console into the backseat. Sprawled herself on top of Naomi and Cole as more bullets struck the car.

"Is he dead?" Naomi asked.

"Yes."

The firing stopped.

"Either of you hit?"

"No."

"Make it stop!" Cole cried.

"Are you hit, Cole?"

He shook his head.

Footsteps approached the Jeep, and in the illumination of an oncoming flashlight, Dee could see clear liquid sheeting down the glass of the rear passenger window.

Already her eyes were burning, the fumes getting stronger.

"We have to get out of the car," she whispered.

"They'll shoot us," Naomi said.

"They'll burn us alive if we stay in. They've shot some of the plastic gas cans on top of the Jeep."

Dee opened the door and tumbled out. The glare of flashlights maxed her retinas and she could see little of who was there, nor could she determine their number amid the afterimages that pulsed purple in the dark.

"Stop right there." A man's voice. Dee stood and raised her hands.

"Please. I have two children with me. Naomi, Cole, get out." She felt one of them, probably Cole, glom onto her right arm.

"They're like me," Cole said.

"What are you talking about?"

"They have light around their head. All of them."

"Get back in your car," the man said, close enough now for Dee to get a decent look—three-day beard, dark navy trousers and parka, aiming an automatic weapon at her face.

He motioned toward the car with the machine gun as others emerged out of the dark behind him.

Dee considered the Glock pushed down the back of her pants. Suicide.

"Bill, check the driver."

A short, stocky soldier put a light through Ed's window.

"Gone to be with the Lord, boss."

"Got your Zippo on you, you chain-smoking motherfucker?"

"Yeah."

"Particularly attached to it?"

"It was my older brother's."

"Cough that shit up."

"Fuck, Max."

The light beam glimmered off the steel as the soldier chucked his lighter to the man who held Dee and her children at gunpoint, Max catching it with his left hand, never letting the AR-15 waver in his right.

Max looked at Cole. "What are you doing with *them*, little man?"

"Do not speak to my son."

"Shut the fuck up."

"What do you mean?" Cole asked.

"You know exactly what I mean. Don't you want to come with us?"

"Why don't you leave us alone? We aren't doing anything to you."

Max looked up at Dee with unfiltered hatred. "Get back in the car."

"No."

"Get in the car or I'll shoot you and your children in the knees and put you in there myself. You can roast healthy or you can roast with shattered kneecaps. It makes not a fucking bit of difference to me so long as I get to watch you burn."

Dee said, "What did we ever . . ."

Max aimed the AR-15 at her left knee.

Split-second choice—reach for the Glock or speak one last time to her children.

"I love you, Naomi. I love you, Cole. No one and nothing can take that away."

"I can," Max said.

She drew her kids into her, Naomi crying now, but she didn't allow herself to avert her eyes from the man who was going to murder them. She stared Max down, wondering if he would think of them years from now on his deathbed in a moment of clarity and regret, wondering if her eyes would always haunt him. But she doubted it as he returned the stare, a malevolent smile curling his lips, Dee's heart in her throat.

The slug mostly decapitated Bill.

A shotgun thundered out of the woods, Max spinning toward the gunfire, several of his men falling, flashlights hitting the ground, muzzle flames spitting out from their machine guns. Dee jerked Naomi and Cole to the ground and dragged them away from the Jeep toward the other side of the road, where they rolled into a ditch.

The gunfire intensified, bullets striking the trees behind them, Dee pushing Naomi's and Cole's heads down, pulling Cole into her chest and speaking into his ear over the shattering noise: "I'm right here, I've got you." She couldn't hear him crying but she could feel his body shaking.

After what seemed ages, the gunfire dissipated.

They lay in the dark, Dee staring into a wall of dirt.

Someone yelled, "Fall back."

Footsteps crunched through the leaves—someone retreating into the woods.

A man groaned nearby, begging for help.

Three reports from a handgun.

An AR-15 answered.

The exchange went on for several minutes, and it struck Dee that the gunfire sounded like the communication of terrible birds. She was tempted to climb out of the ditch and have a look, but she couldn't bring herself to move.

After a while, the shooting stopped altogether.

Footfalls echoed through the forest.

The man nearby pleaded to God.

Someone said, "Jim, right there."

A machine gun ripped up the silence.

Four shotgun blasts roared back.

Footsteps moved closer to the ditch.

"Sure we got all of them?"

A woman answered, "Yeah, there were nine. I count one, two, three, four, five, six . . . ." She laughed. "Where you think you're going?" A single handgun report rang out. "And this one's still hanging in there too."

"No, Liz."

"Why?"

"Please, it hurts so bad."

"You're breaking my fucking heart. Why can't I end this piece of shit?"

"Mathias wants one alive."

"Fine. Driver's dead, but I saw three others get out. Woman, couple of kids."

"They crawled into the woods when the shooting started. May be gone by now."

Footsteps moved across the dirt road and stopped at the edge of the ditch.

The woman yelled into the woods, "Woman with two kids! You out there? We're the good guys, and the bad guys are dead or wishing they were."

Dee didn't move, not wanting to startle anyone, just said softly, "We're right here. Underneath you."

The woman knelt down. "Anyone hurt?"

"No." Dee pushed herself out of the dirt and sat up. "Thank you. They were going to burn us."

"You're safe now." The woman reached out, took hold of Dee's hand. "I'm Liz."

"Dee."

"And who's this?"

"This is Cole, and this is Naomi."

"Hi, Cole. Hi, Naomi."

Liz wore a dark one-piece jumpsuit. Long black hair drawn back into a ponytail under her black beanie. Even squatting down, Dee could see that she was tall and fit, possessing a hard, wiry strength evident in the angular tapering of her jawline.

"You want to come with us?" Liz asked.

"To where?"

Liz smiled. "It's not far."

--- --- ---

Dee held Cole's and Naomi's hands as they followed Liz and the others back through the woods, guided by flashlights. Two of their party stayed behind, dragging the injured soldier whom they could hear groaning some distance back through the trees, Dee feeling the ache, despite everything, to attend to him. It was deep-rooted hardwiring from her medical training that she wondered if she would ever lose.

A quarter mile into the woods, they stopped.

Someone said, "We're at the perimeter."

A voice crackled back over a radio: *"You're clear."*

"We picked up a woman and two children. I'm going to have Liz put them in Number 14. Have someone bring food and water over. New clothes too."

"Copy that."

Dee noticed light glinting off coils of razor wire straight ahead.

One of the men stepped on the wire where it sagged, made an opening for everyone to crawl through. They went on and, after another fifty feet, finally emerged from the woods.

Under the moonlight, Dee could see a number of smaller buildings scattered through the clearing—all satellites of a large, arched steel building.

Liz fell back and walked with them.

"You must be exhausted," she said. "We're going to put you up in a cabin. You're safe here. See those?" She pointed toward opposing ends of the clearing where twenty-foot log towers stood near the edge of the forest. "There's a heavily armed man in each wearing night-vision goggles. They'll be watching over the clearing while you sleep."

They were moving toward a grouping of small cabins now.

"I don't understand. What is this place?" Dee asked.

"It's home."

The cabin was clean and smaller than the shacks at the top of Togwotee Pass. There were two beds and a chair pushed under a desk and a chest of drawers. Sink and shower.

"We cut the generators off at night," Liz said. She opened the top drawer and took out several candles and a box of matches. Soon, candlelight warmed the room.

She came over to Dee and inspected her face.

"You're covered in blood. I'll make sure they bring a basin of water so you can clean up. The showers won't run hot until morning."

"Thank you, Liz."

"I'll leave you guys now. Food should be here shortly."

Dee stripped to her bra and underwear, suddenly aware of how terrible she smelled. She bent down and dipped her face into the basin of water and wiped off the dried blood with a washcloth. Scrubbed her armpits, did a cursory cleaning of her arms and legs.

= = =

Cole slept. Dee and Naomi sat on the other bed devouring the food that had been brought for them—a tray of fruit and cheese and crackers that tasted better than anything they'd ever eaten.

Dee stowed her Glock under the mattress. They crawled under the covers and it took some time before their body heat warmed the air between the mattress and the sheet, Dee spooning her daughter, sleep right around the corner.

Naomi whispered, "Do you think Dad's dead?"

The question felt like someone driving a spike through the ulcer in Dee's stomach.

Tomorrow would be four days without him.

"I don't know."

"Well, does it feel to you like he is?"

"I don't know, baby. I can't even think about it. Please just let me sleep."

SHE'D just fallen asleep when the windows filled with dawn light. Dee rose, pulled the curtains, climbed back into bed. Tried to sleep but her thoughts came frenetic, unstoppable. She got up again and went to the window and peered through the split in the curtain. The grasses were blanched with frost, and a few people were out already.

In the meadow were two dozen cabins like the one they occupied, three larger A-frames, the central steel building, and a number of semitrailers along the edge of the woods, rusted all to hell and cemented with pine needles, as if it had been centuries since their abandonment. Distant mountains peeked above the pine trees, and Dee stood watching the light color them.

$$- - -$$

The main building was fifty feet wide, twice as long, and windowless. Bare lightbulbs dangled from the trusses and the amalgamation of voices caused a hollow, metallic resonance off the corrugated steel. Folding tables had been pushed against the walls, leaving a wide aisle down the middle. Just inside the entrance, a chalkboard stand displayed: BACON & CHEESE OMELET WITH HASH BROWNS.

Liz led them to an empty table.

"We haven't been able to get into town for several weeks, so we've been dipping into our MRE stash."

"What's an MRE?" Cole asked.

"Stands for Meal, Ready-to-Eat. It's an army ration. We bought two truckloads last year."

Dee could feel the stares coming from every direction, tried to focus on the blemishes in the plastic tabletop, ignoring that twinge in her gut like the first day of junior high and the minefield of the cafeteria.

A teenage girl appeared at the end of the table holding a basket filled with small, brown packages, plastic silverware, and a stack of tin bowls.

"Welcome," she said.

- - -

The man who spoke after breakfast was slight and smooth-shaven with thinning blond hair on the brink of turning white. He wore jeans, a plaid shirt, a black down vest, and he stood on a table at the back of the mess hall so everyone could see him.

"No doubt you all heard the gunshots last night. I'm happy to report that Liz and Mike and their team managed to take out the soldiers' checkpoint at the road."

Raucous applause broke out.

Someone yelled, "Freemen!"

Silence returned when he lifted his hand.

"No casualties on our end, and the really good news is that we took one alive. Badly wounded, but alive. Liz and Mike also managed to save three lives during the ambush." He pointed to Dee's table. "Would you and your children stand up, please?"

Dee took Cole's hand and poked Naomi and they all rose. The room grew quiet.

"Thank you," Dee said. She glanced down at Liz. "To you. To Mike, wherever you are, and all of the others who came. My children and I would be dead right now if it weren't for you."

"Why don't you come on up here," the man said.

Dee stepped around her chair and walked down the aisle. When she arrived at the table the man was standing upon, he reached down and opened his hand and pulled her up with him. Slipping his arm around her waist, he put his lips to her ear and whispered, "I'm Mathias Canner. Introduce yourself. Tell us about your journey."

Dee looked out over the crowd—fifty, maybe sixty faces staring back at her. She managed a weak smile.

"I'm Dee," she said. "Dee Colclough."

Someone in the back yelled, "Can't hear you!"

— — —

Later, she walked with Mathias. It was midmorning and the sun had cleared the forest wall. He showed her the well, the greenhouse and chicken coop, the gardens that had already been winterkilled.

"I bought this ninety-acre parcel twelve years ago," he said. "Sold my business and moved out here with several friends from Boise."

"What made you want to do all this?"

"Wanting to live as a free man."

"You weren't free before?"

He waved to the bearded man up in the guard tower holding a sniper rifle. "Morning, Roger."

"Morning."

"All quiet?"

"All quiet."

As Mathias led Dee into the trees, his right hand unsnapped the holster for the huge revolver at his side.

"Roger came to me nine years ago. He was an investment banker pulling down three mil a year and utterly miserable. The electrified razor wire starts fifty feet in and runs through the woods around the entire clearing. We've installed motion detectors at key points and six people walk the perimeter day and night. If I find out you're a spy or that you've lied to me in any way, I'll kill your children in front of you, wait a day, and then kill you."

He stopped and stared at her.

She could hear the hum of the fence just ahead of them and, standing in a patch of light, see the color in his eyes—brown with sunlit flecks of green. Her kneecaps trembled, and for a moment, she thought she might have to sit down.

"I'm just a doctor from Albuquerque," she said. "Trying to keep my kids safe. Everything I've told you is true."

They walked again, moving alongside the fence.

"Ten days ago, we sent someone out on reconnaissance."

"They haven't come back?"

He shook his head. "What's it like out there?"

"It's a waking nightmare that never ends. You can't tell who's affected until they try to kill you."

"They aren't just military?"

"No. They group together and travel in convoys, and they recognize the unaffected on sight. I couldn't tell you how many towns we passed through that have been burned to the ground."

"We had to put five of our own down a few weeks ago. They killed three people before we stopped them. Is it a virus? Do you know what's causing it?"

Dee hesitated.

"No," she said finally. "It all imploded so fast."

They crossed a road—just the faintest depression of tire tracks in the leaves.

"You have vehicles?" she asked.

"Yeah."

She caught movement up ahead—one of the guards cruising the perimeter.

"Two of our women are pregnant," Mathias said. "We don't have a doctor."

"I'd be happy to see them."

They veered back out of the woods into the clearing, moved past a group of children standing in the grass, each with their own easel.

"We're really proud of our school here," he said. "Naomi and Cole are welcome to attend, of course."

— — —

In the afternoon, Dee examined two women with child and checked in on a fifteen-year-old boy with a low-grade fever and rackety cough. It was a relief to engage her mind in her old life again, if only for a short while.

— — —

"I don't like this place," Naomi said. "These people creep me out."

Dee lay in bed in their cabin under the covers with Cole and Naomi, the boy already asleep.

"Would you agree it's an improvement on starving to death?"

"I guess."

Cold air slipped in through the window frame. There was just a hint of color in the sky and the tops of the spruce trees were pro-filed against it.

"Are we staying?" Naomi asked.

"For a few days at least. Get our strength up."

"Is this, like, a militia?"

"I think it might be."

"So they probably believe all kinds of crazy shit about the government and Black people?"

"Don't know, haven't asked them, don't plan to."

"I'd rather just go to Canada."

"Could we take it a day at a time for now? At least while they're still feeding us?"

— — —

The knock at the door came in the middle of the night.

Dee stirred from sleep, sat upright, and looked around. Not a single source of man-made light, and because she'd extinguished the candle before settling into bed, the room was absolutely dark. She couldn't recall the layout of her surroundings or even where she was until Mathias Canner's voice passed through the door.

"Dee. Get up."

She climbed over Cole, her bare feet touching the freezing floorboards.

Moved through pure darkness toward Canner's voice.

No locks on the inside of the door, which she pulled open by the wooden handle.

"Sorry to wake you," Mathias said through the inch of open space between the doorframe and the door. "But you're a doctor." He grinned, and in the starlight, she noticed a dark smear across the left side of his face. "Sometimes you get called in the wee hours, right?"

"Not often. I'm a general practitioner."

"Well, terribly sorry to inconvenience you, but we require the services of an MD."

"What happened?"

"Just get dressed. I'll be waiting right here."

= = =

She followed him through the field, stars blazing over them in the moonless dark. Arrived at a small concrete building at the forest's edge, half-buried in the ground.

Mathias led her down a set of stairs to a steel door.

He pushed it open and a waft of blood and shit and scorched tissue washed over Dee and conjured the memory of her ER rotation. She looked away from it and braced herself and looked again.

The man, or what was left of him, lay toppled over on the stone floor, naked and manacled to one of the metal folding chairs from the mess hall. He was unconscious in a puddle of blood that appeared as black as motor oil in the candlelight.

Liz sat in another folding chair looking sweaty and happy. She held an iron rod across her lap, half an inch wide and wrapped at one end with a bulge of duct tape, the finger-grip indentations clearly visible. A blanket had been spread out on the floor beside Liz, and upon it lay knives, a drill, a bucket filled with ice water, and a small blowtorch.

"I want no part of this," Dee said.

"Do you think the food and water and shelter we're providing to you and your children come at no cost?"

"Why are you doing this to him?" Dee asked.

The disgust must have bled through her voice because Liz answered, "This is the man who was on the verge of burning you and your children before we showed up."

"I know who he is."

"We're collecting information," Mathias said. "Unfortunately, he lost consciousness after Liz hit him several minutes ago."

Dee looked at Liz. "Where'd you hit him?"

"Right arm."

"Would you examine him please, Doctor?" Mathias asked.

Dee approached the man named Max, squatting down at the edge of the pool of his blood, which was still creeping, millimeter by millimeter, across the stone. She touched two fingers to his wrist, felt the weakest shudder of his radial artery. Inspected the mottled bruise that was expanding imperceptibly over the broken bone beneath his right bicep like a cancerous rainbow—red, yellow, blue, then ringed with black. His abdomen was hot and swollen around a bullet hole in his side, which she guessed had nicked his liver.

"She didn't kill him, did she?" Mathias said.

"No, but she did break the humerus of his right arm. He probably lost consciousness from the pain." She noticed Max's legs, fighting back the rise of bile in her throat as she said, "If you burn him any more, he's going to lose so much fluid he'll go into shock and die. I mean, he's going to die of sepsis in the next day or so anyway, but keep burning him, and you'll lose him tonight."

"Good to know."

"Was there anything else you needed from me?" Dee asked, staring at this man who would've murdered her children and yet still cringing for him.

"Max did happen to mention that Cole is affected." Dee looked back at Mathias. "He told us that when you pulled up to the checkpoint and got out, he saw a light around Cole's head."

"That's bullshit. You were torturing him. He'd say anything to—"

"That's possible. In fact, I hope it's the case. But just to be sure, Mike's talking with Cole right now."

Dee started toward the door. As she reached for the handle, something struck her from behind and shoved her up against the cold wall of concrete.

Liz spoke into her ear, "Calm down, Dee."

"I'll fucking kill you if you touch—"

"They're only talking," Mathias said.

"You don't talk to my son without me." She was trembling with rage.

"Fair enough. Let's join them."

— — —

She walked between Liz and Mathias, the woman clutching Dee's left arm in a solid grip that Dee imagined could be crushing if Liz wanted it to be. There was candlelight glowing in the windows of her cabin now, and if she could have broken free she would have run toward it.

They followed Mathias up the three steps to the door.

He pushed it open, said, "How we doing?"

Dee jerked her arm out of Liz's grasp and pushed past Mathias into the cabin. Cole sat on the bed and Mike straddled a chair which he'd spun around in front of the door. Naomi was up too, sitting against the window, and Dee could see in her daughter's face a measure of real fear.

She climbed onto the bed, pulled her son into her arms.

"You okay, buddy?"

"Yes."

"Naomi?"

"I'm fine, Mom."

"Everybody's fine, Mom," Mike said, and something in his tone—a note of rehearsed steadiness and authority—and his clean-shaven face and buzzed blond hair reminded her of everything she hated about lawmen.

"You don't speak to my son without me."

Mike seemed to disregard this jurisdictional instruction, glancing instead at Mathias.

Mathias looked down at Cole. "Tell us about the lights, Cole."

"Don't answer him," Dee said. "You don't have to say a word to that man."

"That's not exactly true, Dee. Do you think I'm incapable of arranging a private conversation with your son? You can answer me, Cole."

Cole turned into Dee's chest, and she could feel his little body shaking. He was trying not to cry in front of these strange people.

Mike said, "From what the boy told me, there was some feature in the sky about a month ago."

"So he's confirmed what Max said."

"Yeah, and apparently the people who witnessed this event became affected shortly after."

"Did you see the lights, Cole?" Mathias asked. Cole wouldn't look at him. "Did he?"

"Says he did, but that his parents and sister didn't."

"There's nothing wrong with him," Dee said. "He's no threat to anyone."

Mathias stared at Dee. "We stay intentionally out of the loop here. We don't monitor the news. Tell me exactly what this event was."

Dee kissed the top of Cole's head and rubbed his back while she spoke. "It was an aurora visible to all of the lower forty-eight, northern Mexico—"

"And you didn't see it?"

"It wasn't like the news was going crazy over it. No more coverage than a large meteor shower. We had wanted to stay up for it,

but it happened so late, Jack and I just didn't manage to drag ourselves out of bed."

"But your son saw it."

"Cole slept at a friend's house. They set their alarm and woke up
at three in the morning and watched it."

Mathias smiled. "You lied to me."

"I was afraid you'd—"

"You've brought someone who's affected into our community."

"My son is not affected."

"So you say. But Cole has admitted to seeing the lights and Max
saw the light around his head. How exactly is he not affected?"

"I'm his mother. I know my son. He hasn't changed at all. He
isn't hostile."

"You'll understand, me being responsible for the safety of the
sixty-seven souls who live in this field, if I don't just take your word
on that."

"Then we'll leave," she said.

"I wish it were that easy."

"What are you talking about?"

"You know the location of our compound. You've had a tour of
our security measures. Do you honestly believe I would allow you
to go back out into that warzone with this information?"

"You can't stop us from leaving if we want to."

"Dee." Mathias moved forward, eased down onto the bed. He
ran his hand along her shinbone until his fingers closed gently
around her ankle. "I wrote the constitution we abide by. I invented
our civil and criminal codes of law. I am God here."

"Get your hand off me."

He let go of her ankle, said, "I think at this point, it would benefit all concerned for you and I to step outside and have a private
conversation."

"You go to hell."

He lowered his voice. "Think about your children, Dee." Whispering now: "If you get upset, it's only going to make them more
afraid."

Mike's radio squeaked: *"Mike, come back."*

Mike unclipped the radio from his belt and lifted the receiver to his mouth.

"Can this wait, Bruce? Little tied up at the moment."

"The sensors are returning multiple echoes."

"I know this is a new assignment for you, but sometimes a herd of elk or deer will pass through."

"No, it's not that."

"How do you know?"

"We've had a current interruption in the fence."

"You're telling me someone's cut through the razor wire?"

"I think so, because . . ." His voice trailed off.

"Bruce, repeat. You broke up."

"I'm wearing night-vision goggles and staring south toward the woods . . . there's movement in the trees. A lot of it."

"How many?"

"Can't tell."

"Soldiers?"

"I don't know. They're crawling on the ground."

Mathias stood and grabbed the radio from Mike. "Bruce, we're coming. Put the word out on channel eight and get people into position. Just like we've drilled. If you get a shot, start taking them out."

"Copy that."

Mathias handed the radio back to Mike and started for the door. "Liz, stand guard outside. If they try to leave, shoot them."

Dee brought the candle over from the dresser, down onto the floor where she and Cole were sitting.

"Come on, Naomi, I don't want you near the window."

Her daughter climbed off the bed, said, "We're going to be killed if we stay in here."

Dee crawled over to Naomi's bed and lifted the mattress. She took the gun, ejected the magazine—still fully loaded—then coughed to cover the metallic clatter as she popped the magazine home and jacked a round into the chamber.

"Both of you get dressed," she whispered. "Put on every piece of clothing they gave you."

Dee went to the closet and tugged the three black parkas off the hangers, handed Naomi and Cole theirs, slid into hers.

Then she knelt between them, Cole struggling with the laces of the hiking boots, which were a size too big.

"Naomi, take Cole into the closet and wait until I come back for you."

"How long—"

"A minute, tops."

Dee approached the front door, trying to steady the Glock in her hand.

She spoke through the door: "Liz? You out there?"

No answer.

Dee slid the Glock into the front pocket of her parka and pulled the door open.

"Liz?"

The woman was squatting ten feet away, watching the tree line with her back to the door.

"Liz?"

The woman looked back. "He told you to stay inside."

"I need to talk to you."

Liz stood and started back toward the cabin, a machine pistol attached to a strap around her neck. Her right hand kept it trained on Dee.

The woman stopped at the foot of the steps, two feet below her. "What?"

Dee breathless, lightheaded.

"Isn't there a safer place you can put us? Like maybe that—"

"Mathias wants you here, so you stay here. Now, go back inside or I'll fuck you up."

Dee wasn't sure if Liz would even notice in the starlight, but she suddenly diverted her eyes toward the woods, let her brow scrunch into a subtle furrow. In the time it took Liz to glance back at whatever she thought Dee had seen, Dee drew the Glock from the pocket and had it waiting when Liz looked back, aimed down at her face.

Liz's eyes went wide. "You cunt."

Dee pulled the trigger.

Liz dropped like she'd been poured out of a glass, and Dee stood frozen, staring down at her, awestruck. How short the distance from life and thought to a sprawled shell in the grass. She could have stood there all night trying to wrap her mind around it and been no closer at sunrise. No closer forty years from now, or whenever the end of her days might come.

A spark flared across the field, the report right on its heels.

Other muzzle flashes erupting in the forest like lightning bugs and the night filling with gunshots and yelling.

Dee rushed back into the cabin, found her children still hiding in the closet.

"Time to leave."

Movement everywhere—shadows running through the dark and voices broken by sporadic shots. As she led her children around the side of the cabin, a distant burst of machine-gun fire shredded the front door.

"Stay close," she said, grabbing Cole's hand and pulling him toward the woods. Naomi ran alongside. Fifty yards to cover and they were passing people in pajamas who'd just stumbled groggy-eyed out of their cabins, loading rifles and shotguns.

They reached the woods and Dee dragged Naomi and Cole down into the leaves.

From where they lay, it all looked like chaos.

Clusters of gunfire blazing back and forth.

Muzzle flashes from the guard towers.

No apparent order.

Just people trying to kill one another and not be killed themselves.

"You guys ready to run?"

"Where are we going?" Naomi asked.

Dee stood. "Just come on." She shoved the Glock into her parka. "Give me your hands."

They jogged together through the woods, working their way around the clearing as the firefight intensified.

A hail of bullets eviscerated a pine tree three steps ahead, and Dee forced her children to the ground and lay on top of them.

"Anybody hit?"

"No."

"No."

"There's a hole just ahead. Crawl into it. Go. Now."

They scrabbled the last few feet through the leaves and rolled down an embankment. With starlight barely straggling through the crowns of the trees, it was almost pitch-black in their hole, which was more of a depression, two feet below the forest floor and just spacious enough to accommodate the three of them.

Dee was sweating under her clothes from the exertion, but as her heart began to slow, she knew the chill would come. She pulled her children into her and shoveled as many leaves as she could grasp on top of them.

— — —

It went on all night, broken occasionally by brief periods of silence. Sometimes there were footfalls in the leaves nearby, and once Dee glimpsed two shadows running past the edge of their depression.

Just before dawn, the shooting stopped. A chorus of weeping and pleading soon followed, rising toward a crescendo that was promptly silenced by twenty-five shots, ringing out in tandem, from what sounded like small-caliber handguns.

BY dawn, an eerie silence had settled over the clearing and the woods. The sky was lightening through the trees, and though her children snored quietly, Dee hadn't slept at all. Carefully, she withdrew her arms from under Cole's and Naomi's necks, turned over in the frosted leaves, and crawled up to the lip of the embankment.

Gunsmoke hovered over the clearing like a dirty mist. From ten yards back in the trees, she had a decent view of the soldiers. She counted at least twenty of them milling around in the grass, sometimes leaning down to confirm the dead were really dead.

There were bodies everywhere, and over by the mess hall, two dozen or more lay toppled in a row—women and children.

She backed down into the hole.

Naomi stirred. Her eyes opened. Dee brought her finger to her lips.

— — —

They didn't venture out of the hole. Kept hidden down in the leaves, listening and sometimes watching the soldiers in the clearing. At midday, a commotion pulled Dee back up to the forest floor. She saw Mathias running through the field, chased by a group of soldiers, one of whom stopped, drew a sidearm, and sighted him down.

Mathias fell concurrently with the pistol report, cried out, and amid the fading echoes of the gunshot, Dee could hear the soldiers laughing.

Someone said, "Nice shot, Jed."

She watched them approach, others coming over now. Surrounding Mathias at the back of a little cabin, fifty or sixty yards away.

"What hole did this rat crawl out of?"

"There's a trapdoor in the ground back there, camouflaged with grass."

"Anyone else in there?"

"Just big enough for him."

Mathias was still crying, and someone said, "You're only shot in the ass. Shut the fuck up until we give you something to cry about."

And they did. All afternoon and into the evening, they did. The screams of Mathias blaring through the woods between bouts of what Dee could only hope was unconsciousness. She didn't trust Cole's curiosity, so she held the boy to her chest and covered his ears herself, part of her dying to know what was happening out there, figuring her imagination had invented something infinitely worse than the truth. The other part trying to force her thoughts elsewhere—to a memory or a fantasy—but when the raw and blistering screech of human agony filled the clearing, there was no way to avert her mind from it, or to keep from attempting to picture what they must be doing to him.

As darkness fell, light flickered off the trees above them and streamers of sweet smoke drifted into the woods. For three minutes, Mathias screamed louder than he had all day, and then, at last, was silent.

Cole and Naomi became still, and soon they were both murmuring softly in their sleep. Dee turned over onto her stomach, the stiffness in her joints excruciating after nearly twenty hours in this hole.

She crawled up the embankment and peered out past the trees.

A bonfire raged in the middle of the clearing and some of the men had gathered around it, their faces aglow, while others carried the pieces of the cabin they were using for firewood over to what she now realized was a pyre.

Mathias had been hoisted up in the middle of the blaze, and even from sixty yards away, she could see that the crossbeams that held him were still standing and that in fact her imagination had failed to concoct anything as remotely evil as what they had actually done to the man.

The soldiers' laughter was gleeful and alcohol-infused.

Somewhere out there, a woman wept.

Dee eased back down into the depression and roused her children.

— — —

They crept all the way back to the razor wire, which no longer hummed, and followed it through the trees. The fire was roaring now, shooting flames thirty feet high. From Dee's vantage, she could see one of the soldiers running naked through the grass carrying a burning branch, which he delivered onto the front porch of a cabin.

The soldiers hooted their approval, assembling to watch as the flames licked out along the walls and the roof like molten fingers. Then the voices started up from inside.

"Keep running," Dee said. "Don't listen."

She could hear the people beating on the inside of the door, pleading to be let out, and the soldiers talking back, taunting them. What welled up inside of Dee nearly drove her out into that clearing. Maybe she'd only kill one or two of them before they stopped her, but God, in this moment, nothing would feel so right.

"Mom, look."

Naomi had stopped just ahead at a break in the fence where the soldiers had come through the night before. The razor wire was severed and pushed back.

"Careful, Nay," Dee said, and she lifted Cole in her arms and followed her daughter between the coils of wire.

When they were through, she set Cole down and they all jogged away from the screaming in the clearing.

Naomi was crying now. She stopped, said, "We have to help them."

"Baby, we'd end up dead, just like them."

"Are they hurting?" Cole asked.

"Yes."

"I can't stand hearing it," Naomi said.

"We have to keep moving."

— — —

In a little while, they came out of the woods and onto the road about a hundred yards up from the checkpoint. Dee took the Glock out of her parka and they moved toward the vehicles up ahead.

No light. No movement.

A pair of Hummers still sat in the road and the dead soldiers too.

They arrived at Ed's Jeep.

"Tires are still inflated," she said.

Of all the gas cans fastened to the luggage rack, only one had survived the gunfight with its contents.

"We taking the Jeep?" Naomi asked.

"If the engine isn't damaged."

"Ed's still in the driver's seat, and he doesn't smell good."

Dee went around the back of the Jeep and stood beside Naomi.

"No, Cole, stay there."

"Why?"

"Ed's dead, Cole. It's nothing good to see."

She held her arm over her nose and mouth, could only imagine what the potency might have been in warmer temperatures.

Ed had swollen up against the steering column, his head resting on the wheel. Dee grabbed hold of his left arm. Rigor mortis had come and gone, and the arm bent easily as she heaved Ed out of the car. Finally got him free and he tumbled out of the seat onto the dirt road, his legs still caught up in the floorboard.

"Give me a hand here, Nay. Don't look at his face."

They dragged him the rest of the way out of the car and off the side of the road into the trees. Dee found a couple of extra shirts in the cargo area and she spread them across the driver's seat to cover the sticky, rotting blood.

"It still smells bad," Naomi said.

"We'll keep the windows down. This cold air will scour it out."

They grabbed a few candy bars and crackers from the banker's box. Cole sat in the front passenger seat so Naomi could stretch out across the back, and Dee climbed in and worked the driver's seat forward until her feet reached the pedals. Right away, she could see that driving was going to be impossible. Five bullets had come through the windshield into Ed, and around the puncture holes, each of them had made a circle of fractured glass that destroyed the translucence.

Dee got out and climbed up onto the hood and stomped on the windshield. All she managed to do was punch out a hole in front of the steering wheel where the cracks had weakened the glass.

The engine cranked on the first try. She shifted into gear and turned on the lights and eased onto the gas. They crept forward. The engine rumbled smoothly, no audible sign of damage. The oil and temperature gauges likewise offered no indications of malfunction.

She steered between the Hummers and the dead soldiers and accelerated down the dirt road, wind blasting through the windshield in a freezing stream. The car reeked of gasoline and decay

and the bits of glass she sat upon cut through her jeans, but at least
they were on their own, moving away from the clearing, and, in this
moment, safe.

= = =

Fifteen miles on, the dirt road intersected with an interstate. All
lanes east- and westbound were empty under the stars. She accelerated down the exit ramp, hit eighty after a half mile. At this speed,
the rush of air coming through the windshield dried out her eyes to
the brink of blindness, so she braked down to forty.

Her children slept.

In every direction, no glimmer of habitation.

A mile marker shot past every couple of minutes.

The long vistas and straight trajectory of the interstate gave a
sense of safety—the security blanket of seeing what was coming
long before you reached it.

Just shy of midnight, she turned north onto Highway 89.

Got twenty miles up the road and through a ghost town of
charred houses before exhaustion forced her off the highway at a
reservoir.

She killed the engine and left the kids to sleep—Cole curled up
in the front passenger seat, Naomi in back. She popped the cargo
hatch and dug out Ed's sleeping bag and the road map. Walked
down to the water and unrolled the sleeping bag across the dirt
beside the remnants of another camp—water bottles and potato-
chip wrappers strewn across the grass. Kicked off her boots, zipped
herself in.

She studied the map. By highway, they were roughly 275 miles
from the Canadian border, with one major city—Great Falls—to
deal with. But she could cut around and actually save time.

She closed the map.

No trees in this open country. Sagebrush everywhere and she
could see forever. A range of mountains loomed in the north, the
top thousand feet glazed with snow that glowed under the stars and
the moon.

Soundless.

Windless.

The water so still she could see the stars in it.

She eased back into the sleeping bag and said her husband's name. Tears burned down her face. It had been six days without him. She lay there trying to feel if he was gone. From a purely logical standpoint, it seemed impossible that he wasn't, and she certainly felt apart from him. But for whatever it was worth, and she had to acknowledge maybe nothing, she didn't feel his absence. She felt that Jack was still alive—somewhere, somehow—under the same night sky.

T HE semitrailer reeked of shit, urine, vomit, body odor, blood, and
something even more malignant. Jack leaned back against the
metal wall, his left hand throbbing with such intensity he prayed
to lose consciousness again. With the rear door closed, it was pitch-
black inside and Jack could feel his shoulders grazing the shoulders
of the people he sat between as the rocking of the trailer jostled
them together. The noise was bewildering—the distant big-rig growl
of the V12 Detroit Diesel, the closer rumble of the tires underneath him, a baby wailing, a woman crying, a half dozen voices in
whispered conversation.

A man across from him said, "This is for the guy who just got
put in here. Where are we?"

"A mountain pass in Wyoming," Jack said. "Not far from Jackson. Do you know where they're taking us?"

"Nobody knows anything."

"How'd you wind up here?"

"They picked me up two days ago in Denver."

"Did someone die in here?"

"Yeah. That's what the smell is."

The pressure in Jack's ears released. They were descending

from the pass. What was left of his ring finger dripped on his pants, and he tucked his hand under his jacket and tried to wrap his undershirt around the open wound, felt a surge of white-hot pain that nearly made him vomit when he touched the jagged phalange of his ring finger.

The baby went on crying for what he guessed was thirty minutes.

He said finally, "Is someone holding that baby?"

"I'm sorry." A woman's voice. "I'm trying to calm her—"

"No, I'm not complaining, I just . . . I can't see anything. I wanted to make sure someone's holding her."

"Someone is."

No light slipped in anywhere.

They rolled down what felt like a winding road, and after a while the sharp turns diminished.

Someone shoved a plastic jug of water into his hands, said, "One sip," and Jack didn't even hesitate to lift it to his mouth and take a swallow.

He passed it to the person beside him.

"Thank you." Voice of an older woman.

Every passing moment, he was moving farther away from his family, and the thought of them alone out there, every bit as hungry and thirsty and scared as he was, simply made him want to be back with them or die right now. He tried, but he couldn't stop himself from picturing Dee and the kids inside the pipe, waiting for him to return, beginning to wonder where he was. After a while, when he didn't come back, they'd search the construction site and, soon after, start calling his name, their voices traveling into the forest. Calm at first. He could almost hear them, and it broke his heart. He hadn't told them where he was going. Hadn't known himself. Maybe they'd walk up to the pass, but there'd be nothing there, certainly not him. Dee and Naomi would be getting frantic. Cole as well if he grasped the situation. Would they think he'd abandoned them? Wandered into the woods and somehow gotten injured or killed? How long would they keep looking and what would their state of mind be when, finally, they gave up?

Jack opened his eyes. The diesel engine had gone quiet. The baby had stopped crying. His head rested against the bony shoulder of the old woman to his right and he felt her hand on his face, her whisper in his ear, "This too shall pass. This too shall pass."

He lifted his head. "I'm sorry, I didn't—"

"It's okay, I don't mind. You were crying in your sleep."

Jack wiped his eyes.

The rear door shot up and the light of a sunset flooded the semitrailer, accompanied by a blast of freezing air. Two soldiers stood on the ramp with automatic weapons, and one of them said, "On your feet!"

Everyone began to haul themselves up, and Jack struggled onto his feet as well.

He descended the metal ramp into grass, lightheaded and unstable.

A soldier at the bottom pointed across the open field. "You hungry?"

"Yeah."

"Food's that way."

"Why are we—"

The soldier rammed his AR-15 into Jack's chest. "Get going."

Jack turned and stumbled along with the crowd, everyone moving through an open field and folding into streams of more people filing out of four other semitrailers—two hundred prisoners by Jack's estimate. They looked haggard and addled and he searched for the old woman whose shoulder he'd used for a pillow, but he didn't see anyone who met his mind's imagining of her.

In the distance, Jack spotted several buildings, and though it was impossible to be certain in the low light, they appeared to be surrounded by small airplanes and private jets.

Everywhere, soldiers were directing prisoners toward a collection of tents a quarter mile away.

"Hot food and beds!" someone yelled. "Keep moving!"

Jack looked for the man who'd cut his finger off, but he didn't see him.

They crossed the asphalt of a runway, the tents closer now, and straight ahead, less than fifty yards away, stood a mountain of dirt and a bulldozer.

Jack smelled food on the breeze.

On ahead, people were stopping near the pile of dirt and he could hear soldiers yelling. They were lining up the prisoners shoulder to shoulder.

A soldier shoved him forward, said, "Stand right there and don't fucking move."

"Why?"

"We have to inspect you."

"For what?"

"Shut the fuck up."

Jack stood in a line of ragged-looking people, some of whom had begun to cry.

The soldiers were backing away now, Jack's head swimming with the smell of whatever was cooking across the field.

As he glanced back toward the tents, his eyes caught on the hole of freshly turned earth that he and the other prisoners were standing at the edge of.

He looked at the bulldozer again.

By the time he understood what was happening, the two dozen soldiers who'd herded them into the middle of the field were raising their AR-15s.

Someone said, "Oh my God."

Several prisoners took off running, and a soldier squeezed off four controlled bursts. They fell and the others began to scream, some trying to flee, and one of the soldiers yelled and they all opened fire at once.

The noise was tremendous. Slap of bullets into meat. The schizophrenic madness of the machine guns. The screams. All down the line, people were tumbling back into the pit, the muzzle flashes bright in the evening and the soldiers edging forward, still firing.

It felt like someone punched him in the shoulder, and then Jack was staring up at the clouds, which were catching sunlight on their underbellies, people falling into the pit all around him, blood spray everywhere and the smell of shit and urine and rust becoming prevalent like the sensory embodiment of terror itself, warm blood leaking all over him, down into his face, appendages writhing all around him. Then the shooting stopped and there came a moment of silence before the sound of a hundred dying people faded in. If Jack had believed in hell, he couldn't have imagined it sounding any worse than this chorus of agony—groans, moaning, weeping, screaming, people dying loudly, dying quietly, some cursing their murderers, some begging to be saved, or begging for an end, some just asking why.

A realization slowly dawned on Jack amid the horror—*I'm still alive.*

A voice lifted out of the open grave, "Oh God, please finish me."

Jack's shoulder was burning now.

He could see the soldiers standing at the edge of the pit, Jack thinking only of his children as he pulled several bodies over him, and then the machine guns erupted with a new blaze of fire, and he could feel the bodies that shielded him shaking with the impact of the bullets.

This time, when the guns went quiet, the groans were half what they had been.

Jack's entire body trembled.

He willed himself to be still.

Soldiers above him were talking.

"—don't serve meatloaf again. That's some rancid shit."

"I love the mac and cheese though. Don't disrespect."

"You got a crawler over there."

Two bursts from the machine gun.

"All right, boys, who drew cleanup?"

The light was abandoning the sky, and there was little in the way of groaning now, just desperate breathing all around him.

"Nathan, Matt, Jones, and Chris."

"Well, fucking get to it, boys, and before you lose your light. We're going to party tonight. God, this is going to be a pretty piece of grass next spring."

Jack could hear the soldiers walking away, the sound of distant voices, and still some movement in the pit.

As one of the bodies on top of him began to twitch, a noise rose up at the far end of the pit, followed by another and another, and then a fourth, much closer to where he lay.

He watched one of the soldiers climb down into the pit. They held a chainsaw with a three-foot guide bar, wore a white vinyl apron and a helmet with a Plexiglas faceplate. Starting across the top layer of bodies, they slashed at anything that moved.

Jack tried to lie still, tried to ignore the radiant pain in his shoulder.

The body on top of him sat up, and in the low light, Jack could see her long, black hair falling down her back. She was crying and he reached up to pull her down, but the soldier with the chainsaw had already seen her and was wading over through the bodies.

The woman screamed as the soldier swung his giant chainsaw.

She fell back onto Jack and the blood flowed, blinding him, choking him, and he lay there unmoving as the soldier passed by, the noise of the chainsaws growing softer.

Someone yelled, "Jones, look at this guy. Untouched. Didn't even catch a bullet. Yeah, keep playing dead, motherfucker."

A chainsaw wailed, followed by three seconds of the most horrendous screaming Jack had ever heard.

The soldiers wandered through the pit for another ten minutes, and then the chainsaws went quiet and their voices slipped out of range.

Jack didn't move for a long time. The blood that covered him grew sticky and cold and not another sound dared to lift out of the open grave.

His shoulder throbbing.

The clouds had gone dark and the sky was almost devoid of light.

He finally pushed the headless body off him and sat up.

Near the tents, a bonfire raged and there were fifty or sixty men gathered around it, their laughter and voices carrying across the field.

Jack crawled onto the surface of the pit. There were a few people still barely hanging on, groaning as he moved across them, one man begging for his help. The pain in Jack's shoulder made it nearly impossible to set his weight on his right arm, but he finally reached the back edge of the pit and climbed out into the grass.

He kept moving on his stomach across the field through the strange and fleeting grayness between twilight and night. A hundred yards out from the pit, exhaustion stopped him. He still had a ways to go to reach the trees, but he couldn't catch his breath. Lying on his side, he watched the bonfire and the soldiers, the reflection of the flames gleaming off the shine of their black leather boots.

Jack crawled again.

Another twenty minutes and he passed through the wall of trees, stopping ten feet inside the forest. Retched his guts out, though there was nothing left but the sip of water he'd taken hours ago in the back of that trailer.

He dragged himself to the nearest spruce tree under an overhang of branches.

On the cusp of pitch-black darkness now in the shadow of the forest.

He touched his right shoulder. It was painful and hot, though not as bad as the last bullet he'd stopped. Couldn't see the wound, but running his hand along the back of his shoulder he could feel the exit hole—a circular flare of exploded skin.

Despite the pain, he felt a detachment from himself that was so intense it verged on out-of-body, like a filter setting up between what had happened in the field and his emotional connection to it. He felt a beautiful step removed, watching himself listening to the soldiers. Watching himself lie down on his side on the moist ground with his back against the tree trunk. Watching his eyes close as the devastation that was this day sat perched beside his head with the patience of a gargoyle, waiting to crush him.

———

At some point in the night, a noise from the field woke him. It took Jack a moment to connect it with the growl of the dozer. Through the branches of the spruce tree, he could just make out the lights on top of its cab blazing down into the pit as the scoop refilled the grave with earth.

He shut his eyes, but another sound wouldn't let him sleep—a crunching like the snap of trees during an ice storm. He realized what it was, what it could only be—the bones of those inside the pit, breaking under the dozer's weight.

JACK woke to stomach cramps and the splintering brightness of sunlight coming through the branches. He crawled out from under the tree, lightheaded and sore, wondering how much blood he'd lost during the night. The exposed bone of his left ring finger hurt more than his shoulder.

The meadow was abuzz with soldiers, many of them closer than he would've liked, and some of them with dogs.

He struggled to his feet and started into the forest.

No sense of direction.

Just a dense pine wood that seemed to go on and on.

By midday, he hadn't crossed a road, a water source, or anything resembling civilization, and as the light started to fail, the forest began to climb, until in the twilight, he found himself on a steep, wooded hillside.

He sat down.

Shivering.

Nothing left.

WOKE colder than he'd ever been in his life, covered in frost, and curled up on the mountainside, watching the torturously slow progression of sunlight climbing the hill toward the spot where he lay.

When the sun finally washed over him two hours later, he shut his eyes and faced its brightness, letting the warmth envelop him. He stopped shivering. The frost steaming off his clothing. He got up and started to climb.

— — —

Somehow, he went on.
    Hands and knees.
    Mindless hours.
    Always climbing.
    Endless.

— — —

Late afternoon, he lay on a hillside covered in aspen trees. If someone had told him he'd been climbing this mountain for a year, he
would've believed them. He was losing control of his thoughts. The
thirst was fracturing his mind. It occurred to him that if he didn't
get up and start walking in the next ten seconds, he wasn't going to
get up again. Could feel himself on the edge of not caring anymore.

— — —

In the middle of the night, he stumbled out of the forest into a
clearing that swept another thousand feet up the mountain to his
left and shot down a narrow chute between the spruce trees on his
right. The sky was clear, the moon high, everything bright as day. A
golf course, he thought. A steep golf course. Then he noticed the
tiny lodge halfway up the hill. The metal terminals that went up the
mountain. The cables strung between them. He stared downslope,
saw a sign with a black diamond next to the word "Emigrant."

Jack's legs buckled.

He sat down, then lay down, the side of his face in the cold,
dead grass, staring down the steep headwall. He could see three
mountain ranges, the rock and the pockets of snow above timberline glowing under the moon.

He closed his eyes, kept telling himself he should get up, keep
walking, crawling, roll down this fucking mountain if he had to,
because stopping was death, and death meant never seeing them
again.

Saying her name aloud tied a hot wire of pain around his throat,
which felt full of glass shards. So dry and swollen. He said the
name of his daughter. The name of his son. He pushed himself up.
Sat there dry-heaving. Then he got onto his feet and started down
the mountain.

— — —

Jack was a dead man walking two hours later and a thousand feet
lower when he arrived at the foot of the dark lodge. He had to crawl

up the steps and pull himself upright again by the wooden door handles. They were locked. He went back down the steps and pried out one of the rocks that lined the sidewalk.

So weak it took him four swings to even put a crack through the big square window beside the doors. The fifth swing broke through and the glass fell out of the frame. He climbed through into a cafeteria, perfectly dark except for where moonlight streamed through the tall windows. The grill in back was still shuttered for the season. He limped over to the drink fountain, his mouth beginning to water. Pressed the buttons for Coca-Cola, Sierra Mist, Orange Fanta, Country Time Lemonade, Barq's root beer, but the machine stood dormant.

He made his way between the tables toward a common area that accessed a bar and a gift shop. Both were locked up. He moved out of the long panels of moonlight into darkness. Straight ahead, he could just make out a pair of doors. As he moved toward them, they vanished in the black, but he kept on, hands outstretched, until he ran into a wall.

He pushed and the door swung back. Couldn't see a thing, but he knew he was in a bathroom because he smelled the water in the toilets. Ran his hand along the wall, found the switch, hit the lights. Nothing. Heard the door ease shut. He moved forward to where he thought the sinks might be and stepped into a wall. Turned around, becoming disoriented as he moved in a different direction. He touched a counter, his hands frantically searching for the faucet. Cranked open the tap, but nothing happened.

He opened a stall door. Dropping to his knees, his hands grazed the cold porcelain of the toilet. Inside the bowl, his fingers slid into the chilly water.

He didn't think about where this water had been or all the people who'd sat on this toilet and pissed and shit and vomited into it, or the industrial-strength chemicals that had been used to clean the bowl. He lowered his face to the surface of the water and drank and thought only of how sweet it tasted running down his throat.

A RAZOR line of light. For a long time, Jack just stared at it. His face against a tiled floor. Cold but not freezing. Piecing together where he was, how he'd arrived here, beginning to face the fact that he wasn't dead. At least, he was mostly sure he wasn't.

He crawled out of the stall. The raging thirst was gone, but the hunger pangs doubled him over when he stood, his feet so badly blistered he was afraid to see the damage.

He groped for the paper-towel dispenser.

Cranked out a length of paper, tore it off.

Then he pulled open the door, the light like a railroad spike through his temples.

He limped out into the lobby, which looked almost like civilization in the daylight, sat down and went to work making a bandage for what was left of his ring finger.

— — —

He was already pushing open the front doors when he realized what he'd just walked past. Stepping back inside, he half expected it to have vanished, like a mirage, but there it stood.

He rushed into the cafeteria and grabbed the rock he'd used to break the window. Back in the lobby, he threw it through another pane of glass.

He reached in and pulled out everything he could get his hands on—bags of potato chips, candy bars, crackers, cookies—until the vending machine was emptied and its contents spread across the floor.

He ripped into a bag of Doritos.

The chips were stale, leftovers from last season, but the intensity of the flavor made his mouth water. He sat in the warm sunlight that poured through all the glass around the front entrance. Finished the bag and opened another that was filled with processed onion rings he would never have ingested in his former life.

They were gone in a moment.

He drank his fill of water from the toilet and urinated for the first time in days.

Then grabbed the plastic garbage bag from the trash can under the sink.

He loaded two dozen snack packages into the bag and slung it over his shoulder.

There was a giant mirror across from the vending machine. He'd noticed it a little while ago, and now it called to him.

The reflection was no one he knew, his face as thin as an ax blade, beard coming in full, and he was the color of rust, covered in dried blood like some zombie-vagrant.

Outside the entrance to the resort, he came across a bicycle rack and a single abandoned mountain bike standing between the bars. The tires were low and there was bird shit all over the seat, but it looked otherwise in working order. He climbed aboard and tied his bag of food to the handlebars.

He coasted down the sidewalk, through the empty parking lot, turned out onto a country road, and then he was speeding along at 35 mph down the winding, faded pavement.

— – —

Ten miles on and several thousand feet lower, Jack braked and brought the bike to a stop. Up ahead, a herd of range cattle was crossing the road, and he waited for them to pass. He'd ridden down out of the alpine forest and now the foothills of the mountains were bare and the air had become almost warm and redolent of sage.

— – —

He rode on, still cruising east and dropping. The foothills lay a mile behind him now, and the mountains fifteen, and the land was barren and open and the sky immense.

The ride turned strenuous when the grade of the road leveled out, but it was nothing compared to walking on blistered feet or crawling up a mountain.

— – —

In the evening he was twenty miles out from the mountains and turning north onto Highway 89, his quads burning and his face glowing with wind- and sunburn.

A mile and a half up the road, he caught the scent of water on the breeze, thinking he'd grown hypersensitive to the smell as of late, some recent adaptation born of nearly dying of thirst.

He crested a small rise and there lay the reservoir, the water like ink under the evening sky and the sun just a chevron of brilliance on the ridgeline of those mountains he'd ridden out of.

Abandoned the bike on the grassy shoulder and descended the slope to the water's edge. Fell to his knees. Drank.

He ate a supper consisting of a Butterfinger candy bar, two

packages of Lay's barbecue potato chips, and a Famous Amos chocolate chip cookie.

Curled up in the grass by the water, already cold, but at least he wasn't hungry or thirsty. He watched the sun go behind the mountains and the stars begin to burn through the growing dark, reeking of the dried and rotting gore that covered every square inch of his person.

He was crying before he realized it, hot tears running down his face. Alive now, and on track to stay that way for the time being. There were choices to make.

Head south back into Wyoming, maybe meet up with his family on the way. But they'd been separated now almost five days. They might've been picked up or found transportation or come upon some fate he couldn't bring himself to imagine. Would Dee try to find him, or focus on getting Naomi and Cole across the border into Canada?

He took his phone out of his pocket. The battery had been dead for weeks. He typed in Dee's number on the dark screen and held the phone to his ear.

"Hey, baby. I'm at this lake in Montana about thirty miles north of Bozeman. It's beautiful here. So quiet. I'm watching the stars come out. I hope you and the kids are okay. I've had a hard few days."

Out in the middle of the lake, a fish jumped.

"I think I'm going to keep heading north toward Great Falls, our old stomping grounds. I have such sweet memories of that city and you.

"I don't know how to find you, so please stay open and make smart choices. I'm not leaving this country without you."

The ripples from the middle of the lake were just beginning to reach the shore.

He put his phone back into his pocket.

The water became still again.

He let his eyes finally close.

THE sound of wind in the grass. Sunshine on his eyelids. It didn't feel cold enough to be first light. He sat up stiff and so sore. An act of willpower just to stand. It was late morning, the sun already high, and he walked up the grassy slope into the middle of the highway. The vistas north and south were endless. Nothing going. Nothing coming. Just silence and an overload of open space.

— — —

He stripped out of his clothes and ran naked and gasping into the freezing water. Ducked under and swam until he had to surface, ten yards out from the shore. He swam back and grabbed his clothes and carried them out into waist-deep water, rinsed the blood and filth out of everything, and used one of his shirts to scrub himself clean.

— — —

Jack rode north up the highway, soaking wet. Rode hours. Until his clothes had dried out and he had nothing left. He stopped in the early evening, no idea how far he'd ridden, but he hadn't passed a car or a house all day. The world looked much as it had twenty-four hours prior. High desert. Big sky.

He felt very small, very alone.

TWO miles into his day, coasting down a long, gentle grade in the dawn light, Jack braked and came to a stop in the road. He squinted, trying to sharpen his nearsightedness into focus. Couldn't tell how far. A mile. Maybe two. The calculation of distance was impossible in this country.

He knew this: it was a vehicle parked in the road. One of its doors open.

For ten minutes, Jack didn't move, didn't take his eyes off the car.

He began to pedal up the road again, stopping every few hundred yards to view things from a closer vantage.

It was a late-model minivan. White. Covered in dust and pockmarked with bullet holes. Some of the windows had been shot out, and there was glass and blood on the pavement. All four tires low but intact. Utah license plate.

Jack stopped ten feet from the rear bumper and climbed off the bike.

The smell of death was everywhere.

There was a girl in the sagebrush. The sliding door of the minivan was open, and it looked as though she'd been gunned down running, her long blond hair caught up in the branches. He wasn't going to get close enough to see how old she was, but she looked small from where he stood.

A woman sat in the front passenger seat, and her brains covered the window. Twin teenage boys lay slumped against each other in the backseat.

— — —

Jack climbed in behind the wheel. The keys dangled in the ignition. Fuel gauge at a quarter.

He turned the key.

The engine cranked.

— — —

He pulled the boys out of the back and their mother out of the front and laid them all down in the desert. Didn't want to, but he couldn't just leave the girl face-up and naked, entangled in the sage.

He stood for a long time staring down at them.

Midday and the flies already feasting.

Jack started to say something. Stopped himself. It would've meant nothing, changed nothing, been solely for his benefit. No words could put this right.

— — —

He drove north, keeping his speed at fifty. A CD in the stereo had been playing the Beach Boys, and Jack let it go on playing until he couldn't stand it anymore.

— — —

He passed through a small, burned town, and fifteen miles north, on the outskirts of another, had to swerve to miss someone walking alone down the middle of the highway.

He stopped the car, watched a man staggering toward him in the rearview mirror, his defective gait unfazed, as if he hadn't even noticed the car that had nearly hit him. He didn't carry a gun or a backpack, nothing in his hands, which he held like arthritic claws, his fingers bent and seemingly frozen that way.

Jack shifted into park.

The closer the man got, the more wrecked he looked—deep purple with sunburn, his dirty white oxford streaked in blood and missing one of the arms entirely, his loafers disintegrating off his feet.

He walked past Jack's window and kept going, straight down the double yellow.

Jack opened the door.

"Hey."

The man didn't look back.

Jack got out, walked after him. "Sir, do you need help?"

No response.

Jack drew even with him, tried to make eye contact, then stepped in front of the man, who stopped finally, his gray eyes staring off at some horizon beyond even the scope of this infinite country.

"Are you hurt?" Jack said.

His voice must have made some impact, because the man met his eyes.

"I have food in the car," Jack said. "I don't have water, but this road will take us through the Little Belt Mountains. We'll find some in the high country for sure."

The man just stood there, his entire body trembling slightly. Like there was a cataclysm under way deep in his core.

Jack touched the man's bare arm where the shirt sleeve had been torn away, felt the sun's accumulation of heat radiating from it.

"Come on. You'll die out here."

He escorted the man to the passenger side and installed him in the front seat.

"Sorry about the smell," Jack said. "It ain't pretty, but it beats walking."

The man seemed not to notice.

— — —

They sped down the abbreviated main street of another slaughtered town. Mountains to the north, and the road climbed into them. Jack glanced over at the man, saw him touching the gore on his window, running his finger through it, smearing it across the glass. A bag of potato chips and a candy bar sat in his lap, unopened, unacknowledged.

"I'm Jack. What's your name?"

The man looked at him as if he either didn't know or couldn't bring himself to say. His wallet bulged out of the side pocket of his slacks. Jack reached over, tugged it out, flipped it open.

"Donald Massey of Provo, Utah. Good to meet you, Donald. I'm from Albuquerque."

Donald made no response.

"Aren't you hungry? Here." Jack reached over and took the candy bar out of Donald's lap, ripped open the packaging. He slid the bar into Donald's grasp, but the man just stared at it.

"How about some music?"

Jack turned on the Beach Boys.

— — —

They rode up into the mountains, Jack hating to be on a winding road again. All these blind corners meant you could roll up on a roadblock before you even knew what hit you.

In the early afternoon, they passed through a mountain village that was very much a ghost town before anyone had bothered to burn it. A few dozen houses. Couple buildings on the main strip. Evergreen trees in the fields and on the hills, the smell of them coming through the dashboard vents, a welcome change.

On the north side of town, Jack pulled over and turned off the engine. When he opened the door, he could hear the running water in the trees and smell its sweetness.

"You need to drink something, Donald."

The man just stared through the windshield.

Jack lifted a travel mug out of the center console.

– – –

He rinsed the residue of ancient coffee out of the mug and filled it with water from the stream. Headed back to the van, opened Donald's door.

"It's really good," Jack said.

He held the mug to Donald's sun-blasted lips and tilted. Most of the water ran down the man's chest under his shirt, but he swallowed some of it.

"We'll reach Great Falls in the afternoon. It's a big city. I used to live there."

Impossible to know if the man registered a word he was saying.

"I got separated from my family five days ago." Jack glanced at the man's left ring finger, saw a gold wedding band. "Were you with your family, Donald?"

No response.

Jack sipped the water, grains of sand from the streambed catching on the tip of his tongue.

"Let me guess what you do for a living. My wife and I used to play this game all the time." Jack studied the man's loafers— nothing much to look at now, but they suggested wealth. Couple hundred dollars off the shelf. He inspected the tag on the back of the man's collar. "Brooks Brothers. All right." He looked at Donald's hands. Covered in blood and still clutched like claws, but he could tell they weren't the hands of a man who earned his living working outdoors. "You strike me as an ad man," Jack said. "Am I right? You work at an advertising and marketing firm in Provo?"

Nothing.

"I bet you'd never guess my vocation. Tell you what. I'll give you three . . ."

Jack stopped. Felt the cold premonition of having missed something. He almost didn't want to know, but the fear couldn't stop his curiosity.

He opened the glove compartment, rifled through a stack of yellow napkins, plastic silverware, bank-deposit envelopes, until he came to the automobile liability policy, protected in a plastic sleeve. He opened it, stared down at the small cards that identified the coverage, the policy limits, and the named insureds.

Donald Walter Massey.

Angela Jacobs Massey.

Jack looked at Donald.

"Jesus Christ."

They went on through the mountains, Jack trying to pay attention to what was coming in the distance, but all he could think about was Donald, wondering what had happened back down the road. Couldn't imagine the man fleeing. He wouldn't have left his family. Had the affected purposely left him alive? Murdered his family in front of him and then sent him down the highway on foot?

Jack looked over at the man who now leaned against the door, wanting to tell him that he'd taken care of their bodies, or at least done what he could, shown them respect. He wanted to say something beautiful and profound and comforting, about how even in all this horror, there were things between people who loved each other that couldn't be touched, that lived on through pain, torture, separation, even death. He thought he still believed that. But he didn't say anything. Just reached over and laced his fingers through Donald's, which barely released their incomprehensible store of tension.

Jack held the man's hand as he drove out of the mountains and he did not let go.

In the early evening, the city lay several miles in the distance. The sun low over the plains beyond. Everything bright, golden. The way Jack dreamed of this place.

He disengaged his hand from Donald's, the man still sleeping against the door. The gas-gauge needle hovered over the empty slash, and he was debating whether to head into town or take the bypass when he saw the first sign—a billboard that had once advertised a casino, now whitewashed and covered in black writing:

YOU ARE NOW UNDER SNIPER SURVEILLANCE
STOP IN THE NEXT 400 YARDS

Jack took his foot off the gas.

Another billboard, same side of the road, one hundred yards farther down:

300 YARDS TO STOP
COMPLY OR YOU WILL BE SHOT

Jack looked in the rearview mirror, saw several vehicles trailing him, no idea where they'd come from.

200 YARDS
TURN OFF YOUR VEHICLE AND . . .

He could see a roadblock in the distance, set up at a fork in the highway. More than twenty cars and trucks. Sandbags. Staunch artillery.

He passed vehicles on the shoulder that had been shot to hell and burned.

DO NOT FUCKING MOVE

The cars behind him were close now, one of them a Navigator with the moonroof open and two men with machine guns standing on the backseat, ready to unload. Jack brought the minivan to a stop, put it in park, and turned off the engine. He looked over at Donald, started to rouse him, then thought, Why wake a man just to be killed?

Six heavily armed men strode up the middle of the highway toward the minivan. One of them brought along an emaciated, blindfolded human being on a leash.

They didn't strike Jack as military, didn't carry themselves so cocksure.

The greeting party stopped thirty yards out from the front bumper of the minivan, and the tallest of the bunch raised a bullhorn to his mouth.

"Both of you, out of the car."

Jack grabbed Donald's arm. "Come on, we have to get out."

The man wouldn't move.

"Donald."

"You have five seconds."

Jack opened his door and stepped out into the highway with his hands raised.

"You in the car, get out or—"

"He doesn't hear you!" Jack yelled. "His mind is gone."

"Down on your stomach."

Jack got down onto his knees and prostrated himself across the rough, sun-warmed pavement. Listened to the sound of their footsteps coming toward him, and he didn't dare move or even raise his head. Just lay there with his heart throbbing against the road, wondering, from a strangely detached perspective, if this was how and where it would end for him.

The men stopped several feet away.

One of them came forward and Jack felt hands running up and down his sides and then his legs.

"Clean."

"Check the other guy. You, sit up."

Jack sat up.

"Where's Benny?"

One of the guards produced the blindfolded rail of a man. He was naked and beaten to within an inch of his life, bruises covering his body and face, his hands cuffed, a chain linking his ankles above his bare feet.

The tall man pointed a large revolver at Jack's face and asked him his name.

"Jack."

"Is there a bomb in your van?"

"No."

The one who'd frisked Jack peered over the front passenger door, said, "This one's completely checked out."

The tall man stared at Jack. "Jack, I want to introduce you to Benny." Benny's handler gave a hard tug on the leash, dragging him within a foot of Jack. "So here's the deal. If Benny likes you, I'm going to blow your brains out all over this road. If he doesn't, we'll talk." He looked at Benny and said, as if speaking to a dog, "Ready to do some work, Benny?"

Benny nodded, salivating.

"I'm going to take your blindfold off now and show you our new friend."

Benny urinated on the pavement.

"If you're a good boy, I'll give you some water and a treat. Are you a good boy?"

Benny made a sound that wasn't human, and then the tall man nodded to his handler, who pulled off the blindfold.

The wild man crouched in front of Jack. Eyes ringed with black and yellow bruises but still a deep clarity and intensity in them. He was inches from Jack's face. Smelled like he'd been bedding down in his own shit, and he seemed to be staring at something on the back of Jack's skull.

Jack looked up at the man holding the revolver. "What the fuck is—"

Never saw the thing move, but Benny was suddenly on top of him, trying to tear Jack's throat out with his teeth. It took three men to drag him away and several jolts from a cattle prod before he finally collapsed in the road and curled up moaning in the fetal position.

Jack scrambled back toward the van, trying to catch his breath, the man with the revolver moving toward him, saying, "It's all right. This is good news. If Benny had crawled into your lap and started cooing, you wouldn't be with us anymore."

"What is that thing?"

"Our pet. Our affected pet. He checks out everyone who tries to come into the city. I'm Brian, by the way." He offered a hand, helped Jack onto his feet.

"Is the city safe?" Jack asked.

"Yeah. We figure there's ten, fifteen thousand people still here. Many have left, gone north for the border. But that's a rough trip. We've got all the roads into town protected."

"No affected in the city?"

"Nope."

"How's that possible?"

"It was cloudy the night of the event over this part of Montana."

"You haven't been attacked?"

"Not by any force that stood a chance. We've got five thousand armed men ready to fuck shit up on a moment's notice."

Jack looked around, the RPMs of his heart falling back toward baseline.

"Has a woman with two children passed through in the last five days?"

"I don't think so. You have a picture?"

"No."

"Your wife and kids?"

Jack nodded.

"We haven't had much traffic. You're the first person to even come up this road in three days. Are they coming here to meet you?"

"I don't know. I don't know where they are. We were separated in Wyoming." He looked at the rest of the crew. "Any of you seen them? Fourteen-year-old girl, seven-year-old boy."

Nothing but headshakes.

"My boy is affected," Jack said. "He isn't symptomatic or violent, but he saw the lights. Would you let him in?"

"How is it possible he isn't like the others?"

"I don't know, but he isn't. His name is Cole."

"We'll keep an eye out for them," Brian said, "and if he isn't hostile, we'll let your family through."

"You swear to me?"

"We don't kill kids." Brian pointed toward the windshield at Donald. "Friend of yours?"

"I picked him up this morning outside of White Sulphur Springs, just walking down the middle of the road. He needs medical attention."

"Well, there's shelters set up at some of the schools. You might find a doctor at one of those."

"There's an air force base here, right?"

"Yeah, but it's been on lockdown since everything went to hell. I guess it's understandable—they've got the silos holding the Minuteman missiles."

— — —

Jack had passed through the outskirts of Great Falls a handful of times in the last ten years, during those long driving trips to see his father, when his old man had still lived up in Cut Bank. But he hadn't been in the city proper since he and Dee had left to start a life in Albuquerque, sixteen years ago. Thought this might be the most peculiar circumstance under which to experience the emotion of nostalgia.

Driving the quiet streets, he found it haunting to see the darkness fall upon a city that had no light to raise in its defense.

In the blue dusk, he passed an ice-cream shop he and Dee had frequented on Friday nights, all those years ago. But everything else, at least what little he could see of it, had changed. He drove to a hospital and cruised past the emergency room entrance—dark and vacated. Went on.

There was no one out. The streets empty. The geography of the town might have been an asset, might have stoked his memory had there been streetlights to guide him. But it was as dark as the countryside in these city limits. He drove for thirty minutes, dipping into the reserve tank, rambling in search of anything that resembled a shelter.

= = =

The engine had already sputtered once when he saw the soft smears of light in the distance. The form of a building took shape, and he recognized it—a high school. People were milling around the steps that climbed to the main brick building, the cherry glow of their cigarettes barely visible in the dark.

Jack pulled to the curb and turned off the minivan.

He was thirsty again.

"Donald," he said. "We're at a shelter. They might have hot food. Clean water. Cots. I'll find a doctor to look at you. We're in a safe city now. You'll be taken care of."

Donald leaned against the door.

"Don? You awake?" Jack reached over, touched the man's hand.

Cool and limp.

His neck gave no pulse.

= = =

Jack climbed the steps to the school. Inside, candlelight flickered off the lockers. It smelled of body odor and rancid clothing. Cots stretched down the length of the hallway. He heard hushed conversations and snoring. Somewhere, a baby cried.

He walked a long corridor, cots on either side and open suitcases—barely enough room for him to make his way without trampling someone's filthy laundry.

Five minutes of negotiating the crowded hallways brought him to the entrance of a gymnasium, where a woman sat at a folding table, reading by candlelight. She looked up at Jack with the no-bullshit demeanor of a mathematics teacher or principal.

"You're new," she said.

"Yeah."

"Do you live in Great Falls?"

"Albuquerque. I'm looking for my family. My wife is Dee. She's short, auburn hair, beautiful. Forty years old. My son is Cole, and he's . . ." As he said Cole's name, he thought about Benny and the roadblock at the edge of town.

"Sir?"

"He's seven. My daughter is Naomi and she's fourteen. Looks a lot like her mother."

"And you think they might be here?"

"I don't know, we were separated. But they might have come to Great Falls."

"Doesn't ring a bell, but we've got over two thousand people here. Look, I wish I could offer you a cot, but we're maxed out and I don't know when more food is coming. The air force base had been trucking in MRE rations, but we haven't seen them in five days." She sounded tired and emotionless.

Jack glanced into the gymnasium—a sprawl of sleeping bodies.

"There a morgue around?" he asked. "I've got a dead man in my car. Guy I picked up this morning who didn't make it."

She shook her head. "I don't know what to tell you. We're in a bit of chaos here."

"If you see my family, tell them Jack was here looking for them."

- - -

He drove to a nearby park that took up a single city block. Unbuckled Donald's seatbelt, pulled him out of the front passenger seat, and dragged him away from the car. He made it as far as a boulder that was surrounded by flower boxes whose contents had wilted, laid Donald down in the grass, and folded the man's hands across his chest.

Sat with him for a long time in the dark. It didn't feel right just leaving Donald here alone. Thinking there was something more to be done, though he had no idea what.

After a while, he said, "This is the best I can do, Don. I'm sorry.
I'm sorry about everything."

And he got up and walked back to the van.

— — —

Drove fifteen blocks toward the river, the engine sputtering, cylinders misfiring. He'd wanted to make it to the water, but that wasn't
going to happen.

The feeble moonlight was shining off the columns of the civic
center several blocks ahead. When he saw them, he realized where
he was and brought the minivan to a stop in the middle of the
street. Sat staring in disbelief toward the square, little to see in the
powerless dark but the five-story block of the Davidson Building.
Wondered how it had not occurred to him until this moment to
come here.

Jack put the van back into gear and cranked the steering wheel.
Drove over the lip of the sidewalk into the middle of the square
between two rows of potted evergreen trees.

He turned off the van. Sat in the dark and the quiet, listening to
the engine cool. He was in a dark plaza, buildings on either side of
him, joined by a skywalk. There was a fountain nearby, dormant.

So much as he remembered it, even after all this time.

He opened his door and stepped down onto the concrete. It was
cold. There were clouds scudding through the light of the moon.
Silence like this was one thing in the wilderness, a completely different matter in the city. No cars out, no people, not even the hum
of streetlamps or powerlines. Too dark. Too quiet. Everything
wrong.

It hit him. Pure exhaustion. The emotional expenditure of another day in hell. He felt the call of sleep, and the promise of a few
hours of unconsciousness, of checking out of all of this, had never
sounded better.

The minivan still smelled like death.

He cracked all the windows and laid the front seat back as far
as it would go.

WHEN his eyes opened, he was staring through the windshield at the windows of an office building thirty feet above him. A sheet of clouds reflected in the dark glass. He sat up. Hungry. Cold. Opened the door and stepped down onto the plaza.

Eighteen years ago, there had been a coffeehouse a block from here, and he could almost smell the memory of their French roast, feel how the heat of it had steamed into his face on mornings just like this.

He walked toward Central Avenue. Strange not to know the day, but he was certain it was near the end of October now. The sky certainly looked it, and the steel chill in the air felt it. Clouds soft and pregnant, debating whether to snow or drop cold rain.

Up and down the avenue, not a single car on the street. A few of the stores had been looted, broken glass on the sidewalk. Nothing moved but some dead leaves scraping across the road.

- - -

Jack went back to the minivan and looked inside. Don's youngest daughter had been sitting in the third row, from what Jack could tell. It looked like she'd made the space her own—iPad, books, a stuffed penguin that had been dragged around forever.

He lifted a drawing pad out of the floorboard, stared at a half-finished sketch of countryside that looked remarkably similar to the Montana waste where he'd stumbled upon this van. She had talent. All she'd used was a black magic marker to suggest a sharpened mountain range, miles of sagebrush, and the road that shot a lonely trajectory through that country. He wondered if she'd been drawing when her family was ridden down. A line stopped abruptly at the summit of a mountain, the downslope never finished, and the black marker she'd used still lay uncapped on the carpet.

Jack picked a cigar box off the floor and raised the lid.

Markers, pastel pencils, miniature bottles of acrylic paint, charcoal, brushes, erasers, and a sterling silver etched locket.

He couldn't bring himself to open it.

He was all morning writing her name. Big block letters on the sliding door, the black Sharpies showing up well on the minivan's white paint. He used up three markers coloring in the letters, then took a bottle of white acrylic paint and brushed her name onto the plate-glass windows of the surrounding buildings.

Dee's name could not be missed, even from fifty yards away.

By early afternoon a light mist was falling, and he sat in the front seat behind the wheel, watching the beads of water populate the glass.

Drifted off and when he woke again it was dark and a harder rain falling. He crawled into the very back and stretched out across the young girl's seat. Wrapped himself in a blanket that still carried her smell. He was hungry but figured he should start rationing his bag of junk food, which was down to twelve packages.

The rainfall on the minivan roof was a good sound. He thought about his family until it hurt too much, and then he went to sleep.

THUNDER is what it sounded like in his half-conscious state, and it made the windows tremble. Jack tugged the blanket away from his face, lay there listening to see if it would come again, thinking he might've dreamed it.

It came again. Not thunder. This was a deeper, focused sound, and it didn't roll across the sky.

He crawled out of the backseat and pulled open the side door.

Walked through the plaza into the street.

Late morning. A low cloud deck. The pavement wet.

He heard it again. Far off. Perhaps beyond the city. He'd never heard it before, not in real life, but he knew it was the sound of bombs exploding.

--- --- ---

The plate glass on the first floor of the Wells Fargo bank had been smashed out some time ago. Jack stepped through into the lobby. Dark, silent. He looked at the vacant teller stations. The velvet rope lines. Signs for commercial and residential mortgage departments. A water fountain stood against the wall between the restrooms. He walked over and turned the knob. Nothing. He went into the women's restroom and tried the faucet. Nothing. There was water in the toilets, but he wasn't at that point just yet.

= = =

He crossed the plaza to the Davidson Building. The entrance doors were locked. The glass intact. He uprooted a baby fir tree from a concrete planter that must have weighed fifty or sixty pounds. When he'd finally hoisted it up, he ran toward the doors and heaved the planter at the glass like an oversize shot put.

= = =

He took his time stripping branches from the fir tree, relieved just to have something to occupy his mind. When he'd finished, he took off his outer shirt and tore it into long strips. Raised the hood of the minivan, unscrewed the cap to the oil tank, and dipped the pieces of his shirt inside. He tied the oil-coated cloth around the end of the stick. No idea if this would even work. He'd seen someone do it on a survival show once.

= = =

He held the glowing orange coils of the van's cigarette lighter to a dry corner of the fabric.

A flame appeared, crept across the cloth, and then the end of Jack's torch ignited.

It burned beautifully.

= = =

Jack arrived on the fourth-floor landing, firelight flickering off the concrete walls of the stairwell. He opened the door and stepped out into a carpeted hallway. Moved down the corridor, brass name-

plates catching torchlight. Stopped at a window with the words
FINANCIAL ADVISORS stenciled across the glass. In the firelight, he
could see a waiting area, several chairs, a small table stacked with
magazines. Jack tried the door. Locked. He set the torch on the
fire-retardant carpet, grabbed the metal trash can standing beside
an elevator, and hurled it through the glass.

— — —

Through the office windows, daylight filtered in. Down the length
of a wall, he studied a photographic series of grinning salesmen. He
carried his torch into a breakroom and opened the refrigerator. A
dozen cups of undoubtedly spoiled yogurt. Something wrapped in
tinfoil. A Styrofoam box of leftovers that smelled like a rotting corpse.
     A water cooler stood nearby.
     He lodged the torch in the sink and knelt down on the floor.
Held his mouth under the tap and drank until his stomach ached.

— — —

He entered a corner office and sat in the leather chair behind the
desk. Propped his feet up and stared at framed photographs—
a soccer team of boys in green uniforms; a family (sunglassed and
screaming) on a raft in the midst of whitewater; three beer-flushed
men, arm in arm, in the fairway of a golf course. He swiveled
around in the chair and rolled toward the window. A half mile to
the west, he could see the Missouri. The water gray-green under
the clouds. Plains beyond. Down in the plaza, the minivan stood
glazed in rainwater.
     A plastic inbox tray rattled on the glass top.
     The building shook.
     A few seconds later, he heard the blast.
     Miles away, south of town, black smoke lifted off the prairie.

— — —

He carried the half-filled canister of water down the stairwell and through the lobby.

Outside, a light rain fell, the air cold enough to cloud his breath.

He climbed into the minivan and curled up in the backseat under the little girl's blanket. Shut his eyes.

Rain hammered the metal roof.

My day, he thought. Fire and water.

- - -

Black of night, he shot awake.

Not only explosions but gunfire now. Inside the city limits.

He climbed into the front seat and peered through the windshield.

The sky lit up—cushions of cloud overhead and snow falling out of them.

Darkness.

The delayed boom of whatever artillery shell had just exploded.

A brighter flash toward the horizon.

Then black.

J ACK watched the sky lighten through the glass, his hands still clenching the steering wheel as they had for the last two hours. Like listening to a hurricane come ashore and the intensifying terror of the eye wall creeping closer.

The sound of war coming.

He straightened in the seat, pushed open the door, stepped outside. Snow clung to everything, and he brushed it off the minivan's sliding door to uncover Dee's name.

Realized he was crying. What if the guards hadn't allowed Cole into the city? Would Dee have even risked an entry this close to the border? No. She'd have gone around, tried to rush the kids across. They might even be in Canada by now. They might be dead in Wyoming. Might be anywhere. But not here. Not with him.

He sat down in the snow.

They weren't coming.

They weren't coming.

They weren't—

The jackhammer pounding of a machine gun broke out several blocks away.

He staggered out into the street, which was lined with two- and three-story buildings and trees with a few orange leaves still desperately hanging on.

Three blocks down, muzzle flashes blossomed from a top-floor window.

The firing went on for a full minute.

When it stopped, silence fell upon the city.

Specks of snow seemed to hang weightless in the air.

Jack walked back to the minivan, suddenly hungry, but even more tired, and he was asleep seconds after his head hit the seat cushion. He slept so hard it seemed like barely a minute had passed, and then he was awake again and a noise like Armageddon right on top of him.

He peered over the back of the seat, saw people running through the square, twenty feet from the van. They were dressed like civilians and wearing clothes so tattered they appeared to be molting. The three men bringing up the rear held shotguns at waist level. They were backpedaling and firing and Jack could see the abject fear in their faces laced with the mad rush of adrenaline, something screaming at him to get the fuck down, but he couldn't tear his eyes away. The shotguns thundered and one of the men collapsed and then the small platoon streamed into the Davidson Building.

For fifteen seconds, nothing.

No sound. No movement.

Then a company of black-clad men swarmed into the square, some of them taking positions behind the planters, a handful charging into the building.

Jack got down into the floorboard and flattened himself against the carpet, pulling the blanket on top of him as machine guns erupted all around him, men yelling over the mayhem, the shotguns booming down out of the building, pellets and rounds chinking into the side of the minivan, and then a window exploded, glass everywhere, and the van sank to one side, a tire punctured.

A man began to scream nearby, and Jack covered his ears and squeezed his eyes shut and he was saying her name. Could feel his lips moving, though he couldn't hear the words, not even inside his head, over the terrible noise.

An explosion blew out every window in the van.

When Jack's ears stopped ringing, he heard footsteps pounding the concrete. Someone shouted, and the next time he heard gunshots, they were distant, muffled.

He waited another minute, then slowly sat up. Brighter in the van with the tinted window glass shot out. A half dozen men lay scattered across the plaza, one of them still crawling.

On the fourth floor of the Davidson Building a black crater smoked, ragged flames cutting through.

Jack made his way into the driver's seat and eased the door open.

Gunshots inside the Davidson Building.

He stared at the bank. Twenty yards away. *Get inside. Find an office. Crawl under a desk. Wait for silence.*

He glanced back toward the Davidson Building. A man stepped out of the lobby and walked into the square. He was looking at the minivan. Jack ducked as far as he could under the steering wheel. More voices. Orders being shouted. Fading away now. He eased up into the seat again and peered through the shattered windshield. The black-clad men had lined the civilian platoon up in the middle of the street. They were making them get down on their knees at gunpoint.

A man in a red bandanna stood facing the kneeling men. Jack could just hear his voice. He was telling them he would be pleased to shoot each of them in the head, felt certain they would in turn be grateful for this outcome. However, if even one of them resisted, his unit would spend the rest of the day torturing them to death.

A handful of the civilians wept. He could see their shoulders bobbing. But no one moved.

Red Bandanna went to the first civilian, pulled a handgun from his holster, and shot him between the eyes.

He went on down the line, stopping midway to reload, Jack watching the heads of the condemned snapping back, bodies toppling, found himself morbidly drawn to study the unimaginable bracing of the next one to die. And the next. And the next.

Ultimate tension, then emptiness, then ten people lay dead on the snow-dusted street where ten had knelt living just thirty seconds before. The soldiers left them there, drifting on down Central Avenue toward the river, in a formation that made Jack certain they were military.

When the last man had slipped out of view, Jack breathed again.

Staying here, in this plaza, wasn't going to work. Not with the city under siege.

As he lifted his head off the steering wheel, the man in the red bandanna reappeared around the corner of the Davidson Building. He was walking back into the square, straight toward the van. Jack's heart raced, a hot spike of panic flooding in.

He slammed his shoulder into the door and barreled out of the minivan at a dead run toward the bank, waiting for the gunshots, the shattered windows rushing toward him.

Just as he reached them, he heard three shots squeezed off, and he was inside, untouched, turning left now, bolting up a set of stairs into the mortgage department, which was dark except for the crumbs of daylight filtering in through the offices that overlooked the plaza.

Jack stopped.

He could hear the man's footfalls in the lobby down below.

Now running up the stairs.

Jack moved into a maze of cubicles, his world getting darker with every step he took away from those windows.

He crawled under a desk. Couldn't see a thing. Breathless. He shut his eyes, tried to calm himself, and when his heart finally slowed, he heard the footsteps—soft and slow—moving toward him.

He took long, slow inhalations through his nose, and even in the dark chill of the bank, lines of sweat were running down his sides.

The man let out a sharp breath. Couldn't have been more than a few feet away.

His footsteps trailed off into the black, audible only when his boot tread caught on the carpet—an imperceptible scratch.

Jack's legs burned. He'd crammed himself up underneath the desk, the wood digging into his backbone.

Five minutes passed without a sound.

Ten minutes.

Twenty.

Then an hour was gone, maybe longer. Impossible to know.

He leaned forward, rocking slowly back onto his hands and knees, his feet tingling with an excruciating numbness. Crawled several feet into the dark, his knees popping as he stood.

He glanced over his shoulder, saw the barest thread of light sliding around a corner. Wondering, Should I crawl back under the desk, wait a few more hours? Maybe the man with the red bandanna had gone to get a flashlight. Maybe he'd left with no intention of returning.

Jack moved between the cubicles, back into the light.

He stepped into the hallway.

Back down the stairs, through the lobby, where he stood in that glassless window frame, looking out across the plaza.

Snowing again. Nothing moving. The minivan riddled with bullet holes. Some of the dead lay beside their weapons, and he felt a subtle charge at the prospect of getting his hands on a gun again.

Ten steps into the plaza, Jack bent down to unwind the strap of a machine gun that had tangled around the arm of a dead man.

Froze as his finger touched the strap.

An icy prickle down the center of his back.

What he'd heard was the sliding door to the minivan easing open.

Jack let go and stood, turning slowly.

Red Bandanna sat in the floor of the van, lighting a cigarette.

"Finally." He took a deep drag. "Didn't want you to see the smoke."

He climbed out and started toward Jack, motioning him away from the dead man with his pistol.

"The fountain," he said.

Jack crossed the plaza, never taking his eyes off the man, as if that somehow kept the balance of control in his favor.

The fountain was a circle of old concrete, fifteen feet across, with a stone feature rising out of the middle that had once circulated water. Most of it had long since evaporated, and what remained was stagnant and filled with disks of ice.

The men sat five feet apart.

Jack saw that the man's hands were covered in dried blood that was cracking on his skin like an old oil painting. He looked out at the plaza—the minivan, the dead, the blood on melting snow.

In proximity, the soldier looked nothing like Jack had imagined. A kinder face. Three-day beard. Thoughtful eyes. Curls of black hair slipping out from under the bandanna. His fatigues weren't black, as Jack had first thought, but some pattern of night camouflage comprised of dark blues. Might have been Jack's age, perhaps a year or two younger.

He stared at Jack while he smoked, his handgun resting on his leg, trained on Jack's stomach.

"Is Dee alive?"

Jack didn't respond.

"Where's your family, Jack?"

"How do you . . . ?"

When the man smiled, Jack felt the eerie prickling of recognition.

Jack said, "Kiernan."

"I saw her name all over this square, and it didn't even click with me until I was walking away."

"What are you doing here?"

"Me and some Guard buddies from Albuquerque defected. We've been heading north, just like you, killing and fucking and ravaging. Time of my life. Are you expecting Dee and the fam? Because we can wait. I'd be totally down for that."

"I haven't seen them in days."

"You got separated?"

Jack nodded.

"Where?"

"Wyoming. Where's your family, Kiernan? I seem to remember Dee telling me you had children."

Kiernan took another drag. "Rotting in our backyard back in New Mexico."

"I'm sorry."

"It's okay. I killed them."

Jack could feel, even in the light of everything he'd seen, a new horror at this.

Kiernan smiled. "Smoke?"

"Not in years."

Kiernan tugged a crumpled pack of Marlboro Reds out of an inner pocket, offered it to Jack. "Treat yourself. I don't think it really matters anymore. Do you?"

Jack's hands shook. He plucked a crooked cigarette from the pack along with the lighter. It took him four attempts to fire the tobacco sprigs hanging out of the end. Kiernan got another cigarette for himself.

"So why are you *here,* Jack? In this square, out of all the places in the Wild, Wild West? I'm literally dying to know."

Jack said nothing, just pulled the smoke into his lungs. It burned sweetly.

"You think Dee's going to find you here? That it?"

Jack exhaled, felt the nicotine hit pulling him deeper into himself, sliding a filter between this moment and his perception of it. A dulling of the fear.

"Ask you something?" Jack said.

"As long as your cigarette's still burning."

"When you're trying to fall asleep at night, do you see the faces of your wife and kids?"

"Sometimes."

"How do you not kill yourself?"

"That you could even ask that is a perfect demonstration of why you're all being slaughtered. Now answer *my* question. Why are you here?"

The idea of lunging at Kiernan occurred to Jack, and with it a monster dose of weakness and fear that slashed through his nicotine rush.

Kiernan smirked. "You'd never pull it off. Not on your best day and my worst. Answer my fucking question."

"I'm here because this is where I ran out of gas."

"Why do you want to piss me off?"

Jack smoked.

"In all my travels north," Kiernan said, "I was always looking for your green Land Rover. Always chasing you and Dee, even though I never expected to actually find you."

"What's it like?" Jack said.

"What is what like?"

"To have become . . . whatever you are now."

Kiernan thoughtfully considered the question. "All our life we spend wondering, you know? Now it's all about knowing."

"You were blind but now you see?"

"Something like that."

"What do you know now that you didn't know before?"

"You taught philosophy, right?"

"Yeah."

"Then you know . . . words just fuck up true meaning. Even if I could make you understand, I wouldn't."

"Why?"

"Because you didn't see the lights. Just so I'm clear . . . you have no way to contact Dee, but you think she's going to show up here. Why? Was it prearranged in the event you two were—"

"I've been here three days. She's not coming."

"She could be dead."

"It's all I think about. How many children did you have?"

"Three."

Jack flicked the ash.

"Did you look into their eyes while you murdered them?"

"I was crying. They were crying, asking what they'd done. My wife was screaming. Horrible day. I need to know why you're here before your cigarette's gone. The curiosity will eat at me."

"I told you. Ran out of gas."

Kiernan shook his head. "You're going to make me threaten you, aren't you?"

"Fuck your lights and fuck you."

Kiernan let his cigarette slip out of his hand, hiss out in the snow. He stood, lifting his shirt so Jack could see the sheathed Ka-Bar.

"When I open you up and start pulling stuff out and feeding it to you, you will talk. You will tell me everything I want to know and more. You'll curse Naomi and Cole with your last breath and beg me to do the same to them."

Jack still had an inch of tobacco left, but he threw his cigarette into the pool.

"You can't touch it, and you know it, and it kills you, doesn't it?"

"What are you talking about?"

"Even if I could make you understand, I wouldn't."

Kiernan holstered his pistol, unsnapped the sheath, and drew the Ka-Bar.

"One last thing," Jack said. "You and your batshit-crazy friends have fucked our world, but you've also made me a better father. You made me love my wife again, and for that I thank you."

Jack stared down into the pool, waiting for whatever was going to happen next.

The ice melted and the water turned clear and the fountain began to rain. He looked up. The sky now a bright, almost painful blue. It was midday in the square, a dozen people eating lunch out in the autumn sunshine.

Jack sat with an iced coffee, ten minutes left on his lunch break.

She sat at that same table fifteen feet away, engrossed in a text-book, a tray of half-eaten salad pushed aside. Third day in a row she'd eaten lunch in the plaza. Third day in a row he couldn't take his eyes off her.

He'd walked up to women he didn't know and asked for a date. No big deal. He was good-looking, tall, and confident. But something about this girl had put him off his game. She was gorgeous, sure, but it was more than that—maybe the white lab coat fucking with him (already fantasized about that), maybe the intensity with which she read—never moving except to turn the page or brush away a strand of loose auburn hair that contained honest-to-God strands of gold.

Yesterday he'd spent the whole hour building up the nerve. Had finally stood with five minutes left, his mouth completely dry as he approached. In proximity to her table, he'd caught a whiff of something—shampoo or body wash—and he knew he'd only make a fool of himself. Walked right on past into the Wells Fargo bank and just stood watching her through the glass until she finally packed her book into a tattered Eastpak and went on her way.

Now there were five minutes left in this hour. A repeat of yesterday. He'd fucked around and put himself in the same position.

He stood quickly and started toward her table, trying to get there before he had the chance to talk himself out of it again. He was three feet away from her, wholly uncommitted to any of this, when the tip of his sneaker caught on the lip of a concrete slab.

Jack went down hard and fast, and when he looked up from the ground he was staring at the rivulets of his iced coffee running down her leg and dripping off the hem of her lab coat.

"Oh my God," he said, picking himself up. "I'm so sorry." As he got back onto his feet, he saw that he'd somehow managed to drench her book, her white coat, her skirt, even her hair—maximum damage inflicted with a single cup of iced coffee.

She glared up at him, possibly more shocked than he was, Jack mumbling, trying to string together a coherent sentence that finally came together as "I'm a total idiot."

The anger in her eyes melted away. She wiped the coffee from her face and looked down at her coat, and all Jack could think was that she was even more beautiful at point-blank range.

"I'll pay to replace the book and the coat and—"

She waved him off. "It's fine. You all right? That looked bad."

He'd have a black bruise on his elbow by nightfall, but in this moment, he felt no pain. "I think I'll live, once I get past the devastating humiliation."

She laughed. Like nothing he'd ever heard. "Oh, come on, it wasn't that bad."

"Actually, it was."

"No, it—"

"I was coming over here to ask you out."

Her face went blank.

Longest moment of his life.

"Bullshit," she said finally.

"Excuse me?"

"You're just fucking with me."

Jack smiled. "Would you grant me a do-over?"

"A what?"

"A do-over. Let me have another shot at this."

He couldn't tell for sure in the brilliant afternoon sunlight, but she might have blushed.

"Sure," she said.

"I'll be right back. It'll go better, I promise."

Jack walked to the fountain, his heart beating so fast he could barely breathe. He sat down and looked over at the table. She was watching him now, and she'd taken off her sunglasses. He started toward her again, stopping at her table with his back to the sun, so she sat in his shadow.

"Hi, I'm Jack," he said.

"Hi, Jack, I'm Deanna. Sorry about this mess. Some asshole spilled his coffee on me."

And she smiled, and he looked into her eyes for the first time. Had never felt anything like it. Up until this moment, he thought he'd experienced pure attraction, but all those other times, other women, had been lust—he saw that now—and this wasn't that. Not *just* that. There was an energy present, something combustive between them that hit him in the solar plexus. She had eyes that were dark blue but also luminescent, and later, when he thought of them, their color and clarity would remind him of a lake where he'd often camped with his father in Glacier, so deep but so clear the sunlight shot all the way down to the stones on the lakebed and made the water glow.

But he barely noticed the intensity of her eyes in that moment. It was all electricity, a terrible current, like looking into the future, everything prefigured—a life together, a daughter, a mortgage, a son born two months premature, the death of Jack's mother, an automobile wreck that would take Deanna's parents on Thanksgiving night eight years from now, moments of indescribable happiness, long winters of depression, a slow drifting, a betrayal, fear, anger, compromise, stasis, but when it all lay stripped to the bone, whatever mysterious alchemy had been present in this moment would be present always. Untouched by their failures. Everything changed, and nothing.

This is what he saw, what he sensed on some primal frequency, when he looked into his wife's eyes for the first time on a fall day in the American west that was so perfect it would always break his heart to think of it.

And it was what he still felt, eighteen years later in the same city square, when his eyes met Dee's again.

She looked unreal, moving among the dead like a ghost toward the fountain, emaciated, tears riding down her cheeks.

Kiernan must have seen the glitch in Jack's attention, because he glanced back just as Dee raised an old revolver.

"What are you doing here, Kiernan?" she asked.

"Waiting for you, love."

The gunshot reverberated between the buildings.

Kiernan stumbled back and sat down beside Jack. He was still holding the knife, and Jack grabbed it and stood facing him. Blood ran down the man's face out of a hole through his left eye.

The blade of the Ka-Bar passed through his chest plate with no effort, and Jack buried it to the hilt. Kiernan toppled back into the icy pool, a cloud of murky red surrounding him, the weight of his boots and fatigues pulling him under as the one good eye blinked frantically.

Jack turned and Dee was there. He pulled her down into the snow and he was on top of her, kissing her, like drinking water again, like breathing, and they came apart, both crying. He held her face in his hands and wouldn't let go for fear that she would vanish, or he'd wake up and realize it was *him* dying in the fountain and these were his last thoughts.

"You're here, aren't you?" he said, and he kept saying it, and she kept telling him that she was, that she was real, the kids were safe, and they would soon all be together.

– – –

"You didn't have problems getting Cole into the city?" Jack asked. They were walking up Third Street North toward the library, each holding two machine guns taken off the dead men in the square like a pair of bad action-flick heroes.

"We drove in last night," Dee said. "The barricade had been destroyed. We almost didn't make it. Bombs going off everywhere. Gunfights on every block. A couple of really close calls. It's a full-scale war on the east side of town. Thousands dead."

They passed a law office that had been hit with a mortar shell. Wet paper plastered across the sidewalk.

"How'd you know to come to the square?"

Dee smiled. "How did you?"

"I'd gone to the shelter looking for you. No one had seen you or the kids. I drove downtown, out of gas, desperate, and then the headlights shone on the Davidson Building. Today was my third in the square. I didn't know if you'd try to come here or just get the kids across the border. For all I knew, you were dead."

"When I saw the mileage sign for Great Falls, I knew that, if you were alive, if you had any strength left in your body, you'd come here."

"So you have a car?"

"Yeah."

"You should've tried to cross the border."

"Not without you."

Machine guns chattered a dozen blocks away.

"I came here this morning," Dee said, "but it was crawling with soldiers."

"Did you see what I wrote on the car?"

"I started crying when I saw it. Lost it. I hid until the soldiers left, but then Kiernan came back to kill you. I watched him chase

you into the bank. I thought . . ." She shook off the wave of emotion. "You were in there so long."

Half a mile away, a bomb exploded.

"Come on," she said. "We better run."

- - -

Jack knelt beside the sofa in the historical archive room of the
Great Falls Public Library. Dee shined a flashlight on the ceiling,
and in the refracted light, Jack looked down at his children, sleeping head-to-toe. He put his hand on Cole's back.

"Hey, buddy. Daddy's here."

Cole stirred, eyes fluttering. They opened, got so wide Jack
knew the boy had given him up for dead.

"Is it you?" the boy said.

"It's me."

"I dream about you every night and you talk to me just like this,
but every time I wake up, you're not there."

"You're awake, and I'm here."

He drew the boy into his arms.

"Why are you crying?" Cole said.

"Because I'm holding you, and I didn't think I ever would again."

Naomi sat up at the other end of the couch. When she saw her
father she burst into tears and lunged toward Jack. He grabbed her,
now holding both his children in his arms, and he could not think
of a time in his life when he'd been more overloaded with joy.

- - .-

Dee wouldn't take his word for it that he was okay. She made him
strip and examined every square inch of his body with the flashlight, starting with the recent gunshot wound to his right shoulder.

"How's it feel?"

"Pretty sore these last few days."

"It's infected."

She took him into the bathroom and cleaned the wound as well as she could with a few paper towels and antiseptic hand soap.

"We have to try and keep it clean until we get some real bandages over it."

She held up his left arm.

"What's this?"

He slowly unwound the filthy bandage covering what was left of his ring finger.

Dee gasped when she saw it.

"Soldier at the top of Togwotee Pass cut it off."

She grabbed the flashlight off the sink and shined the light on the jagged phalange and the scab trying to form across it.

"Your ring finger," she said, her eyes welling. "Your ring."

"I know. But I'm here, and you're here, and that's all that matters."

— — —

While the kids slept, he and Dee lay on another sofa and talked as night fell. Soon it was pitch-black except when light flickered through the tall windows of the archive room—like watching a rainless thunderstorm. Even the most distant detonations shook the building's foundation and made dust rain down from the ceiling.

— — —

Jack drifted off, and when he woke again he was still holding Dee on the couch. Her ear against his mouth. He didn't know if she was sleeping, but he whispered anyway. Told her how his heart was so full, how if they ever got someplace safe, he would spend every waking moment making her happy, loving her, loving Cole and Nay. Fuck the life they'd walled themselves in with. He didn't care if they lived in a trailer in the middle of nowhere. Let them be poor. Let them scrape by. He just wanted to be with her, every second of every hour of every day. Wanted to see her old and slow and gray. Watch her hold their granddaughters, their grandsons.

– – –

Jack sat up. The building shook, books falling off the shelves. His ears ringing. Dee was up too, her lips moving, but he couldn't hear anything, and then the sound came rushing back—the kids were screaming, Dee shouting. He got to his feet, the room brilliantly lit through those tall windows by the flames consuming a building several blocks away, burning with such intensity he could feel the heat through the glass.

He opened his mouth to say something, but a fast-building roar stopped him, something approaching, the noise of it getting louder and closer. And then it was right on top of them, like God scream- ing, and in the flamelight, Jack could see his children covering their ears, eyes wide with terror.

Then it was gone, and the room filled with enough silence for the sounds of distant machine-gun fire to filter in.

Jack turned to Dee, said, "We're leav—"

A flash of scalding white light. The windows blew out and something hit Jack in the chest that was neither force nor sound but a terrible fusion of the two, and he was lying on his back, his molars jogged loose, telling himself to get up, check on the kids, but his legs were slow to respond.

The ringing in his ears had become a jackhammer.

He sat up, eyes still struggling to adjust after that blinding deto- nation.

The building across the street had taken a direct hit, and in the twisting flames, he could see steel girders sagging, melting in the heat.

He was unstable on his feet.

Dee looked all right. She was sitting up, stunned, her eyes open, blinking slowly.

Cole and Naomi lay in fetal positions on the floor, still bracing, covering their heads and trembling. Dee was suddenly beside him.

He tried to say something to her but couldn't hear his own voice inside his head. Dee grabbed his face and pulled him close enough to read her lips.

— — —

He slung the machine-gun straps over his neck and carried Naomi down the staircase, Dee leading with the flashlight, Cole draped over her shoulder.

On the second-floor landing, Jack heard that sound again, muffled now but racing toward a violent climax, and then the building shook with such intensity he couldn't believe it resisted collapse.

Everywhere on the ground level, shelves had toppled, books strewn everywhere. The shock wave had exploded the wall of windows at the entrance, and they passed over mounds of shattered glass into a nightmare world. Black smoke poured from the ruins of whatever had stood across the street, and at the pinnacle of a flagpole, the United States and Montana State flags had begun to burn at the fringes.

Dee led Jack to a Jeep Cherokee that was parked out of sight between the building and a hedge. She tossed him a ring of keys and opened the rear passenger door and set Cole inside. Jack handed Naomi over, and after Dee had gotten their daughter in and shut the door, he put his lips to his wife's ear.

"How much gas?"

"Enough to reach the border."

"You have to be my gunner." She nodded. "Shoot any fucking thing that moves."

Jack climbed in behind the wheel and cranked the engine, his mind running hot, trying to orient himself in the city. There were essentially two routes north—I-15 to Sweetgrass or Highway 87 to Havre.

He shifted into gear and eased the Jeep through the steaming grass onto the pavement, the heat from the building across the street so intense that sweat was running down his face.

He punched the gas, wind and smoke streaming through the

windshield. The glass had been shot out, and that was going to make driving at high speeds infinitely more difficult.

By the time he rolled up on the next intersection, he'd decided to try the highway north out of town. He glanced over at Dee, who already had the machine gun shouldered and pointed out the window. Glanced into the backseat, saw his children down in the floorboards, didn't know if they could hear him, but he yelled, "Do not lift your heads for any reason!"

Jack turned onto Third Avenue North and gunned the engine. In the distance, tracer fire streamed into the low cloud deck, giving the eastern sky a radioactive burn.

They were doing eighty down the street, and he could barely see a thing in the absence of headlights and with the wind and smoke rushing into his face.

They shot through several dark blocks where nothing had been touched, Jack driving blind. He had reached to turn on the headlights when muzzle flashes erupted all around them like a swarm of fireflies, bullets striking the Jeep on every side and the racket of Dee's machine gun filling the car as she fired back and screamed at him to go faster.

They sped away from the gunfire.

One block of peace.

Jack uncertain whether his hearing was improving or if they were coming up on another battle, but the sound of gunfire and exploding mortar shells became audible over the groaning engine.

At the next junction, he looked down the intersecting street and saw a tank rolling toward them, flanked by a pair of Strykers.

A quarter mile ahead, a succession of ten closely staggered explosions lit up four city blocks, and Jack could feel the road shuddering underneath him, everything illuminated brighter than day, as if the sun had gone supernova, and he could see people drawn to the window frames of almost every building they raced past—doomed, gaunt faces awash in firelight.

In the rearview mirror, he saw that one of the Strykers had launched out ahead of the tank. From it issued several splinters of light and a low-frequency, concussive report, like someone pounding nails. Two 50-cal rounds punched through the back hatch, one of them obliterating the dashboard.

They had reached the blast zone, and up ahead, the road vanished into towers of fire. Jack swung a hard left and drove up a side street parallel to an elementary school that had been carpet-bombed into molten rubble. The street teemed with people on fire who had fled the building, fifty of them he would've guessed, and their collective screams as they literally melted onto the pavement made Jack pray for deafness.

He was trying to go around them, but they kept stumbling in front of the Jeep, and that Stryker was coming, nothing to do but drive through them, over them, Dee screaming, "Oh dear God," and then she started shooting.

— — —

Two blocks from the school, Jack spotted the sign for the highway, and he veered onto the road and pushed the gas pedal into the floorboard.

The street was empty and they were screaming north, all the fire and death now confined to the rearview mirrors.

They shot across a river, through the northern outskirts of the city, and then Jack finally turned on the headlights.

They were pushing 100 mph now into a vast and welcoming darkness.

— — —

North of town and nothing but black, endless prairie. Even forty miles out, they could still see the glow of everything burning and the tracer fire arcing through the sky.

Jack had found a pair of sunglasses under the parking brake and he wore them against the wind, driving northeast now, the speedometer pegged and the noise like standing under a waterfall. But he didn't mind. The brutal wind meant that every passing second that city was falling farther behind and the Canadian border rushing closer.

Jack had just glanced at the ruined dash, wondering about the time, when he noticed a line of deep gray—just a single shade up from black—lying across the eastern horizon.

D EE awoke in the front passenger floorboard, cramped as hell, cold, and staring up at her husband, who wore sunglasses, his hair blowing back, face ruddy with windburn and the glow of what she hoped was a sunrise. It was so loud and the Jeep rode rough—either the shocks had given out or they were no longer traveling on a paved road.

She watched him. Even with a heavy beard coming in, he looked so thin, and her heart was swelling. She'd lost him, felt the awful vacuum of their separation, and now she had him back, sitting three feet away. For once she knew what she had, the kind of man he really was, even in the face of all this horror. Knew she didn't need another thing for the rest of her life except to be with him.

Jack must have felt her stare because he looked down at her and smiled.

She climbed into her seat. They weren't driving on a road anymore. It was grassland, as far as she could see in every direction. Not a building in sight. No sign of civilization.

Jack brought the car to a stop and killed the engine.

The silence was astounding.

She looked into the backseat. Naomi and Cole lay curled up in their respective floorboards. She held her hands against their backs, confirmed the rise and the fall.

"Where are we?" she asked.

Her voice sounded muffled inside her head, and Jack's came back equally distant: "North of Havre. I think the border's about ten miles that way." He pointed through the gaping windshield toward a horizon of grass, everything glazed with frost.

"Why'd you stop?" she asked.

"Engine's been in the red for a while now. Plus, I have to pee."

— — —

Jack stood pissing the frost off the grass in the massive silence. White smoke trickled out of the Jeep's grille, and he could hear something hissing under the hood, wondering if he'd fried the water pump pushing the Jeep as hard as he had. He'd been taking it slow and easy since leaving the paved roads north of Havre, hoping it'd be the safer route.

He walked back to the Jeep. Dee had set a few bottles of water and a pack of crackers on the center console.

They shared a meager breakfast, watching the sun come up.

— — —

It took an hour for the engine to cool, and then Jack cranked the Jeep and they went on, his attention focused on the temperature gauge, the needle climbing much faster than he would've liked, passing the halfway point after only a mile, edging into the red at two.

After three miles, the engine made a terrible sound, Jack fearing he'd killed it because smoke was pouring out of the grille.

He got out, raised the hood.

Wafts of smoke and steam billowed out, and it smelled bad too, like things had cooked that shouldn't have.

He left the hood raised and walked around to Dee's door.

"That doesn't look good," she said.

"It's not. We're going to have to wait until it cools down again."

Two hours later, the engine had stopped smoking, and when Jack engaged the ignition, the temperature gauge dropped almost back to baseline.

The kids were awake and thrilled to discover the bag of junk food Jack had scored at the ski area. Cole's smiling mouth was smeared with chocolate.

Jack shifted into drive and watched their progress in tenth-of-a-mile increments, the landscape scrolling by so slowly.

After one mile, the needle had almost touched the red again, and smoke was creeping out of the engine, the wind driving it up the hood and into the car.

Jack stopped once more, turned off the engine, and this became the architecture of their day—drive one mile. Overheat. Wait two hours. Drive another mile. Overheat.

Rinse.

Repeat.

In the late afternoon, they were stopped at the edge of a gentle depression. The hood raised. No wind. White smoke coiling up into the sky. Dee dozed in the front passenger seat, and Jack lay with his children in the soft, cool grass, staring up into the sky.

Cole was snuggled into his chest, the boy asleep, Naomi on his other side.

"How far are we?" Naomi asked.

"Two or three miles."

"You really think there are camps across the border?"

"Won't know until we get there."

"What if there aren't? What if it's no different on the other side? It's just an imaginary line, right?"

"Somewhere north of here, there's a place where we don't have to run anymore, and we will drive or walk or crawl until we get there."

Behind them, something chinked against the side of the Jeep.

Naomi said, "The first thing I'm going to do—"

A shot rang out across the prairie. Long ways off.

Jack sat up.

"Was that a gun?" Naomi asked.

"I think so."

Jack glanced back at the Jeep. Because of its dark color, he didn't notice the bullet hole right away, but he did see that Dee was awake, sitting up now.

"Mom's up," he said. "Let's get out of here."

He got onto his feet and walked over to Dee's door.

She was pale, and she was looking at him with a brand of fear in her eyes he'd only seen twice before, in the throes of childbirth. It was a look of pure desperation, like she'd committed herself to something that she couldn't bear to finish.

"Baby, what's wrong?"

She looked down, and he did too.

Her seat was full of bright-red arterial blood and she was squeezing her right leg.

"Oh God," Jack said.

"Dad, what's wrong?"

"You and Cole run to the other side of the car."

"Why? What—"

"Just do what I fucking tell you!"

A bullet struck the rear passenger door a foot from Jack. He slid his right arm under Dee's legs and lifted her out of the seat.

The report reached them as he carried her around the smoking grille, Dee moaning as he laid her in the grass on the other side of the Jeep.

"What happened?" Naomi asked.

"She's shot."

She covered her mouth with her hand and Cole started to cry.

Jack's hand was slicked with warm blood that was dripping off the ends of his fingers.

A round zipped through one of the back windows.

"Nay, Cole, get behind the tires and lay flat against the grass." He looked down at Dee. "You have to tell me what to do."

"It nicked the femoral artery. You have to stop the bleeding right now or I'll go into hypovolemic shock and die."

"Okay, how do I do that?"

"Wrap something around my leg."

Jack ripped open his button-down shirt and pulled his arms out of the sleeves as another bullet hit the Jeep.

Dee cried out as he lifted her leg and ran one of the sleeves underneath it.

"How tight?" he asked.

"Cut the circulation off."

He slid the loop to the top of her thigh and bore down on the knot, then put his foot on it while he cinched it down. He kept watching Dee's right hand, which she'd been pressing into the wound, trying to stop the blood that pulsed between her fingers with every heartbeat.

"Is it working?" he asked.

She blinked several times, staring into the fading sky, her eyes glassy.

"Yeah," she said finally. "I think so."

"I'll be right back."

He opened the rear passenger door and scrambled into the backseat. Reaching into the cargo area, he grabbed two AR-15s and a pair of binoculars, diving back outside as another gunshot resounded across the prairie.

Then he crawled around to the back of the Jeep, lay with his chest heaving against the ground, and brought the binoculars to his eyes, pulling the prairie into focus.

Endless grass, waving in the wind.

A backdrop of clouds going dark as night fell.

A jackrabbit standing on its hindlegs.

He made a slow scan of the horizon. A pickup truck scrolled into view—an old, beat-to-hell Chevy with equal parts paint and rust. He lowered the binoculars to gauge the true distance—a mile, possibly more. Then he glassed the truck again.

A woman stood in the bed staring through the scope of a high-powered rifle that she'd braced against the roof. The rifle bucked, soundless. A bullet hit the other side of the Jeep with a hard ping, like it had struck one of the wheels.

The report was slow in reaching him. While the woman loaded another long, brass-tipped cartridge, he panned down the prairie, starting when he saw them.

The men were already so close they took up the entire sphere of magnification—three of them in hunting camouflage, a man perhaps five years his senior and two teenagers who shared a strong resemblance.

The teen boys carried pistols and the man a double-barreled shotgun. Their faces were flush from running.

Jack lowered the binoculars. They were less than a hundred yards away.

He took up one of the machine guns, wondering how much ammo remained.

Looked back at Dee, the children huddled around her.

"They're coming," he said.

"How many?" she asked.

"Three of them."

"I can help shoot," Cole said.

"I need you to stay with Mama."

Jack crouched behind the right rear wheel, his finger sliding onto the trigger. He eased himself up until he could just see through the panels of spiderwebbed glass. The footsteps had become audible, swishing through the grass. The men would be upon them in seconds.

He crouched behind the tire again, shut his eyes, took three deep breaths.

Came suddenly to his feet and swung out around the corner of the Jeep with the AR-15 shouldered, the three men already scrambling to raise their weapons.

They vanished behind the burst of fire, the steady recoil driving into his shoulder, and then the magazine was evacuated, the barrel smoking, the men cut down fifteen feet from the Jeep.

A bullet struck the taillight by Jack's leg, and he was back around the other side by the time the gunshot reached them.

"Are they dead?" Cole asked.

"Yeah."

He lifted the other machine gun out of the grass.

"That one's empty," Dee said. "We're out." He couldn't stand the pain in her voice.

Knelt down behind the tire again and raised the binoculars. The light was going fast. It took him a moment to find the truck again, and when he had, he saw it wasn't alone. Two others had pulled up alongside it, their doors thrown open, and now he counted eight people, heavily armed, in heated discussion.

"What do you see, Jack?"

"There's eight of them now. Three trucks."

"We have to go."

"Where? We'd get a mile, maybe two, before we broke down again."

"Then what?"

"We fight."

The people were climbing into the trucks.

"They're coming," he said.

Dee was struggling to sit up.

"You shouldn't be moving."

"It doesn't matter. Give me a hand."

He pulled her onto her feet, her right pant leg soaked with blood. She used him for support, groaning as she limped over to the Jeep and opened the driver's-side door.

She climbed in behind the steering wheel.

"Dee, the car will break down."

"Jack. Just let me do this."

He felt something inside of him turn cold.

"No."

Dee looked past him to their daughter. "Naomi, take Cole and gather up the weapons from the dead men. Hurry."

"Mom."

"Right. Now." When the children were gone, she said, "I'm not going to make it."

"Yes, you are. We're going to get you help when we find—"

"We're all going to be dead in five minutes."

"Dee—"

"Listen to me. It's dusk. Soon, it'll be night. Let me take the Jeep. The trucks will follow my lights. Think they're chasing us all down. By the time they catch up to me, it'll be dark, and you and the kids . . ." Her voice broke. "You'll be safe."

"But we're almost there, baby."

"You run all night, Jack. Promise me you won't stop."

Over the roof of the Jeep, in the blue dusk across the plain, he could see three points of approaching light.

"No," he said.

"You ready to watch our children die?"

Naomi and Cole were coming toward them.

He grabbed her face and kissed her. There were tears running down their faces, but they wiped them away as the kids arrived.

"Those trucks are coming," Naomi said.

Jack took the handguns from her and set them in Dee's lap.

"We're going due north," he said. "You come to us."

Dee looked down at Cole, her eyes glistening again. "Got a hug for Mama?" The boy handed Jack the shotgun and leaned into the Jeep. Dee pulled Cole into her and kissed the top of his head. Then she looked at her daughter. "Nay?"

"What are you doing?" Naomi asked.

"Mom's going to run some interference for us."

"We're not staying together?"

Jack grabbed Naomi's arm, his chin trembling. "Hug your mother, Nay."

Naomi looked at Jack. She looked at Dee. She wrapped her arms around her mother, and as she sobbed into her chest, Jack heard the distant grumble of the approaching trucks.

"Come on." Jack pulled Naomi away from Dee. "Take your brother into that depression and lie down in the grass at the very bottom. I'll be right there."

"Dad—"

"Just go."

Naomi gathered herself. "All right, Cole, come on."

Dee watched her children run off down the hill into the dark.

"Let *me* take the car," Jack said.

"Will you stop wasting our last moment?"

He nodded.

"Do you know what I'm going to think about?" she said.

"What?"

"That day we had up at the cabin. That perfect day."

"Wiffle ball in the field."

She smiled. "Please get our children someplace safe. Make this mean something."

"I swear to you I will."

"I have to go now."

It was too dark to see the trucks, but their headlights were close enough to have separated into six points of light.

Jack kissed his wife once more and buried his face into the softness of her neck and breathed her in one last time. Then he looked into her eyes until she pushed him away and pulled the door closed and cranked the engine.

He got down in the grass and he was crying as the Jeep rolled away, picking up speed. After ten seconds, the taillights cut on. The engine sputtered and hacked across the prairie.

Jack watched the approaching trucks. They were still moving toward him, getting louder as the Jeep dwindled away. No course diversion yet.

He glanced back into the depression, couldn't see his children, and when he looked forward again, the trucks were turning, all of them, their headlights blazing east.

He lay there watching the lights move across the plain, the engines becoming quiet.

The Jeep disappeared.

The trucks vanished.

Then he was lying on the ground, and there was no sound but the wind blowing through the grass. Lifting the shotgun, he rose to his feet. Couldn't see a thing under the cloud cover. He wouldn't have seen anything regardless with the tears streaming down his face. He called out for his children in the darkness.

In the rearview mirror, Dee watched the trio of headlights pursuing her. The temperature gauge was pegged, and in the Jeep's head-lights, she could see streamers of smoke pouring out of the engine. Her leg throbbed. She kept steady pressure on the gas pedal, trying to maintain her speed at twenty, but the engine was losing power, cylinders misfiring, RPMs erratic.

At 1.2 miles, the RPMs fell off and the engine seized with a vio-lent clanging under the hood. Dee finally eased her foot off the accelerator, let the Jeep roll to a stop and die.

She turned the key back in the ignition.

Short of breath.

Her heart pounding.

The headlights were getting brighter in the rearview mirror, the ominous symphony of their engines already audible.

She couldn't feel her leg anymore, didn't know whether that was owing to the loss of blood flow or the adrenaline surging through her.

Her hands trembled as she lifted the guns out of her lap.

One of the trucks blew past and kept going.

She turned, looked back between the seats.

The other trucks had stopped fifty feet back, their brights blaz-ing into the Jeep for what seemed ages.

At last, she heard a series of distant door slams, and then the lights went dark.

Dee tossed the guns into the passenger seat and opened the center console, fingers probing until they grazed Ed's pocketknife. Her thumbnail found the indentation in the steel and she pried open the longest blade and sawed through the fabric of the shirt Jack had tied around her leg.

The feeling returned—a flood of needles and heat—and she reached down between her seat and the door until her hand touched the lever. As the seat tilted back, the lights of the third truck appeared a quarter mile out through the windshield, moving in her direction.

She could hear voices now, and she could feel the blood spraying out of her, a warm pooling in her seat, the smell of iron filling the car. Already she was lightheaded and breathing fast and breaking out in a freezing sweat.

Her arms slipped down to her sides and she was trying to find that day in Wyoming in the mountains, but her thoughts kept tangling. The footsteps approached, and she was so lightheaded she could barely think at all.

And as flashlight beams swept across the Jeep, she landed upon the image that she wanted to be her last, clinging to it as the dizziness behind her eyes began to spiral and echoing voices screamed at her to get out of the car.

Sunrise on a prairie.

Three figures—a man, a boy, a young woman.

They're tired and cold. They've walked all night, and they're still walking, just a few steps from the crest of a hill.

They reach the top. Breathless.

The view goes on forever and the man pulls his children close and points. At first, they can't see what he's trying to show them because the sun is exploding out of the horizon in radials of early light.

But as their eyes adjust, they find it—a city of white tents spread across the plain.

Thousands of them.

Trails of smoke rise into the morning sky, and a band of soldiers have already seen them. They're climbing the hillside toward her family, hailing them, and one of their number carries the blue-and-white flag of the United Nations.

She wants to follow them—has never wanted anything more—but they've already started down the hillside without her, slipping away now, and she loses them in the blinding light of the sun.

— — —

They'd been running in the dark for three minutes when Cole dug his heels into the ground.

"Come on," Jack said, pulling his arm, "we aren't stopping."

"We have to."

Cole wouldn't move. Jack let go of Naomi's hand and scooped the boy up in his arms and started jogging again.

Cole screamed, his arms flailing.

"Goddammit, Cole—"

The boy grabbed Jack's hair and tried to bite his face. Jack dropped him in the grass.

"He's turning into one of them!" Naomi screamed.

"Look at me, Cole."

"We *have* to go back." The boy was crying now.

"Why?"

"To get Mom."

"We can't. It's too dangerous."

"But it's over."

"What are you talking about?"

"The lights aren't here anymore."

Jack knelt down in the grass, his boy just a shadow in the dark.

"This is not the time to fuck around."

"I'm not! I don't feel it anymore."

"When did it go away?"

"While we were running. I can still feel it going out of me."

"I don't even know what that means—"

"You have to go get Mom. The bad people won't hurt you."

Jack looked at his daughter.

"Let's go," she said. "If there's even a chance, we have to. Right?"

"Listen to me," Jack said. "Do not move from this spot. It might be tomorrow morning before I come back, because I don't think I'll be able to find you in the dark."

"What if you don't?" she said.

"If I'm not back by midmorning, you keep going north until you find help. Cole, look at me." He held the boy's hands. "If you're wrong about this, you might never see me again. Do you understand?"

The boy nodded. "But I'm not wrong."

= = =

Jack ran across the prairie, tearing through the dark, no idea if he was headed in the right direction, and nothing to see but gaping blackness.

After five minutes, he stopped and bent over, his heart banging in his chest.

When he looked up again, he saw a cluster of red lights far across the plain, and over the rocketing of his pulse, he thought he heard engines.

He was still gasping, realized he wasn't going to get his wind back, so he started running again, working up to as much of a sprint as he could manage. Sweat ran into his eyes, and when he wiped the sting away, the car lights had disappeared.

He stopped. Didn't hear the engines anymore.

Just an ocean of soundless dark.

Seven flashes exploded through the black, and for a fraction of a second, he saw Dee's Jeep and the three trucks surrounding it. He was much closer than he thought, just a few hundred yards out, and he was running again, the last stretch blazing past in a rush of terror, pain, and self-doubt, thinking he should have stayed with his children. He was going to see his wife dead, get himself killed, and never see any of them again.

He stopped twenty yards out from the vehicles, so far beyond the boundary of his endurance. It sounded like sirens ringing inside his head, the darkness spinning. He leaned over, puked into the grass, straightened up again, and staggered past the trucks toward the Jeep.

The driver's-side door had been thrown open, the stench of nitroglycerin strong in the air, and he was moving through a haze of smoke, waiting for the gunshots, the attack.

He stopped when he saw them, not understanding what it meant, figuring he must be missing something.

Seven people were sprawled in the grass around the Jeep, each of them dead from a headshot, their guns lying within reach or still in hand.

In the light that spilled out of the Jeep, he saw the eighth member of the party crouched down against the right front wheel, tears streaming down his face, the long barrel of a large-caliber revolver jammed between his teeth.

When he saw Jack, he pulled the gun out of his mouth.

"I can't do it," the young man said. He offered Jack the gun. "Please. Kill me."

Jack was still panting, his legs burning. He reached forward, slowly, as if sudden movement might cause the man to rethink his offer, and then snatched the revolver.

The man said, "Where are you going?" as Jack hurried around to the open door and looked into the Jeep.

The driver's seat had been reclined and Dee lay back on it, unmoving, her eyes closed, blood still pumping out of her leg. The shirt he'd tied around her thigh had been severed.

He set the gun in the floorboard and reached in, taking up both ends of the bloody shirt sleeve and cinching it down even harder than before.

"Dee." He touched her face. "Dee, wake up!"

Outside, the man was crying, begging for Jack to end him.

Jack rushed back to him.

"Which of those trucks is yours?"

"Oh my God!" the man cried. "My daughter!"

Jack knelt down, held the revolver to the man's knee.

"My wife needs medical attention. Do you have keys to any of these trucks?"

The man pointed beyond the Jeep. "The Chevy. Here." He dug a pair of keys out of his jeans, handed them to Jack.

"What happened to me?" the man asked.

"I have no fucking idea."

"You have to kill me. I can't stand knowing what I've done."

"I'm not going to kill you, but I will take your mind off it."

He pulled the trigger and the man screamed, clutching his knee.

Jack raced back to Dee and lifted her out of the car, stumbling away from the Jeep and the shrieking man, and it was all he could do to carry Dee those fifty feet to the truck.

It was a powder-blue Chevy. He opened the passenger door and laid Dee across the vinyl, then limped around and hauled himself up into the cab.

The third key he tried started the engine, and he hit the lights, shifted into gear, and floored the gas pedal.

They sped across the prairie. He held Dee's hand, which was growing cold, saying her name over and over, an incantation, a prayer. He had no idea if she even had a pulse, and still promising things he had no business promising—that they were almost over the border, almost to safety, where a city of tents awaited them, a refuge with doctors who could fix her.

She'd made it this far, she could surely hang on just a little longer, live to see the end of this and whatever new life they made, live to forget the worst of this, to see Naomi and Cole forget the worst of this, see her children grow up strong and happy, because they had so many more years the four of them, so many experiences to share that didn't involve running and fear and death, and please God, darling, if any part of you can hear me, don't let this be the end.

He will wipe every tear from their eyes.
There will be no more death or mourning or crying or pain.

—Revelations

THE team disbands as the light begins to fail, but she lingers in the pit, gently brushing the dirt from the rib cage of a skeleton she's just uncovered in the last hour, lost in her work. The distant hum of an airplane breaks her concentration, and she looks into the sky, sees the twin-engine turboprop catching sunlight on its descent.

She climbs out of the pit and walks over to the showers. Pulls the curtain. Strips out of her boots, her elbow-length rubber gloves, her clothes, and stands naked under the heavy spray of water, letting it pound away the reek of decomp.

— — —

In fresh clothes, she starts across the field.

The airplane is parked in the distance, the cabin door opening.

She breaks into a run.

The old man coming down the stairs of the plane is already smiling. He drops his bag as she runs into his arms, and they embrace for the first time in six months on the broken pavement of the runway.

When they come apart, she looks up at him, thinking, Was his hair this white last Christmas? But he isn't looking at her. He's staring across the field, an intensity coalescing in his eyes.

"What's wrong?" she asks. "Dad?"

He can barely speak, eyes shimmering with tears, his voice just a whisper.

"This is the place."

= = =

They cross the field, moving toward the pit.

"They pulled the trucks up to here," he says. "A half dozen tractor trailers. There were tents set up over there"—he points—"right about where yours are. They told us there was hot food and beds waiting." He stops. "Is that the smell of . . . ?"

"Yeah."

"It was right about this time of day too. Dusk. There was a beautiful sunset."

He continues walking, the stench growing worse with every step, until at last they stand at the edge of the grave.

She watches his face. He's somewhere else—nineteen years in the past.

"They lined us up right here," he says. "Grave was already dug."

"How many people?"

"Maybe two hundred of us." He closes his eyes. She wonders what he sees, what he hears.

"Do you remember where you stood?"

He shakes his head. "I just remember the sounds and what the sky looked like, staring up at it through the bodies that had fallen on top of me."

"Did they use chainsaws?"

He looks down at her, startled by the question.

"Yeah."

"We were curious about how some of the bones had been bisected."

The man eases himself down into the grass. She sits beside him.

"You've been down in the grave?" he asks.

"I worked there all day. That's what I do."

She leans her head against his shoulder and holds his hand, touching the platinum band he still wears on the nub of his left ring finger.

- - -

The team builds a bonfire after supper.

Someone strums a guitar. Someone rolls a joint. A bottle makes the rounds.

Naomi sits between her father and Sam, the Australian team leader, feeling contemplative off two swigs of whiskey and staring into the flames, the cold of the night a wonderful contrast to the eddies of heat sliding up her bare legs.

Usually, those thirty days on the run through hell are as unreachable as if they had happened to another family. But sometimes, like tonight, she feels plugged back into the raw emotion of it all. It's a closed circuit, which, if she isn't careful, still has the power to shock and break her.

Her father is a little drunk, Sam more so, and she tunes back into their conversation as Sam loosens his tie and says, "Curious to know what you think about the Great Auroral Storm."

"I've read some wild theories," Jack says.

"Talking about mine?"

"You really believe these auroral events contributed to the massacres and extinctions in human history?"

"I think there's some compelling solar abnormality data on that, yes. Do I think it's possible the Cro-Magnons wiped out most of the Neandertals forty thousand years ago following a similar phenomenon? Absolutely. Natural selection at its darkest."

"So who got selected in this one?" Jack asks. "Who won? Us?"

Sam laughs. "No."

"The affected?"

"Most of the affected selected themselves out when they committed mass suicide."

"Then who?"

"Your son," Sam says. "People like Cole. Those who witnessed that terrible light show and either didn't kill, or did and resisted the crushing guilt. That's who won."

Jack said, "I have a close friend back home in Belgium, in the humanities department where I teach. A priest. He thinks the aurora was God testing us."

"Those who saw the aurora? Or those who ran?"

"Both," Jack says.

"Well, it all comes down to purification in the end."

"You say that like it's a good thing."

"On a human level, no, but in terms of our DNA, it's a different ball game. Remember, the barbarians finally took Rome. It was awful and violent, but Rome had become a corrupt, ineffectual, soft culture. Genetically speaking, it was a positive thing."

"Or," Jack says, "maybe sometimes we just need to kill each other. Maybe *that's* our perfect state of being."

Sam pauses to smoke, and when he finally exhales, says, "It surprises me that you would want to see this place again."

"You should be examining my bones in that hole," Jack says.

"That's what I'm saying."

"This was a horrible place, no question, but a miracle also happened here. I somehow survived. I never want to forget that."

Naomi is buzzed and getting tired. She stretches her feet toward the fire and lays her head in her father's lap. Soon he's running his fingers through her hair, still debating with Sam, and she's almost asleep when something vibrates near her head.

Jack reaches into his pocket, takes out his phone.

"I forgot, didn't I? . . . Yes, here safe and sound, sitting by a fire . . . Difficult, but good . . . Yes, I'm glad I came . . . That's still the plan. We'll meet you both tomorrow evening . . . She's right here, but she's sleeping . . . I'll tell her . . . I won't forget. I'll do it as soon as we get off . . . Good night, darling."

Jack slides his phone back into his pocket. Naomi is almost asleep now, in that cushioned bliss between consciousness and all that lies beneath. She feels her father's hand on her shoulder, his breath against her ear.

"Naomi," he whispers. "Your mother sends her love."

ACKNOWLEDGMENTS

Run is a novel of firsts. First new novel I self-published (back in 2011). First novel I wrote that allowed me to become a full-time writer. First novel that showed me the way to the emotion-driven, speculative stories that would come to define my identity as a writer. This is also the book that brought David Hale Smith, my wonderful literary agent of almost fourteen years, into my life. I'd like to thank him for his counsel and guidance, along with Alexis Hurley, Naomi Eisenbeiss, and the team at Inkwell Management for your enduring, resounding support. A very special thank-you to Julian Pavia, my editor of almost ten years, and to everyone at Ballantine Books for giving *Run* its first official publication in the United States, and to Wayne Brooks and Francesca Pathak at Pan Macmillan for publishing *Run* and so much of my backlist in the UK. It truly means the world to me. And last, a tremendous bear hug to my readers who found this book all those years ago, embraced it, and in doing so gifted me a career doing the only thing I've ever wanted to do.

BLAKE CROUCH is a bestselling novelist and screenwriter. His novels include *Upgrade, Recursion, Dark Matter,* and the Wayward Pines trilogy. He's helped several of his projects make their way to the screen, most recently acting as head writer and showrunner for the Apple TV+ adaptation of *Dark Matter,* starring Joel Edgerton and Jennifer Connelly. He lives in Colorado.

Blakecrouch.com
X: @blakecrouch1